NIGHTSHADES

JANUARY RAYNE

Graphics: Adobe Stock
Graphic Designer: Dallas Ann Designs
Chapter Artist: Mon Reyes

This is a work of fiction. Shallow Cove Dimensions is a world I have created. My imagination ran wild and will run untamed with no reins. Only whips and spankings when asked for. Unless otherwise indicated, all the names, characters, businesses, places, events, and incidents in this book are either the product of the author's imagination or used in a fictitious manner. Any resemblance to actual per- sons, living or dead, or actual events is purely coincidental.

Fang v__v bang on fangbangers

 Formatted with Vellum

Also by January Rayne

Shallow Cove™ Dimensions

The Eternally Series:

Book 1: Eternally Hers

Book 2: Eternally Damned

Book 3: Carnival of Creeps

Book 4: Eternally Cursed

Book 5: Eternally Rare

Book 6: Eternally Lost

Dead Man's Ranch Series:

Book 1: Kentucky Nights

Shallow Cove™ Dark Dimensions

The Monster Stalker Series:

Book 1: Honeysuckles

Book 2: Snapdragons

Book 3: Hollyhocks

Book 4: Nightshades

DEDICATION

To your sweet little dreams.
When I'm done with you,
you're never going to want to fall asleep again.
Pray for rest.
Because this monster cock is going to
give you nightmares you'll never forget.

Author's Note

This is a work of fiction. Shallow Cove Dimensions is a world I have created. My imagination ran wild and will run untamed with no reins. Only whips and spankings when asked for. Unless otherwise indicated, all the names, characters, businesses, places, events, and incidents in this book are either the product of the author's imagination or used in a fictitious manner. Kickstarter backers who wanted a death in the book are listed by first name with their permission. Any resemblance to actual persons, living or dead, or actual events is purely coincidental.

SPOTIFY PLAYLIST

Scan here to listen to the playlist
of Nightshades:

A Note from Shade, Our MMC:

Heads up: Listen, Little Dream, everything in this book is fiction. If you find it hard to believe that any of this would happen in real life, you're right. Nothing about this story is believable. The author who created me let her imagination run wild. If you knew her, it would make sense. Invading her nightmares scares *me*.

Content Warnings From The POV of Shade:

La-lala-la-la-laaa.

You'd better read these trigger warnings because you do not want me to give you a nightmare and find out your greatest fear. I am not a kind man. I am not a gentleman. I am not someone you dream about.

I'm someone you *scream* about.

The following are in this book for your own mental health, Little Dream. Read them.

Somnophilia, NC and CNC, gore (a lot of it), graphic violent sexual and oral scenes, forced pregnancy, stalking, murder, domestic violence (between my parents), self-harm, cutting with glass, child abuse (me as a child), paralysis, drugging, skinning, self-in!icted gunshot, breath play, blood play with consumption, parental death.

I know. It's more than usual, but I'm not the usual MMC January typically writes about. I'm much darker; even she didn't like it when I got into her head.

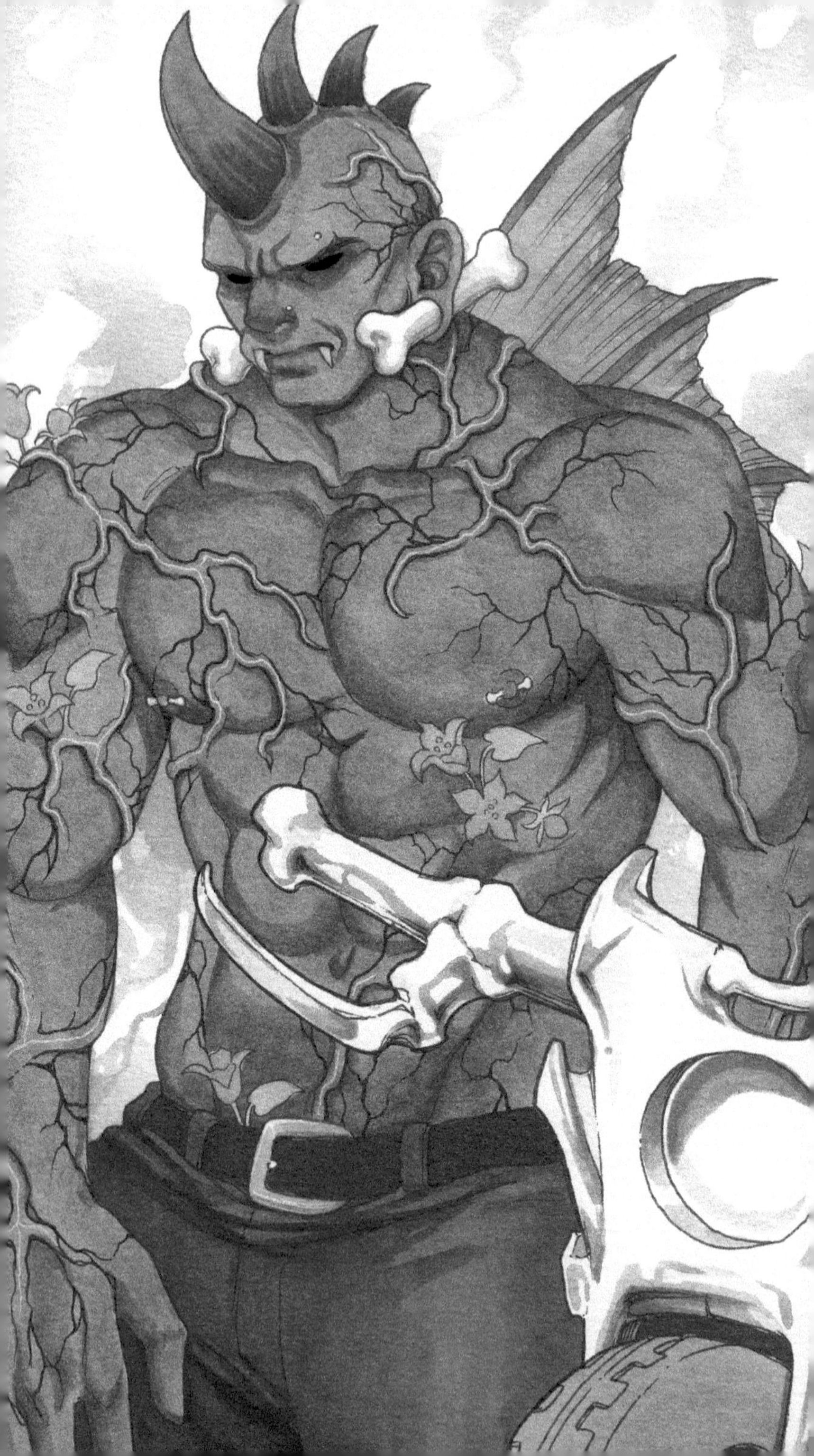

Six months ago

I was always told that nothing good happens in the dark. All the bad and scary things that make people lock their doors take place at a devilish time of night.

It's why I stay in the dark. It's why I hide myself in the shadows where I belong.

I am what everyone fears.

It's my six-foot-six-inch frame. It's the full-body tattoos. It's the black out of my eyes. I am judged, tried, and more often than not, tested to see if anyone could ever win against me.

I am not kind. I hold no patience. I am not a good man.

What I look like on the outside is how I feel on the inside—chaotic and full of rage. I'm the Sergeant at Arms, the leading enforcer for the motorcycle club Shallow Sinners. We're one percenters. The kind the world fears and hates.

And we make most of our moves in the dark.

The vibrations from the motorcycle humming between my legs have my cock hard and my blood filled with lust. Even the sound of the exhaust strokes the Jacob's Ladder and Prince Albert piercings I have.

I pull into the lot in front of the clubhouse, the music pounding against the walls. The laughter is almost as loud as the glass bottles breaking. Party must be going well if I can hear all that from outside.

Off to the right, I see one of the members fucking his old lady against the wall. Her skirt is hiked around her hips, panties pushed to the side, and her moans are echoing through the woods that surround us.

I've buried many bodies in these woods. It's my own personal graveyard.

My trophies.

Bad people deserve even worse deaths, and that's why the Devil created me.

The front door to the clubhouse swings open, slamming against the wall. Another chip of cement where the door handle meets the side of the clubhouse falls to the ground. I've been telling Prez for the last few years that this place needs a remodel, but he doesn't want to invest.

It will be too late when this shit hole crumbles around us.

"Hey, Nightmare," Chelley, one of the biker bunnies, shouts for me in her thick New York accent.

I don't bother getting off my bike yet. I love the feeling of her between my legs too fucking much. "What do you want, Chelley?" I know what she wants. I don't typically fuck the biker bunnies. I'm more interested in killing than fucking, but tonight, I think I'll make an exception.

I killed a man who was raping his kid. I think that deserves celebration.

She blows a big pink bubble from the chewing gum she's smacking, then pops it with one of her sharp fingernails. "Want to meet me in the back? I can show you a good time, Nightmare."

She and the other ten bunnies inside right now.

Taking a cigarette from my pocket, I place it between my lips, light it, and inhale as deeply as I can before blowing out the smoke.

"Go on, then." I lean forward, crossing my arms on the handlebars. "Go get ready for me. I'll be there in a minute."

"I'll get ready for you, baby," she purrs, biting the corner of her lip. "I've seen what you're packing. You aren't going to be easy to take."

"No," I grunt in agreement. "I won't be. And I'm not going to lick a pussy that don't belong to me neither. So go get ready." I blow out another thick cloud of smoke, staring her down with black-filled eyes. "I don't have all night."

Chelley blows another bubble, walking down the sidewalk in her red high heels before disappearing into the dark.

I turn off the bike, swing my leg over, and kick the stand with my boot. Already, my hard cock begins to fall limp from not feeling the vibrations of the engine. Not even the sounds of one of my MC brothers fucking his wife causes my dick to stir.

If she isn't screaming, if she isn't crying, if there isn't the least amount of terror involved, I can't get it up. I need pain. I need fear. I need to see them question if their life is flashing before their eyes.

I'm different than the rest of the MC. They don't crave violence the way I do, but they don't run away from it either. Sometimes, I catch a glow in their eyes, or one of them will growl, but I tell myself I'm imagining it.

Must be the side effect of my psyche breaking.

Another familiar growl sounds from the two fucking. She has her hand over his mouth while she buries her face into his neck. Every thrust becomes more desperate.

Flicking my cigarette on the ground, I stomp the embers out with my steel-toe boot and start my stroll into the dark to meet Chelley. I'll be able to fuck her. I just need to think about the way that rapists blood felt on my hands when I gutted him.

"Excuse me! Excuse me. So sorry to bother you. Do you mind helping me out?"

A voice I don't recognize comes from behind me.

I stop in my tracks, sighing at yet another inconvenience. "I do mind. I have plans. Keep walking that way." I point behind me, back towards the entrance. "The clubhouse will help you." I take another step when something sharp pokes me in my side.

"Sorry. I don't want the clubhouse, Nightmare. I only want you."

The voice becomes distorted, and my vision begins to sway. I lose my balance as if I've drunk an entire bottle of gin.

"You're going to be perfect for the experiments. I can't wait to see what you get turned into. We've been watching you for a while now, and we love your...tendencies."

I do my best to spin around, but that only causes my balance to be worse. "I'm going to fucking kill you," I growl on a slur.

"I look forward to you trying."

My eyes roll to the back of my head as the drug he dosed me with takes full effect.

"Timber," he says with a little too much glee. "The bigger they are, the harder they fall."

Everything fades into the same darkness I've lived in my entire life.

Present day

I'm not the same man I was when they locked me in here.

I'm much worse.

I'm angrier. Stronger. Taller. My temper is shorter. There are so many changes made to my body that I can't comprehend. I don't understand what happened to me, but what I do know is that I'm going to get out of here.

The humanity in my soul is numb. I no longer feel that small speck of reason that tells me to stop, that makes me question if what I'm doing is right.

It's gone.

And I'm so thankful.

Nothing will stop me from becoming the nightmare everyone has thought me to be. I'll be worse.

"Sha-ade," one of the scientists sing-songs into the intercom system.

I growl as I tilt my head up, staring into the bulletproof, shatterproof windows that line my enclosure as if I'm some prime time special they watch every night.

"You know the drill," he tsks. "Stand please. We think you have reached your max form."

Ah, yes.

My form. The one they have changed with DNA that does not belong to me. After being tied down day after day and experimented on, I suppose they finally got what they wanted from me.

According to the scientists, I am part rhino, nightmare, nightshade, vampire, and anglerfish.

I believe them.

There are a few that are obvious. My fangs prove I'm a vampire. I crave blood as well. So much fucking blood. My mouth waters at the thought. Now, I'll never have to waste a drop of it like I did in my human form.

I always wanted to know what the iron-infused liquid tasted like, and now, I'll be able to drink it whenever I want as soon as I get out of here.

Even now, I crave it.

I'm going to drain every fucking person here and leave their bodies to turn to dust.

My rhino traits are the first thing anyone will notice about me. I have a long horn on my forehead with smaller ones lining my hairline. While my skin is just as tough as a rhino's hide, the color is different. I'm a very dark green. My tattoos are still there, but now there are plant-like roots covering my entire body where my veins would be. Small leaves with shiny black berries are spotted along my body, but mostly my neck and shoulders. I've noticed that when I get angry, the berry blooms into a purplish flower, and if anyone gets close enough to smell it, they become paralyzed.

A few scientists have learned that the hard way.

The anglerfish DNA is one of the hardest to accept. This specific fish is known for the light that hangs from its forehead, giving light in absolute darkness to attract prey. Only female anglerfish have the light. The scientists here spliced that DNA so many times in order to get the desired...appeal.

I'm not sure how my light will be beneficial, considering it is at the base of my cock, which is now hidden inside a mouth of sharp teeth, leaves, and roots. I guess, in a way, when I have an erection, the mouth opens, and I bloom. The leaves part to allow my cock to grow to its full length, which has doubled from the experiments.

It's the nightmare DNA that leaves me confused. I have yet to be able to see what that side of me can do.

"I said to stand!" The speaker crackles, and the interference from his yell causes high-pitched noises to echo in the chamber I'm kept in.

I stay seated on the dirt floor, my arms folded and my elbows on my knees. I chuckle; the dark rasp louder than the speaker ever could be.

"I think I'm done taking orders from you," I sneer, drifting my hands into the soil.

I don't know why. I'm listening to my natural instincts now, and my instincts have never once failed me.

"Shoot him with the tranquilizer. We will try again later to see what all he can do now."

The roots grow from me, slithering through the ground, and the walls begin to tremble.

Soft pops from a gun ring all around me. Roots stretch from my shoulder, shielding me from the drugs they love to pump me with.

I've been their freak show for far too long. I think they are right. I have reached my full form.

Being strong means nothing if you hold no power.

And now, I hold all the power thanks to these mad scientists.

The roots climb up the walls, covering the windows, and I use as much force as I can. A few roots slither their way between the wall and glass, slipping inside to where the scientists are.

I stand, roaring, the roots and leaves flying from me. I tilt my chin to my chest, paw the ground with my foot, and charge, ramming my head into the wall of roots. The small sound of glass cracking has a smirk stretching across my lips.

I wonder if the scientists knew they would never be safe from me. They left me in this cage like some poor animal at the zoo. They thought they could control me, use me, and violate me without repercussions?

No one ever fucks with me and lives to talk about it.

I back away, watching the roots grow and thicken, cutting through the ground like angry waves during a storm. Small black berries and leaves grow from the roots, the flowers blooming one by one.

Growling, I focus on my fury and how I want them to relive their worst dreams before I kill every single last one of them. A black cloud emits from my chest, a force field that surrounds me. Darkness succumbs my soul, tugging me deeper into the depths of Hell.

And I love it. I've never felt more at home.

The darkness has always beckoned me, and now I can relish in the sin of what it brings.

I catch another tranquilizer, a long root wrapping around the dart until it snaps in half.

"Enough!" The lead scientist orders me.

I forgot his name. I never cared enough to learn it. Not once have they ever gotten me to beg or cry for my life. I've never been a beggar, and I don't plan to start now.

"Enough," I mock him in a deep, haunting voice. "Only I get to say when it is enough." I inhale, lifting my arms in the air as the roots swirl around me.

They wait for my command.

I aim my hands towards the windows, the roots slicing the air, and I charge again. With added pressure from my horn and the roots against the windows, the glass shatters at my feet, and I'm left staring at the man in charge.

The man who tried to take my humanity from me.

Not knowing that I never had any to begin with.

"Not another step or you will get a bullet between your eyes," he warns.

He's wearing wrinkled slacks with a shirt that's half-tucked in. There's a mustard stain on the left side, proving how disgusting these people are. They never leave this facility.

Whatever this facility is. I've never seen it from the outside, and I've never seen what the rest of the inside looks like. I've been kept in here the entire time, chained for the longest time, until I convinced them I was no threat.

I've been preparing for this day from the moment I felt the rage of the nightmare within me.

I step forward, despite his little orders he just gave, and the shards of glass don't even penetrate my rhino hide.

He licks his lips, taking a staggering step back. His fellow coworkers flee to the exit, and we can't have any of them escaping before they get what they deserve. I block both doors with roots, then one by one, hold each scientist by their throat, the vise grip on their necks tight enough to leave them gasping for air as their feet dangle off the ground.

The only one left is the man who chained me down, pumped me full of hormones to get my cock hard, and cut the light of my angler fish off over and over again to see if it would regrow.

All in the name of science.

The black cloud surrounding me drifts inside, and the berries begin to bloom. I grin, knowing each and every person in here is about to get poisoned and lose their ability to move.

One by one, their gasps become silent, and their bodies fall limp in the grasp of the roots.

The eerie black smoke enters their bodies through every orifice. Mouth, nostrils, and ears. I'm able to see what they are all afraid of. What their worst fears are.

It finally hits me that the evil fog that escaped me is the nightmare DNA. My worst traits finally have a form, and I couldn't be more pleased.

Right now, their worst fear, the one way they don't want to die, all leads back to me.

"Scream." The nightmare inside me claws at my voice, deepening it to lull them to a sleep-like state.

One by one, each man screams at the top of their lungs when I implant a scene of me hunting them in their heads. A few of the men piss themselves, their legs begging to move, but they can't.

They will never be able to escape me.

Just like they thought I would never be able to escape them.

I look up at my creator and flash a fang. He is frozen in place. The whites of his eyes shine like the moon with how wide and round they are. Jumping up into the room where they watched me, I land in front of him, smelling the beautiful scent of fear.

I lean in, inhaling the bitterness of the sweat clinging to his skin. He is trembling. His badge hangs from his breast pocket, and I rip it free, reading the name of the man who has pushed me into my greatest form.

"Doctor William Travis." I'm unimpressed. I crush his card in my fist, the paranormal strength allowing me to turn the plastic into a small ball.

I drop it on the ground, taking one more step closer to the doctor who made me into what I am.

A tear drips down his cheek just as one of my roots wraps around his throat.

"You thought your actions wouldn't have consequences?" I ask, forcing him to turn around to watch his fellow coworkers die. His knees buckle from the paralysis, and I hold him up, pointing at the man I'm going to kill. "What did he do for you?"

His men are all screaming. Scratches appear on their arms and torso as they try to escape me in their wicked dreams. I've been playing catch and release with them.

I am loving the hope they feel when I have them escape me—only to kill it when I get them in my hands again.

"What did he do?" I roar into his ear so loud, his eardrum begins to bleed.

"He is the one who pumped you full of nightshade, extrapolating the DNA sequences needed from the poisonous plant to see what it would do to your body."

I tilt my head, dragging my new friend until he is standing in front of his fellow scientist.

"What do you think of the nightshade now?" I growl low, watching as more flowers bloom from the black berries bursting over the roots. "Breathe in, Doctor," I snarl. "Let me show you the monster you've created."

The whites of his eyes turn into inky pools of black as the nightmare rages and possesses his soul. An oil-like substance drips from his eyes and nose, staining his trembling lips.

"He is caught in a spider's web," I whisper to my mad doctor. "Spiders, along with me, are his worst fear. There's nowhere for him to go now. He's stuck. What do you want me to do? Let him go? Or let him live?"

"Let him go! Oh god, let him go. He doesn't deserve this. He was just doing his job. He has a family."

Another scream rips through the air from his friend. Bite marks begin to appear on his throat and arms, the web wrapping around his body as if his nightmare is a reality.

He gasps once, twice, until there isn't the faintest sound of his heartbeat.

The black of his eyes dissipates to white as the nightmare flees his system. I snap his neck for good measure, releasing the grip of the root from his neck, and he drops to the floor in a webbed cocoon.

"I had a life too. I had a family," I snarl.

"You didn't have blood relatives. You didn't have anyone who would miss you. We thought your psychopathic tendencies would create the perfect weapon. We have yet to perfect the perfect soldier. No creation has listened to us yet."

"You've done this to others?"

"If I tell you the truth, will you let me live?" His teeth chatter from fear.

"That's fair," I reply.

"There are facilities all over the country. So many experiments are going on that no one knows about. We have endless funding. A few facilities have gone under, but when one fails, a few more facilities take its place. You'll never find them all."

"Who said I want to find them all?" I sling him to the nearest wall, his body vulnerable with how exposed it is. "The only facility I care about is this one. How many people are here?"

"A few dozen," he answers without hesitation.

"And you think you have the power to change these people's lives? Unlike me, were some of them good people?"

William's lip trembles as he nods.

"See. I have a problem with that. I have a code. You only kill the bad ones, Doctor." The roots swirl around his arms and legs, spreading his body out like a star.

"I didn't. I was conducting an experiment. I didn't...I didn't mean to..." A root rips his shirt open. "Oh, god," he cries. "You said you wouldn't kill me. You said—"

I silence him with a mouthful of nightshade. "I lied. Killing you brings me happiness. Killing you is what I've dreamed about doing for months. Killing you, doing to you what you did to me..." I hum in delight, my cock jerking with arousal at the thought of his blood drenching me. "It brings me happiness. Why would you take the word of a monster, Doctor? Especially one that you created to suit your image."

"That's right. I'm your creator. You should respect me."

The root slithers up his body, snaking between his lips to push the nightshade into his stomach. This amount will kill him. The toxin I release from my body is only enough to paralyze when inhaled, but ingested...

I'll need to hurry.

One of the roots wraps around his waist, and I peek to my right to see the other scientists doing their best not to look.

I can't have that.

"Step right up and enjoy the show." I wave my hand, forcing the roots to pull the men closer to me. Straightening their heads, the sinful smoke morphs into fingers, peeling their eyelids back.

"Please. I'm sorry. I'm sorry for everything I did."

"Apology not accepted." Controlling one of the main roots, I go to plunge it into his gut when I pause right before impaling him.

He has made my life absolute Hell.

It's only fair that I return the favor.

I don't want his death to be quick. I've waited too long for this. I want more for him.

For us.

We've come too far to have our relationship end so soon.

Shoving a root down his throat, I force the scientist to gag, vomiting the nightshade I made him swallow.

"Sorry. You're going to have to give me a learning curve," I chuckle, peering over my shoulder to see the other men whimpering from their nightmares.

I stand in front of him, towering over his pathetic form trapped against the wall. "Let me see what you most fear, William." I grip his chin and blow the black smoke down his throat, the nightmare taking over his veins.

"No. No! No! Please, no. No!" he screams, his eyes bleeding to black as the favorite part of me becomes one with him.

Liquid splashing on the ground has me look down, the front of his pants wet with piss.

"Don't be a coward, William. If I can take everything you did to me, you can take what I'm about to do to you." I stare into the shallow pits of his eyes, diving into the worthless muck of his mind. "Let's see what dark, decrepit secrets you hold in here."

I tilt my head when I realize where we are. "A zoo? That's interesting considering the monster you've turned me into. Did you turn me into your worst fear, William?" I tsk, looking around the fake zoo his mind has created.

The enclosures sway from being built by imaginative fear, the bars fading into the sky, proving that this space isn't real.

But I'm going to make it the realest fucking thing he has ever seen.

William has already placed himself in an enclosure, grasping at the bars.

"Let me out! Let me out!" he begs, tears staining his face.

Lions and tigers roar in the distance. Birds chirp and caw to the left of us. The sky is darkened by me, black clouds constantly swirling to keep the nightmare alive and well.

I love to match the mood.

Dark, menacing, and violent.

Three of my favorite flavors.

"Please." He leans his face against the bars, his tears shining against his cheeks, and snot drips from his nose. "I will do everything I can to change you back to human. I'll dedicate my life to eradicating any DNA we have put in your system."

I growl low in my throat, the roots stretch from my veins and reach for him. "What the fuck makes you think I want to change back into a weak human form? You've created the monster I've always wanted to become."

He sucks the snot from the top of his lip. "Then, then, you'll let me go?" William stammers. "Why would you want to kill the man responsible for your upgrade?" He has the audacity to smile at me.

I step closer, my roots gather as his feet, climbing up his body to keep him still. Narrowing my eyes, I pry his mouth open with the roots, silently ordering my power to glide down his throat.

"Because I can, William."

His eyes turn red, and with every inch of his throat that

I claim, he gags and coughs. Spit drips down his chin, showing how pathetic he really is.

"Such a small man to dare to kidnap, drug, and do the unspeakable things you did to me. While I love my new form, your actions are unforgivable."

Somehow, his eyes widen even more. Fear permeates the air as I step into his enclosure. He tries to speak, but the plant taking over his throat makes it difficult.

"You thought I couldn't come inside?" I turn him around, forcing him against the bars. "I control this nightmare, William. You can add to it, sure, but it is me that knows everything you fear, so I can use it against you." I lean forward, smiling next to his ear. "There isn't anywhere you are safe from me. Your death will belong to me, and your grave will be hollow because there will be nothing left of you to bury."

I curl my lip when I suddenly taste coffee. That's when I learn that not only can I feel sensations through the roots, but I can taste. He gags again, and I watch in complete bliss as the roots move through his chest and stomach. His skin bulges and waves the deeper I probe.

"Your death will mean nothing to me," I whisper. "You mean nothing to me. You picked the wrong person to change, William. I was already a bad man, and now, I'm the nightmare people have feared their entire life." I break off a rib from inside him, and he screams in pain, his eyes rolling to the back of his head to pass out.

I yank the roots from his body, along with the piece of rib I've snagged. He collapses on the ground, vomiting again. I jump back to miss the sprays of bile and growl.

"Don't get your fucking puke on me." I kick him in the gut, hearing a few more bones break.

He screams, blood trickling down his bottom lip, and his cries for help are an endless echo chamber.

"No one can hear you, William." I grip him by the throat and slam him against the bars of his enclosure. "It's just you"—I poke him in the chest—"and me." I grin.

I cup my hand over my ear, pretending to focus on the roars of all the creatures in this nightmare zoo. "I think they are getting hungry."

He shakes his head. "Please, no. No. I'll do anything." He crawls to me, clutching onto my right leg. His hand can't even fully wrap around my ankle.

He is a sorry excuse of a man.

The nightmare pins him against the bars, the roots of the nightshade tying his limbs to the enclosure so he can't try to get free.

I lift the rib into the air, imagining a sharper tip, and the plant twines together, breaking the tip of the bone into the angle I had been thinking of. I grin, showing the sharp rows of my teeth.

"I'm going to skin you alive, William. I'm going to feed you to the animals you fear. I'm going to make sure that the way you die is the worst way. Why is that?"

Blood rolls down his chest from his mouth. By the smell of him, he is already dying from internal bleeding. I forgot my own strength when I kicked him.

"Because"—he sobs—"Because of what I did to you. Not for what you turned into, but the process."

"Good. See? You can learn. You're lucky I'm not shoving this rib up your ass, William. Unlike you, I'm not that sick." Placing the sharp bone on his shoulder, I begin to cut, igniting blood-curdling screams from him. "But in ways, I'm so much sicker."

I love my new life.

And I can't wait to bring havoc to the world of people who deserve it.

OVE POLI
EPARTMENT

CHAPTER ONE
LULA

My entire life, I knew I wanted to be a detective. I always dreamed of being in the big city, solving horrid murders to bring justice to victims who can't speak.

Never in my wildest dreams did I go from being a cop in New York City to a detective in a small town. I came here because there was no more growth for me in NYC. I would have had to wait years to be a detective, and I didn't want to, so I applied to jobs all around the country.

When Sheriff Jake Holland called to offer me the job, I knew I couldn't turn it down. Something inside my soul told me to pack up and give this small town a try.

"Detective Sanchez. Are you ready for your first official day?" Sheriff Holland stops in front of my desk, handing me a cup of coffee that does not smell like it has been sitting in the pot all night.

I can get used to this.

"Yes, sir. I'm ready to tackle anything you can give me."

He hooks his left hand on his belt, taking a small sip of his coffee. "Typically, it's pretty quiet, but over the last few years, we have seen an uptick in crimes. I want to emphasize again that this is a small town, Detective. There might not be much for you to do all the time. This typically isn't the first place a detective would come. You are sure this is where you want to be? If not, I can make a few calls and see if I can't get you into a bigger town—maybe even a city. I don't have a lot of pull, but being a sheriff helps."

"I'm here for a reason. I believe that. The universe wouldn't guide me here if I wasn't meant to be here. I'm going to give it a chance."

He showcases his handsome smile. "That's what I like to hear. Let me introduce you to the rest of the force."

If he weren't my boss, I would ask him out for a drink, but I never mix business with pleasure. That's too messy. I've seen what happens when you combine work and personal relationships. They are career killers, and I've worked too hard and have come too far to let a man—of any caliber—ruin what I have rightfully earned.

"Zig. Waylon. Jenkins. Come meet our detective!" Sheriff Holland shouts into the only room of the police station.

A few old desks sit in the middle with stacks of paperwork that file clerks are currently organizing. Unlike the city, there isn't a front desk here. If anyone has a problem here, they can walk in and speak to anyone they want.

Waylon, Zig, and Jenkins stand next to their boss. Waylon is the biggest of the crew. His khaki uniform sleeves stretch over his bulging biceps, which are bigger than my head. He is definitely the muscle on the team. He wears a scowl, seeming pissed off at anything and everything.

"Fellas, I want you to meet Lula Sanchez, our lead detective. She's come from New York City, so please, don't chase her off. And please, no rude comments. I better not see any sexual harassment paperwork on my desk. That goes for you too, Sanchez."

"You won't have to worry about that with me, sir," I state, taking a casual sip of my coffee. I eye the men up and down, showing my distaste. "Respectfully, none of them are my type."

A scoff from the man in the middle has me quirking a brow. "I'm everyone's type. I'm Zig." He flashes a naturally flirtatious smirk, showcasing his dimples. "Well, they call me Zig. My full name is Audacto Zayas." He points to his nametag. "But still, Zig is the only thing I go by."

"Audacto?" I don't know why I sound surprised. "¿Hablas español?"

"Sí. Sí." He nods, fluttering his long lashes that curl. His eyes are feminine in a way. His irises are light green, pairing beautifully with his skin tone. "You like me now, don't you?"

I snort, coffee going up my nose. "No, no, Zig. I don't. I don't fuck where I work. I'm making that clear now."

Zig's eyes twinkle more somehow since turning him down.

Sheriff Holland smacks Zig on the back of the head. "That's what I'm talking about. It's been a while since we have had a lady in the office. You'll have to excuse my officers."

"I didn't do anything. I'm being respectful." Waylon sounds bored and unamused. "It's nice to meet you. I'm sure you'll be a great asset to the team. I'm Waylon." He holds out his giant hand for me to shake.

My hand completely disappears in his. "Nice to meet you, Waylon."

"I'm Jenkins." The third officer gives an awkward wave.

"Glad to have you here. The last few years have been odd in this town."

I sit on the corner of my desk. "Oh? How?"

"Just weird murders we haven't been able to figure out. Our last sheriff quit over it," Zig informs. "It has been a while though so maybe the guy is gone."

My gaze slides to Jake, and he is looking away as if he knows something that no one else does.

"Sheriff, what do you think?" I blow the steam rising from my cup and take a long swig of my coffee, loving how rich it is.

"Don't know. I think our killer is gone. We just have to remain vigilant."

He's lying. He has answers and doesn't want to share them. I have always been great at being able to tell when people lie. From the time I was young, I could recognize the 'tell' when someone was evading the truth.

The Sheriff's? He doesn't like to make eye contact. He is an assertive man. He likes to be in control, and when he isn't, he is lost, which shows in the way his gaze drifts around the room.

I'll be keeping an eye on that.

"Well, I'm here now. We can land this son of a bitch together if he is still here." My phone dings, interrupting my train of thought to see my brother's name flashing across the screen.

My family is furious at me for leaving the city to come here. They have told me a hundred times that they think I am making a mistake. No one was on my side. They didn't care that I wanted to be a detective *now*. My brother, mother, and father wanted me to wait for a job to open up in the city.

I couldn't risk waiting for a maybe. Maybes don't make dreams come true, and neither does waiting around.

I'm not the waiting type.

I chase after what I want. I don't wait for opportunities to come to me—I *make* them.

My family can be upset with me all they want, but I had to do what is best for me, not them. I love and miss them, of course. They are my family. At the end of the day, I have to do what brings me happiness and peace. We get one life, and I fully believe we as people need to start living for ourselves instead of others.

Even if it means disappointing family.

"Nice kicks." Waylon points to my shoes. "What made you wear those instead of high heels?"

I can't help but raise my brows again as I inhale another gulp of coffee. I have to know where the sheriff got it from because this might be the best I've ever had.

Jake slaps Waylon on the chest. "Are you fucking kidding me right now? You don't ask women that, Waylon."

"I didn't mean any harm," he growls.

"Don't mind this cute grump." Zig throws his arm across Waylon's shoulders. "He means well."

Waylon shrugs Zig off with a snarl.

"It's fine. I get the stereotype. A lot of women wear high heels in a professional setting, but I prefer comfort and the ability to actually chase and catch a suspect. I can't do that in heels. The shows on TV are lying to you." I lift my pant leg to show off my Converse. "I have them in a bunch of different colors to match all of my pantsuits."

My stomach grumbles, interrupting this riveting conversation. "I haven't had a chance to tour the town. Where is a good place to get breakfast?"

"Demi's Diner," the four men say in unison.

Jake lifts the coffee. "It's where I got the coffee. You'll love it there. Minus her husband. He is a pain in the ass, but you'll get used to him."

"I guess," Waylon mumbles. "If you consider warts something to get used to. The guy gives me the creeps. I don't know why. He is crazy about Demi, which, at the end of the day, is all we care about."

"Loco." Zig twirls his finger next to his head and whistles.

"He causes the hair on the back of my neck to stand up, and so does his friend, Rhett," Jake says.

"Don't forget about Holly, Fitz's wife." Jenkins snaps his fingers as if he is just remembering her.

"Are these people a problem?" I question with concern, double-checking that I have my gun attached to my hip.

"A problem? No. I don't think so," Zig states, running his hand over his short-cropped hair. "You'll know what we mean when you meet them. Let's head over now and introduce Sanchez to Demi. It's time you know the lay of the land."

I pat the deep pocket of my plum-colored trench coat to check and see if my money clip is there. I don't typically carry a purse. It isn't beneficial on the job, so I've learned to consolidate my needs the best I can.

"Let's go, then." Waylon is already out the door. "I want the smash burger."

"It's eight in the morning, Waylon."

"So?" The big guy huffs. "Breakfast, lunch, and dinner are served twenty-four-seven."

"That actually sounds delicious. I'm in." I hop off the desk and throw my trench coat on. I have my gun on my hip, and my badge is settled right next to it.

"You too? You eat dinner for breakfast? Hay, Dios mío."

Zig shakes his head. "Can't believe there are two of you now."

I roll my eyes, grinning as I follow Waylon outside the station. I think I'm going to like it here. They seem like a solid group of officers.

"Demi's Diner isn't far at all. It's just down the street here. Oh, that ice cream shop to the left? You'll love it. It's all homemade. You'll have to check it out sometime." Jake points to a cute red brick building across the street.

The shop has an arched door with matching windows. Black iron tables and chairs are outside for people to enjoy the day while they snack on delicious ice cream.

I will definitely be stopping there after I get off work to celebrate getting through my first day.

Jake opens the diner's door to allow me to enter first. It is packed. Waiters and waitresses are practically jogging from one side of the room to the other. A girl with bright pink hair finally looks up from her order pad and gives Jake the biggest smile.

"Sheriff! It's good to see you again." She leans against the hostess podium. "Waylon. Zig. Jenkins." Her big blue eyes land on me, and nothing but kindness shines from them.

"Demi. This is our new lead detective, Lula Sanchez. Today is her first day, and I wanted to treat her to the best breakfast in town. Lula, this is Demi. She owns this diner."

"Hi, it's nice to meet you."

"This is amazing! A detective! In our town? It feels like we are going in a good way, Jake. It's so nice to meet you, Detective."

To my surprise, she gives me a hug, standing on her tiptoes to wrap her arms around me.

I don't typically do hugs. I'm not a touchy-feely person.

I like to keep to myself. With all the bad I have seen, it ends up numbing the part of you that craves love and turns you into a person you don't recognize.

There's also a very dark part of myself that I haven't shared with anyone. It's a secret I plan to take to my grave. A symptom of being on the job.

I crave a thrill. I love being afraid. When I'm in the dark and I can't see, my heart beats faster as fear begins to set in. My body comes to life. The unknown of what could happen to me, the random noises echoing in the shadows I can't see, and goosebumps spread across my skin to warn me that danger is near.

I'm addicted to the terror.

"Oh no," Jake exhales the weight of the world from his chest.

"Here we go," Zig groans.

"You're about to meet the bane of Jake's existence," Jenkins whispers into my ear.

"Oh, stop it guys. He isn't so bad." Demi winks at me as if I'm supposed to know what that means.

"What's going on?" I finally ask.

Waylon juts his chin out. "He is what is going on."

I follow everyone's line of sight, and my breath catches. I can't remember how to breathe. My heart begins to race. My palms become sweaty. The excitement and thrill take over my body.

I have a gift that not many have. This ability is passed down to all the women in the Sanchez family. My mami, my mamita, and so on and so forth have all possessed this. It first manifested inside me when I was just a child. I must have been around four or five years old.

At first, I thought I had imaginary friends, and when I

asked my mami about it, she explained that all the women in our Colombian familia had this gift.

I'll never forget when she sat me on her lap. She began to comb my hair to relax me. I was scared by what I saw.

She said, *"Mi Corazón, el mundo se verá diferente ahora. Verás y experimentarás rostros que nunca entenderás, pero que aún así amarás. Nos acercan a lo desconocido, y lo que no conocemos, debemos explorarlo."*

Which translates to, "My heart, the world is going to look different now. You'll see and experience faces you will never understand, but love them anyway. They bring us closer to the unknown, and what we don't know, we must explore."

Jake sighs again, gesturing his arm out lazily before it falls to his side with a hard slap. "Meet Creed. Demi's husband."

Creed possessively wraps his arm around Demi. He curls his lip at me, flashing his fang. "Who are you?"

"I'm the new detective in town. It's nice to meet you."

"I don't care." Creed presses a kiss to Demi's cheek, whispering words into her hair that cause her to blush.

My gift?

I'm able to see the truth that creatures try to hide so they can blend in.

I can see the unknown.

And I see Creed for exactly who he is.

A monster.

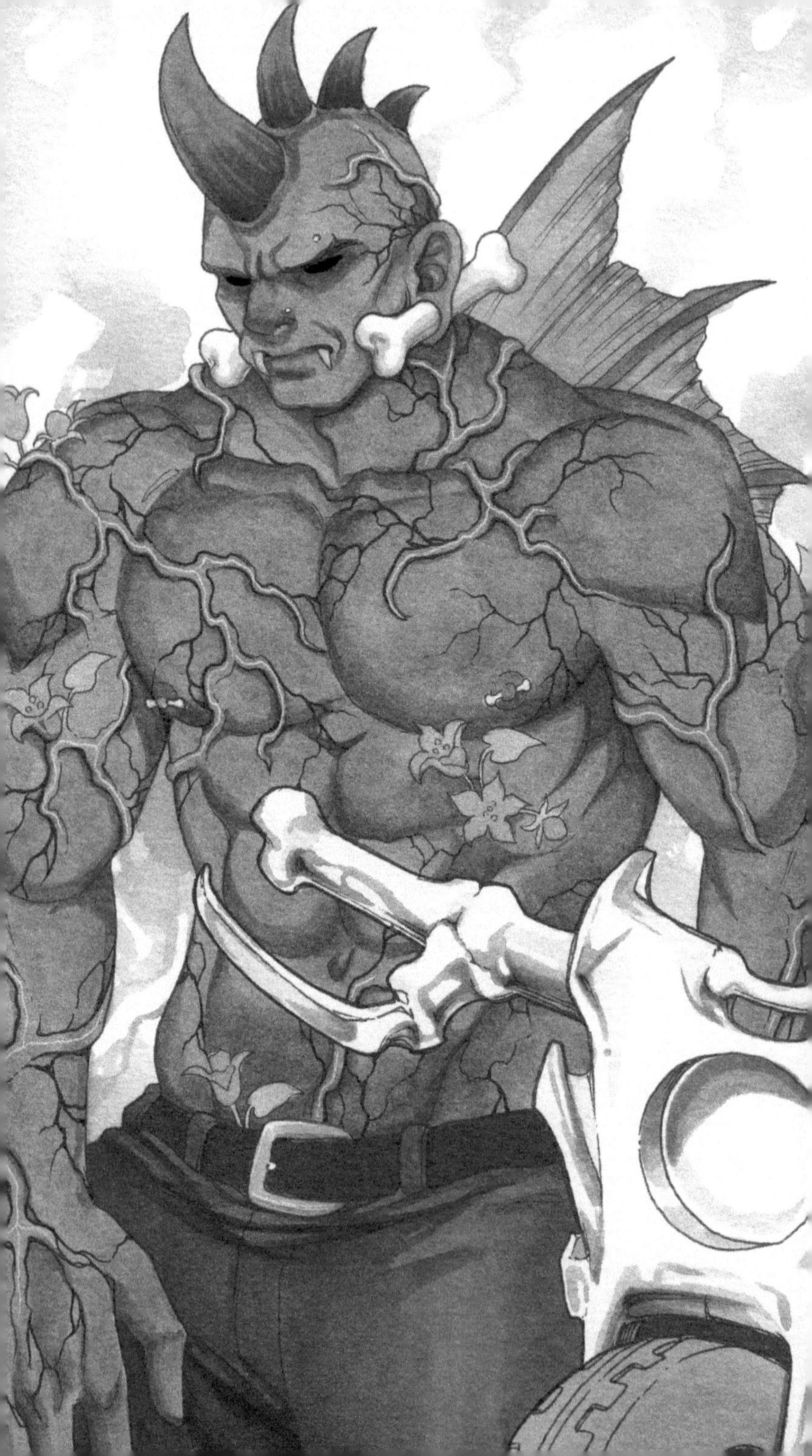

CHAPTER TWO
SHADE

Surviving in a world where I am unstoppable is a dream.

I've gotten to feed on so much fear that my nightmare has gotten stronger. Controlling the darkest parts of me is easy in a world that thrives on greed. No one is innocent, and it has made hunting that much more thrilling.

Vowing to haunt people who have no ethics or morals has worked to my benefit. What's that human saying that I used to hear all the time? There are plenty of fish in the sea?

Only for me, there's plenty of sin.

And so many people need to pay the price.

For instance, I've been following a delicious scent since escaping the institute. It's warm and comforting, a blanket that wraps around the wickedness of my soul to keep the darkness from escaping.

I'm addicted to how this aroma is acting like a lullaby, easing the rage of the evil swarming in my veins. I want to learn more about why this perfume causes the monsters inside me to become drowsy and at peace.

I don't want peace.

I want destruction. I want hatred. I want blood on my

hands and in my stomach. I want to pluck flesh from between my teeth with the bones of my victims.

Following the scent is simple, and when I find it, I'm going to kill whatever or whoever belongs to the smell confounding my mind.

The intriguing scent isn't the only one in the air.

I'm in the middle of the woods, keeping a low profile for now, considering my appearance is far from human. That doesn't bother me. I love lurking in the shadows and becoming what everyone fears.

Bending down, I swipe my fingers through the puddle of blood, snarling. I've been following a poacher for a few days now who has been killing deer illegally.

Would I normally give a fuck about deer? No, but it isn't the right thing to do. People should be punished for the crimes they commit.

Sucking my fingers into my mouth, I immediately spit it out when the taste of rotten trash spreads over my taste buds. Add another reason to the list of why I need this scent to go away. Ever since I smelled it two days ago, I haven't been hungry.

I haven't been able to stomach anything. I immediately throw up, and all that does is enrage me.

About a mile ahead, dogs bark and growl, probably attacking another deer during a season when no one is allowed to hunt.

Black smoke in the shape of an oversized shadow of myself emerges from me, tendrils acting as fog, slithering along the ground to ensnare the killer. Every few feet, another deer lies dead on the ground with its antlers sawed off as close to the skull as possible.

I pat the dead dear, growling at the viciousness of its

death. Not only was he shot, but it has bites all over its body and neck.

That is unnecessarily cruel.

Blurring closer to the hunter, I hide behind a nearby tree, smirking when the nightmare inches closer to the group. The leader is a blonde woman with blue eyes, flanked by two men. Over the last few days, I learned her name is Greta, and the dogs heel by her side, showing how well trained they are.

She squats, sawing off the antlers to the latest kill, and I urge the nightmare forward.

"*La-la-la-la-la-la,*" the malevolent black shadow sings into the cool morning air.

"What was that, Greg?" Greta asks, the grinding of the saw stopping mid-swipe.

"What was what?" Greg asks, twisting and turning to see if anyone or anything is there.

He's tall and a bit scrawny. Breaking his bones would be a pleasure I wouldn't feel guilty about. So thin, it's as if he is daring me to snap his skeleton to see if the bones would penetrate the skin as easily as I think they would.

A low chuckle vibrates my throat. I've been playing with my food ever since I saw them kill three deer in an hour period, and I've been stalking them ever since.

After a day or so, I learned that the nightmare gets into their heads, and they are able to hear the song that reminds me of a horror movie.

"*La-lala-la-la-laaaa.*"

"What the fuck is that? Is that you, Ronald?" Greta hisses, dropping the saw from her hands. Her blonde hair flips over her shoulders when she looks left and right.

"I don't hear anything, Greta," the one called Ronald

chimes in, slinging the rifle over his shoulder. He's shorter with more meat on his bones, and I'm curious how he would beg for his life if he saw me snap his friend in half. "Maybe we should call it. These woods have been creeping me out, and we have plenty of antlers. We even have a few with the velvet still on them. That's going to bring us good money. Come on, let's go."

"No," Greta argues, squatting down to grab the saw again. "We can get a few more."

The grinding of the metal against the antlers causes me to clench my teeth. I growl, pushing my nightmare forward, teasing them with death, and the best part is that they have no idea they will never leave these woods.

I'm going to poach them. I'm going to rip the skin off their bones and use their skeleton in whatever way I see fit. I miss my motorcycle, and their bones would bring a delicious twist to a bike I'll build from the ground up.

I need a project to keep me busy when I'm not feeding on the fear and nightmares of others.

"La-lala-la-la-laaaa."

She stops sawing again, and a grin spreads across my face when Greta looks over her shoulder. "You don't hear that, Greg?" she whispers to her friends, her fear and anxiety kicking up a notch.

I inhale deeply, loving how good her terror smells. I can't wait to get inside her head to see how fucked up her mind is. I wonder what her worst fear is? I wonder how she will die when I have her in the grasp of the evil that rules me.

"Greta, we don't hear anything," Greg exhales on an annoyed breath. "Stop trying to freak us out."

"Seriously. It's getting dark, and it gets creepy in the woods at night."

Greg pushes his friend, causing him to stumble. "Scared, Ronald?"

Ronald trips over a fallen log and lands right on his ass, the rifle misfiring, and a loud crack fills the air.

Mmmmm.

With delicious smoke.

I inhale again, taking in as much of it as I can. The gun smoke wraps around my lungs, and now I crave more.

"Fuck you, Greg. Yes, I'm scared, okay? You guys can't tell me you don't feel it. This hunting trip, something has been off. It's like"—poor little Ronald stands, wiping the soggy leaves from the back of his pants—"It's like someone is following us. I've felt this heavy weight on me, and I've been more scared than usual. Twigs breaking, the sound of footsteps—"

Greg cuts him off. "—Do you hear yourself? We. Are. In. The. Woods. Of course, you're going to hear twigs snapping and footsteps. There are animals all around us. You're being ridiculous."

"Fuck you. I'm listening to myself and my instincts and getting the fuck out of here."

"La-lala-la-la-laaaa."

Greta stands and throws the saw on the ground. "Enough! Which one of you is making that sound? Stop it. It's creeping me out." Emotion catches in her throat. "It isn't funny. Ronald is right. It's getting creepy out here. We should leave."

I'm afraid I can't allow that to happen.

Using my vampiric speed, I bring my head down and ram my rhino horn through Greg's chest. His death is so quick, so sudden, the only sound coming from him is the squelching of his body pouring blood down my face.

I fling my neck to the left, his body flying from my horn.

Greg's useless husk slams against a nearby tree, the chilling snap of his bones breaking is music to my ears.

"Greg!" Greta releases a bloodcurdling scream. "What happened to Greg, Ronald? What just happened?"

She's panicking. Every breath I hear from the expanse of her lungs becomes quicker.

I don't really care for the men who are with her. I only need them out of the way so I can do what I was created to do. They didn't saw the antlers off. They didn't shoot their guns or order their dogs to attack deer.

Unfortunately, they are guilty by association.

The dogs that she has trained to attack whimper when they sense me, fleeing their owner to save themselves. They are smart.

Unlike their mother.

Pawing at the ground, I roll my head over my shoulders, slinging a piece of flesh from my horn as I charge at Ronald. Ramming my sharp spear of keratin through the middle of his throat, wet gurgles rejoice the bitterness living in the valves of my heart.

His blood touches my tongue. Immediately, I smell the worthlessness of Ronald. Weakness is embedded in his blood that I would never want to drink. His weakness might infect me.

I'm worthy of so much more.

"Oh. My. God!" Greta screams when her flashlight lands on me, towering over her with her friend, who hangs on my horn by his throat. It must be such a gruesome sight to see.

"La-lala-la-la-laaa," I sing to her in a deep, slow tone.

The flashlight shining in my face shakes from Greta's hands quaking. Her tears shine against her cheeks like the sun's reflection casting off a glacier.

Just. Beautiful.

Grabbing her friend by the roots of his hair, I pull his body from me without breaking eye contact with her. Roots slither down my body, twisting and traveling across the ground to climb up her body.

"No! No, please! I'll do anything," she begs and sobs, pathetic attempts to save her life.

The roots wrap around her, and the nightshade flowers appear, blooming to release their poison.

"What is happening? What do you want?" Greta sobs, her eyes widening when she realizes she can no longer move.

The roots unwind from the desperate little human, merging with my skin once more.

Greta stands there, almost completely frozen. Small motions occur as she struggles. A twitch of her fingers. The slight shake of her legs. A few whimpers bubbling up her throat.

Awww. That's so cute.

She's trying to scream.

I stand in front of her and tilt my head, allowing her to see into the pitch black abyss of my eyes. My fingers reach for her face, tracing the delicate edge of her jaw. It's going to look beautiful framing the new headlight of my motorcycle.

"Greta. Greta. Greta," I scold with a click of my tongue.

Her eyes fill with salt water, tiny pools sinking her blue irises.

"Sorrowful seas," I whisper in admiration, swiping the tops of her cheeks. "I can't wait to cut them from your face."

She whimpers again, her entire body trembling with a fresh wave of terror. Her eyes spill their water like a dam breaking to fill a lake.

"Does that scare you?" I bend down to get closer,

smelling the fresh scent of deer blood and piss. "Do *I* scare you?" I blink, tilting my head in the other direction.

More tears fall, pairing well with the increased scent of fear. Mmmm, it's like an expensive drink with a gourmet meal.

"Good," I growl. "I'm going to make you feel what you made these deer feel. I'm going to rip your scalp from your skull, so you understand what it is like to have something stolen from you." Tucking a piece of her hair behind her ear, a black cloud swirls around our feet.

"Let me see what you fear most."

The nightmare acts as a snake creeping up her face, the onyx tendrils peeling her bottom lids to slip inside. Her eyes are blue for one last second before my evil intent possesses her.

I drift into her mind, following the screams from Greta. The closer I get to her, the louder they become. I sense her worst fear, a smile belonging to someone unhinged, becomes my face.

Storm-filled clouds escape me, crackling with rage and death. Her screams continue, unknowingly luring me closer to the parts that she keeps secret.

Fuck, I love the way secrets taste. So much mistrust to hold all those wrongs inside a skeleton that can't handle so much deceit. That's what is so special about getting to see what people fear most. More times than I can count, it's one of their deepest darkest secrets that they haven't told a soul.

It's too fucked up.

It's too much.

If the truth leaves your lips, their perception of you might change.

I couldn't care less about perception.

"Your secrets are safe with me," I lie, my hunger growing for her fear by the second.

I lick the neurons firing in her brain, needing to taste more of the fight or flight response firing in her system like fireworks.

"So afraid," I growl in delight, my cock jerks in response.

Not for wanting her, but for wanting her fear.

The murderous shouts of agony have me pushing forward. I have the ability to see into her mind and see in real time, loving that I get to experience deaths by the wicked dreams I enforce.

Her worst fears come to life, the space around us fading into black. A large bonfire is lit, flames reaching for the imaginative sky that doesn't exist.

Greta's cries for help have me look up. She's naked and tied to a long branch like a pig about to be roasted.

The fire isn't big enough to burn her, and that will have to change. Using my shadow self, I throw more imaginary wood onto the fire, wanting the flames to stretch higher.

I want her pain.

I want her pleas for survival.

I want to smell her burning flesh.

"No! Please, I'll do anything!" she screams, wiggling in the restraints she has created for herself.

The scent of her blood has my nostrils flaring. The bark from the tree is scratching the delicate surface of her skin.

"La-lala-la-laa-laaa," my hungry nightmare sings.

Greta vomits. In her mind, gravity forces her puke into the fire, but in real time, it soaks her clothes and chin. She chokes and gags, unable to swallow or spit since she is paralyzed.

"Just think. If only you were a responsible person, I

wouldn't be happening to you. I bet you're thinking that right now, aren't you? I bet you're wondering if you could turn back time, if you could make a different choice, then none of this would be happening." My maniacal, villainous laugh reverberates through the woods and travels through her mind so she can hear me. "You can't turn back time. You have to answer for your crimes, Greta."

"I'm sorry. I'm so sorry. I won't do it again. I'll be done forever. I won't hunt anymore. Please, let me go!" The fire climbs, the whimsical tips of the flames flicker and dance, closing the empty space between the bright orange blaze and her flesh.

From the heat alone, her body is already turning a beautiful shade of pink. I wonder how long before it burns and bubbles her skin off her bones.

Rage swells inside me. "Hunting? Have you learned nothing?" I roar, funneling my fury into the nightmare.

The fire explodes. The better version of me soaks in the smoke, ash, and embers; the nightmare swirling around in circles within the wild, unkept blaze.

I grow stronger as her fear builds.

The scorching heat is finally too much for her skin, and she screams so loud, it echoes into the empty night of her brain.

I love my abilities. I love that her pain is internalized. Her screams in her mind are mere whimpers in her throat as we stand in the middle of the woods.

No one will ever be able to hear the torment I've inflicted. Her death will always be questionable—a case that will never be solved.

Death is poetry, a sweet end to a complicated life. If anything, I'm doing her a favor.

"You're a poacher, Greta. You don't hunt. Killing for

sport, killing to steal, killing in dozens is not hunting. You're controlled by a nightmare, and yet you haven't learned your lesson. What would it take, Greta? What would it take for you to see the errors of your ways?"

She sobs so hard, her body convulses. "I'm sorry." She hangs her head, her long blonde hair falling down her shoulders. "I needed the money. I was desperate."

"And what are you now, Greta? You're just as desperate to live."

My victim nods in agreement; her grunts of discomfort are making me hard. Glancing down, the sharp teeth open, and my cock blooms to its full two and a half foot length—an adaptation from the rhino DNA.

Stroking myself with both hands, I watch in pure fascination as the flames become stronger, growing higher, until there's no more hope left for Greta.

My shadow-self morphs with the fire, turning the wild blaze a searing, unholy black.

"Mmmm," I moan just as another scream clings to her throat.

The possessed fire finally reaches her, cooking her like she fears. She fights the edge of death, refusing to accept her fate.

Her flesh begins to roast, the scent of meat causing my mouth to water, reminding me how hungry I am—but not for Greta. All I want is the scent I've been following for two days.

Once I get my fix, I'll be able to move on to another state. There are plenty of bad people in the world who need to die, and I'm happy to be the executioner since no one else can.

The world turns a blind eye to bad deeds, and I believe I was created to rid the world of them.

One by one, I'll absorb their fears, their deaths, and become the lore everyone has feared since they were children. I'll be the monster under their bed, the creature hiding in the closet, the noise they hear in their house at night.

I'll become the story. I'll change fiction into reality.

The boogeyman is real, and I have become him.

My nose twitches when I smell the burnt hair, causing me to lose my erection. The roots pull the long muscle into the anglerfish's mouth before the sharp teeth close around it.

I laugh so loud, so deep, I know she can still hear me as the fire swallows her body.

Her screams are now silent, and all that's left are the burnt bones and flesh of what she used to be.

Since her brain no longer exists, I can't play with what she fears most, and I have to settle back into the boring landscape of reality. Her body is smoking from the flames, half of her skeleton is showing, and one of her eyes hangs from the socket.

With a soft poke against her shoulder, she falls to the side.

"I did make a promise, didn't I? I can't believe I almost forgot, Greta. Why didn't you remind me?" I squat, digging my claws into her scalp, and yank it apart.

Her hair breaks, and what is left of her flesh begins to tear from the skull.

I begin to break her bones from her body, tearing each limb from the socket and shaking off the chunks of skin that were barely hanging on. The only step left is to find a way to clean the bones completely, so I can use them for the motorcycle I want to build.

If I remember correctly from when I took a few forensic

science classes back when I was human, dermestid beetles are used to eat the flesh to clean them. Those are easy enough to find.

I dump the bag of antlers on the ground and replace them with Greta's bones. She's small, so they easily fit in the oversized duffel bag, especially in bits and pieces.

I'm so excited. I can't wait to have a motorcycle that fits my new form.

Staring at her half-burnt face, I zip the bag shut, toss it over my shoulder, and admire the scene before I leave.

Two dead bodies and a pile of skin are all that's left behind. The cause of death will be obvious, but what caused it? Who?

The police will never figure it out.

Giving the scene my back, I follow the warm citrus scent again through the darkness of the woods, using my vampire speed now that I'm not hunting Greta.

Thunder rolls through the night, lightning veining across the sky. In the next breath I take, rain begins to pour. I tilt my head back, allowing the water to rush down my face. It cleans the blood from my horns, the slight taste of iron ghosting over my lips.

I stop at the edge of a cliff, overlooking an abyss of emptiness, even though the aroma that has ruined my appetite is stronger. It's as if whatever belongs to the delicious scent is right in front of me, yet I can't see it.

I growl low in my throat, the roots spread across the ground as my frustration builds. Lightning pulsates again, illuminating what I thought was an empty space to show a small town nestled in the valley of the mountains.

My claws curl around the edge of the cliff, inhaling that scent again.

Yes. Yes.

The scent is coming from someone in that town.

Flipping over the edge, I sink my claws into the rock, gliding down the steep hill until I hit solid ground. On all fours, I crawl through wet leaves and twigs until I get to the tree line, staring down a black paved road that has buildings on either side.

No lights are on except for a small pink sign in the distance that says 'Demi's Diner', and I don't give a fuck about that place. All I want is to find the source of the scent so I can move on with my life.

Using my vampiric speed, the aromatic scent leads me straight to Cove Police Department. I stay slinked in the alley across the street, curious what is so special about this police station.

The building is made with a light-yellow brick, and it is squished between two taller establishments with red paint, causing the department to stick out like a sore thumb. The window on the front is wide and frosted, so citizens can't see inside.

There's one car parked out front. It's an unmarked blue sedan with tinted windows, so no one can see inside.

With enhanced speed, I also have enhanced hearing and strength. Paired with the strong nature of the rhino DNA, I could cause so much damage.

Keys jingle from inside the station, and a second later, the most beautiful woman I've ever seen walks out. My nightmare begins to sing, wanting to sink into her bones until she fears me.

She uses the glow of her cellphone to illuminate the door to lock it. Not that locking anything would save her from me, but she can try. She looks over her shoulder, her eyes searching the street for the creeping sensation of someone watching her.

Beloved.

Mate.

Mine.

Three words are shouted in my mind from my beasts. I have no idea what the words mean, but what I do know is this woman belongs to me.

She's my Little Dream.

Regardless of how succulent she is, her dreams aren't safe from me either. I can't wait to taste what she fears when she falls asleep tonight.

I'm going to follow her home, and I'm going to give her a taste of what's to come.

The law can't save her now.

Her nightmares are *mine.*

OVE POLI
EPARTMENT

The one other oddity I have learned about this town is how much it rains.

This morning the weather was beautiful. The sun was warm and shining on my face, then out of nowhere, dark grey storm clouds filled the sky. Thunder booms and lightning bolts sound every few minutes. The violent rush of rain pelts against the ground and wind gusts push sheets of water to the right.

I stand on the police department's front stoop under the narrow overhang to keep myself as dry as possible. The wet cold manages to seep through my purple trenchcoat, sending a chill over the surface of my skin.

Staring out into the onyx night, the sensation of someone watching me sends shivers down my spine. I survey the street my car is parked on, searching for any movement in the violence of the storm.

If there is one thing I know about myself, it's that my instincts are never wrong. They have gotten me this far in life. I know when I'm being watched. I know when eyes are on me, and that's the dark thrill I love so much.

I love the pit that grows in my stomach. The unknown of what could happen to me at any given moment has an inkling of fear rattling my bones.

I'm addicted to fear.

I think that is what drives me to be a good cop. Not only do I push past the fear, but I crave more of it. The action of facing a dangerous person always leaves me unfulfilled after. I want the adrenaline to last.

The racing of my heart? The slight sweat of my palms? The way I hold my breath when I'm holding my gun in my hand while doing a perimeter sweep? Chasing a suspect until my legs burn?

Those moments don't even scratch the surface of what I crave, and I don't think there is anything in this world that will be able to give me the fear I want.

Lightning cracks across the sky, the electricity so bright, its glow allows me to see the entire street. In the split second of light, movement in the alley catches my attention.

The files I have tucked under my arm fall to the wet ground as I pull my weapon free from the holster. I step into the rain, aiming towards the alleyway where I thought I saw someone.

I would say it is nothing in a town this small, but after meeting Creed, I know there is more than what meets the eye when it comes to this place.

The rush of raindrops hinders my vision. My hair becomes drenched, and my clothes become heavy with water as I walk down the steps.

Keeping my gun pointed ahead, I look left and right to check for traffic and cross the street. I try to be as quiet as possible, my steps light in the puddles forming in the road.

The street itself is quiet. No people are outside. No cars

have driven by. Street lamps flicker in the heavy rain, strobing the atmosphere with an eerie warning.

Pressing my back against the brick building adjacent to the alleyway, I push my wet hair out of my face. My heart is pounding in my chest. My own breath is hard to regulate as adrenaline rushes through my bloodstream.

A throb forms between my legs, the search for danger igniting the lust that dangerous situations create. Nothing eases the desire until I'm home, my fingers knuckle deep inside my pussy.

Taking a deep breath, I turn and place myself in the middle of the entryway to the alley, aiming my weapon into the darkness. To the left are a row of dumpsters and recycle bins, and to the right are broken-down cardboard boxes that are now soggy from the rain.

"I'm Detective Lula Sanchez from the police department." I pull out my gold badge from my pocket, hoping whoever is in the alley can see it so they aren't afraid of me. "If you need help, please show yourself. I'll put my gun away to show you I'm not a threat." I tuck the weapon into my holster, raising my hands to show I'm here with pure intentions.

I wait for someone to reply, to show themselves, but it's only me standing here alone with the plummeting splashes of rain against the pavement.

"If anyone is here and you need anything, all you have to do is go across the street and ask for me by name, okay?" I raise my voice to shout over the abusive amount of rain. I place a hand against my chest, giving myself a light pat when I introduce myself again. "Ask for Detective Lula Sanchez, and I'll help you. I promise, okay? I can't help you if you hide. I understand you're scared, but I won't hurt you. I'm only here to help."

I wait, standing there in drenched clothes while the rain hinders my vision. I lick my lips, the cool water drenching my dry throat. The longer I stand here in the dark, the more I know I'm not alone.

Someone is here. I feel their eyes on me, analyzing me, drinking me in. It's almost like a thick grime slithering over my body, violating me from head to toe.

A cracking noise has me turning my head, whipping out my cellphone to turn the flashlight on to see what it is. I jerk the light back and forth, shining it on the walls on either side of me.

My breath comes out in quick, chilled clouds as I shine the light against the dumpster.

A long vine or maybe roots creep on the side of the dumpster.

I blow out a breath, relieved and sad; the sound didn't belong to a person.

"I'm going to leave!" I shout just as a loud roll of thunder shakes the atmosphere, silencing my attempt to communicate. "You can come into the station tomorrow and ask for me if you want. I'll be there at eight in the morning." I scan the alley one last time, holding my breath when my mind thinks the bags of trash lining the ground are a body.

There's no one here. I'm psyching myself out.

"Hay, Dios mío," I say to myself, pinching the bridge of my nose at my own actions. I can't believe I've run into a dark place, alone, without backup, again.

It's another reason why I left New York City. My captain was tired of me running into the unknown without my partner to keep me safe. He didn't understand that I didn't want to be safe. I didn't want a safety net.

There will always be a part of me that wants to be caught.

I begin to walk away, my shoes squishing with every step I take since my socks are drenched to my skin.

"Lula-lala-la-la-laaa."

I pause mid-step, turning my chin to my shoulder to see if I heard my name like I thought. A few long seconds pass without anything but the steady pounding of rain.

"You are being ridiculous, Lula," I say to myself, looking left and right down the street before I cross it.

One car drives by, its headlights so bright, I have to lift my hand to cover my eyes. Once the coast is clear, I step onto the street, needing to get into my car and head home. The time has gotten away from me, and it is much later in the evening than I initially thought.

"Lula-lala-la-la-laaa," is breathed on the back of my neck.

My skin rises in goosebumps, and the need to run for my life screams inside my soul.

I spin around, my hand on my weapon, but no one is there. It's just me standing in the middle of the road in the middle of the night and imagining wild scenarios because I'm sleep-deprived.

Leaning against the side of the car, I pat my pockets for the keys when it hits me that I had the files in my hand before I felt someone watching me.

"Fuck," I curse, jerking my head up to the files spread out on the front steps of the police station. "No. No, no, no." I dash to the steps, gathering every single piece of paper that fell from the files when I drew my weapon from its holster. "This can't be happening. Not on my first day." I don't bother inspecting them. There's no time to waste. I shove the scattered papers into the folder, uncaring if the information becomes mixed together. I can always separate everything once I dry out the papers. "Why do you always do that? You sabotage yourself just to chase a ghost that is never there," I scold myself, holding up a piece of paper that is so wet, water drips from the corners.

I groan in frustration. "This can't be happening." It's my fault. It always is, but these files have to be saved. I spent the entire day researching and studying old case files that were never solved. Not because the sheriff couldn't handle it, but they didn't have the resources to dedicate to solving these cases with such a small police force.

After going through the cabinet of 'Unsolved Mysteries', which is what Zig calls it, I plucked four files and studied every single sentence in them belonging to the alleged suspects.

Once the files are tucked under my arms, I dig my hand into my pocket and press the unlock button of my car, then run through the rain.

Opening the driver's side door, I peek at the alley one more time, and the sensation of someone watching me is still there. Not wanting to waste any more time in the rain, I slip into the car and slam the door, not pressing the lock button.

"Lula-lala-la-la-laaa."

I freeze when I hear the creepy song again. It reminds me of the children in horror movies who sing in the dark, only this voice is much deeper. It cracks and breaks, almost as if there is a constant growl or a foreign object is caught in their throat.

Glancing into the rearview mirror, a pair of black eyes stare back at me, and I scream at the top of my lungs. I turn around to look at the creature who broke into my car, but nothing is there.

No one is there.

"You are losing it tonight, Lula." I blow out a breath mixed with disappointment and relief that no one is in my vehicle.

I'm ready to go home, take a hot shower, and go to sleep.

The ride home is quick since the town is so small. I follow the same main road, passing Demi's Diner on the right. Jake wasn't lying when he said they had the best food and coffee in town. I could see myself eating there three times a day.

I crank the speed of the windshield wipers, needing one more additional speed with how fast and hard this rain is falling. At this rate, I won't be able to see the road at all.

The tall trees blend together in the night, appearing to be dark holes in the world instead of a forest. A bolt of lightning allows me to see the long road, and someone or something standing in the middle of it.

The closer I get, the more I realize he isn't going to move. My eyes widen, unable to see what he looks like between how dark it is and the heavy flow of rain. I slam my fist on the horn, pressing the middle of my steering wheel in long beats to warn the guy to get out of the way.

I can't brake. I'm going too fast, and the tires will slide against the pavement with how wet it is.

"Move! Muévete! Move out of the way!" I scream at him even though he can't hear me.

I yank the steering wheel, swerving to the left. That familiar thrill buzzes my body, and the panic and fear sprinkle on top. The terrifying moment the car fishtails, I try to correct myself, turning the wheel left, then right as the metal box changes direction.

The tires hit the grass, continuing to skid. I fly over the

ditch. I can't see out the windshield. The rain is still slamming against the glass, blurring whatever is hopefully not in my way, but all motion has to end, right?

Marilyn Manson's voice creeps through the speakers, life still moving on even if I'm seconds away from impact. The car becomes darker; the windows covered by a shadow. Metal creaks, the frame crunching, and I come to a sudden hard stop.

The momentum has my head smashing against the steering wheel, sending me into the darkness of sweet dreams.

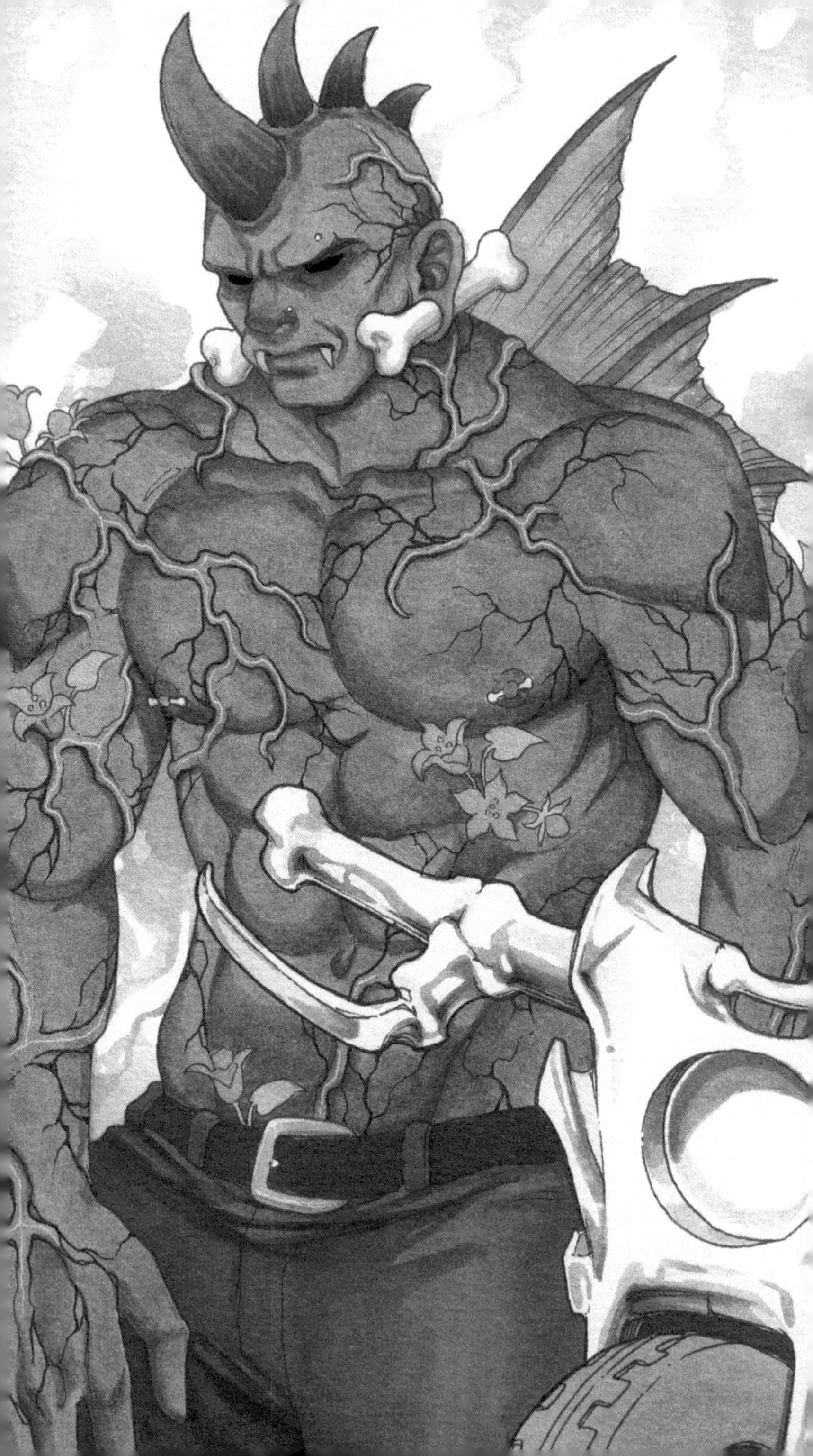

CHAPTER FOUR
SHADE

I'm frustrated that I want to save the *creature* in the car that decided to swerve off the road instead of hitting me.

Humans.

I can't believe I used to be one. She was going the speed limit—like a responsible adult—and taking too long to get home, so I decided to stop her. If she had risked my life, hit me, and driven away, none of this would have happened. I wouldn't have to save her life from ceasing to exist.

That bothers me.

I don't give a shit about anyone else. Why do I give a fuck about her? Even angry, I can't stop myself from being curious. I lower her vehicle to the ground as gently as I can.

When she was in the alley and Lula was close enough for her scent to spread across my taste buds for me to taste, every beast gripped onto my skeleton like prison bars, shaking to be set free.

Mark her.

Claim her.

Fuck her.

Kill her.

Bring her back to life.

Mine. Mine. Mine.

It's all that I could hear.

Curious, I drop to all fours and walk to the side of the car, where I smell her scent drowning the air I breathe in.

She's bleeding.

Forgetting my own strength, I rip the driver's side door from the hinges and throw the metal into the woods. The glass belonging to the window shatters when the door crashes into a nearby tree.

I stare at her unconscious form, tilting my head left to right as I examine this creature.

"You know what I find interesting about you, Little Dream?" I drag my claw across her face, leaving a slight scratch as I tuck her long, dark, wavy hair behind her ear.

She's so beautiful. Too beautiful for a world that's so dark. I dislike that I'm drawn to her light.

It annoys me.

She has a small nose that slightly curves at the tip. Her lashes are thick and curl so much that they almost reach her eyebrows. Lula's cheekbones are high with a defined jaw.

I rub my claw across the plump clouds of her lips, my cock stirring behind the anglerfish teeth. My eyes drift down her body, her clothes still soaked and forming to her every curve.

"You are delectable, aren't you?" I growl, licking the edge of my teeth when my claw rips a button from her blouse. Her cleavage shows, tempting me to do more than stare. "You are beautiful. I never thought I'd find anything beautiful again besides death."

Leaning closer, I inhale her, allowing the aroma naturally pouring from her into my body. Underneath the citrus warmth of her unconscious, something else lingers. It's the same scent from the alley, and I remember it surprising me.

"You were so afraid, Lula, and yet while you searched for me in the night, you were aroused. By the smell of it," I inhale again, "You still are. What am I supposed to do with you now? You're out here, in the open, vulnerable, and for the taking." I lean in closer, my tongue flattening against her cheek, then lick up to her forehead to gather the blood dripping from the cut on her temple.

The anglerfish's mouth opens, my cock hardening from how good she tastes.

"You taste better than fear, Little Dream." I haven't been able to stomach anything except the singular drop of blood from Lula that I just stole.

My hunger has been slightly curbed, but I need more.

I need so. much. more.

"I'm so hungry for you, Lula. You've been haunting me for days, taking my attention away from the matter at hand, and that isn't fair to me. You have interrupted my plans. I'm angry at you for that because I don't understand why I seem to want you more than the destruction I want to cause," I growl, wanting her to hear in her subconscious just how much she annoys me.

"You captivate me too." My gaze falls to her breasts, the lace edges of her bra showing from where a button plucked free.

My mouth waters, wondering what she's hiding under all those clothes. Her white blouse is sheer from how wet she is from the rain. I'm able to see the deep olive of her skin peeking through the damp material.

Temptation to strip her bare and see how much she can take has seeded itself in my mind.

"Hey, what's going on over here?"

A deep snarl vibrates in my throat, the nightmare singing to enter the intruder's head.

"I'll be back, Lula." I lick the wound on her head again, wanting more blood, humming in approval from how delightful she tastes. "Don't even think about going anywhere," I whisper into her ear. "Lula-lala-la-la-la." I can't help but sing, needing her to know how haunted she is going to be for the rest of her life.

A light bounces off the side of the car until it lands on me, the hulking form curling over a woman's body.

Mate.

Mine.

Beloved.

The three words are thundering in my thoughts, shouting into the void of my heart.

"Holy shit. The Devil has come," the stranger's voice shakes, the light becoming erratic as it lands on me.

I look over my shoulder, smirking at the man who has no idea that he is about to die. If he hadn't been a good person to stop and check on a sweet, innocent woman who was unconscious in the car, his death could have been prevented.

The rain is steady, the flashlight capturing how hard the drops are falling from the onyx clouds.

I stand to my natural height, towering over the small human who calls himself a man. He tilts his head all the way back, mouth open in shock, and the flashlight points up to my face.

He drops the flashlight, the hard plastic clattering to the ground. The bulb bursts, casting us in the night with the hiss of rain.

A dark chuckle escapes as I watch him tremble in fear. He surprises me, though. I expect him to remain frozen in place, like most do when they see me. He backs away, then steps to the side to round the front of his car.

"I won't...say...a word," he stammers, his teeth clattering together. "Your secret is safe with me." He opens the driver's side door and slips inside.

The windshield wipers squeak from left to right. He doesn't even shut the door before he slams on the gas. The tires spin against the wet pavement, smoke billowing from his back tires. In four large strides, I'm behind the vehicle and grip the bumper with one hand, lifting the backend off the ground.

His eyes meet mine in the rearview mirror, the rain unable to drown the scent of his fear. Lifting the car into the air completely, he screams at the top of his lungs, and I swing the car over my head as if it were a baseball bat, then slam it onto the ground.

The road cracks from the force, and large chunks fly into the air, making the road impossible to drive on. His head smashes against the steering wheel, causing the horn to blare through the night.

I walk around the car, punch through the driver's side window. The glass tries to cut into me, but the tough hide of my rhino skin prevents it. Gripping him by the back of the neck, I yank him outside, dragging his face along the broken, jagged edge of the window.

He screams, his fear an unexpected, tasty treat, and yet his scent doesn't even compare to Lula's. While his is bitter and sharp, hers is sweet and smooth—a dessert that's a guilty pleasure.

"Please," he begs, bloody drool dripping from his mouth. "Please, don't. Please. I'll leave you alone. I won't say anything. I won't tell anyone. I promise. I swear. No one will believe me anyway."

I smell his truth. He isn't lying.

But I don't care.

His good-intentioned soul means nothing to me.

I lift him by his throat, his feet dangling off the ground. His eyes are level with mine. Shards of glass are embedded in the right side of his face. Blood drips, flowing down his jaw onto my hand.

Before I smelled Lula's blood, I would have drunk him dry. No blood would have gone to waste. Now, I curl my lip in disgust. The only red nectar I want belongs to the lovely little dream in the other vehicle.

"You've interrupted me with my mate. That is unforgivable. She is mine. No one interrupts me with what is mine." I take my other hand and dig my claws into his lower back, igniting loud cries of help from him.

Roots grow over my body, then stretch across to his chest, slithering up his face. Nightshade berries bloom, forcing him to inhale the poison on his next breath.

His body becomes deadweight, but his eyes remain alive, round and wild.

"What do you fear the most?" I tilt my head, wanting nothing more than to turn his sweetest fantasies into a nightmare that would kill him.

A whimper sounds, but it doesn't come from the man in my grasp. I turn my head, listening to Lula's breathing to make sure she's still unconscious.

She settles a few seconds later, the whimpering easing to silence.

"I don't have time to play with you like I want," I sneer, the roots swirling around his neck to replace my hand.

He gurgles something, but I don't care enough to figure out the words. His face is red, the blood trapped in his face from how tightly the roots are squeezing him.

If I had a camera, I'd take a picture so I could remember this moment forever.

My claws dig into his lower back, and I rip the skin, tearing it in half. I bury my hand inside and wrap it around his spine, the bones having no clue they are about to be pulled from their home.

He is still attempting to yell, but only a mouse could hear the small, little yips escaping him.

"Wrong place. Wrong time. That's all." A fresh new wave of fear feeds me. "It will be over before you know it." I flex my claws into the side of his face and drag them down, ripping his flesh open so much, I can see his molars and jawbone.

"La-lala-la-la-laaa."

"Ignore that." The nightmare emerges from me, stretching over me, which has this stranger peer up to the black, ominous clouds. "He's hungry for more of your terror." I lean in, brushing my lips against his cheek as I speak. "But your terror isn't good enough for me." My eyes slide to Lula's car. "My standards have changed."

My nightmare screeches in protest as I yank the man's spine from his body. Blood pours like a waterfall onto the pavement and my bare feet. Unraveling the roots from his throat, the body drops to the ground. His lifeless eyes stare at me, his cheeks still wet from tears.

No one ever knows when they are going to die. That's what makes their death a little sweeter. The plans they had for tomorrow will never come. All their hopes and dreams have come to an end.

So sad.

Anyway.

"I won't be needing this." I place the spine onto his body, giving his torso a small pat. "You seem to need it more." I smirk at my own joke, then step over him and head back to my mate.

I need to figure out what that word means. With how strongly I feel towards Lula, I'm assuming it means I belong to her too.

"Sorry about that, Little Dream. I never want us to be interrupted again. I feel very protective—no—possessive of you, Lula. You've been possessing my mind for days. You belong to me. I know you don't understand that, but you will, Detective. You're good at piecing things together. You'll figure me out before you understand what's happening to you." I reach over to the passenger seat, searching for her purse to get her address.

I'm not finding it.

I pat the pockets of her purple coat, growling in approval when I feel something inside her pocket. Slipping it out, she surprises me with a money clip that holds one credit card, her license, and cash. I reach back in her pocket and pluck out her keys.

"You look so pretty in your license photo. No one looks that good in a damn picture." I'm annoyed with her beauty.

How the hell is she going to stomach staring at me?

Too fucking bad. She's going to have to get used to it.

Grabbing her phone, I type her address from her license into the GPS app. When it gets done loading, the time to her house is only three minutes.

"You were so close to being free of me tonight. And what a travesty that would have been for you." I wrap my arms around her and throw her over my shoulder, snag her coat and the files under it, then speed to her house by following the directions on the map.

The air is cool from the storm, the fog rolling over the

ground. With every exhale, my breath turns to vapor, and all I hope is that Lula is breathing it in.

It doesn't take long to get to her house. I stand at the bottom of the steps, staring at the red-painted front door. The porch wraps around, and a swing is to the right by the door, while a few rocking chairs are to the left. The grass is a little overgrown, and something about the house itself seems empty.

She hasn't made it home. It's missing the touch of her beauty.

I climb up the steps, the wood groaning from my weight. Opening the screen door, I accidentally rip it from its hinges.

"Fuck." I put the key in the lock, careful not to break it and leave her vulnerable. "I'll fix that." I step into the foyer, the blood on the pads of my feet slick against the hardwood floors.

A coat rack is the only object to the left with a simple pair of shoes tucked beside it. I toss her coat onto it, rocking the rack on its legs.

I have to bend down to walk through the archway that leads to the living room. A small yellow sectional couch sits next to the fireplace. No boxes frame the room. It's as if she just moved in, but there's no way to prove it. There's a coffee table, too, that has seen better days. It's worn, the finish rubbed off, and the corners chipped. I toss the damp files on the surface, allowing me to readjust Lula in my arms.

Peering around the room, the only thing on the wall is the TV that is mounted. No pictures. No art. No decorations of any kind.

Her house is bare.

"Did you just move here? Why don't you fucking own

anything, Lula? I don't like this. I'll steal you everything you could ever want. How do you live like this?" I have to pass through the kitchen to get to the bedroom.

Out of curiosity, I open the cabinets to find them all empty except one.

One plate. One bowl. One mug. Her silverware is right next to them too. A fork, a spoon, a butter knife, and a steak knife.

Only one of each.

Opening the fridge, I snarl when I see an almost-empty jug of milk and a half carton of eggs to the side.

That's it. That's all that is in her huge stainless-steel fridge.

"Little Dream," I growl in warning. "You aren't taking care of yourself. I don't like that. I will feed you. You have to be strong for me, or I'll kill you. I'm serious. I probably will. I think it would bother me too." I stare down at her, her eyes closed, and her chest rising and falling, proving she is still alive from the accident I caused.

She's...softening me in ways that I don't like.

"Yes, it would most definitely bother me." I brush a long strand of hair from her face so I can see her.

She hums, nestling her face into my chest.

It softens me even more.

I growl in distress from the new feeling of warmth spreading across my chest when I stare down at her. I'm not sure how I feel about being forced to care about this human, but I know I'll do everything in my power to protect her.

She's mine now.

Opening the nearest door, an empty room is revealed. Nothing is in here except dust.

"Detective, we are going to have to talk about this," I warn.

I try another door, revealing another room with—shocker—nothing fucking in it.

"Do you even live here?" I grumble, trying another door which opens to a bathroom.

Even the bathroom is empty. There's no shower curtain, no towels, no toothbrush. I begin to worry, wondering if this is even Lula's home, when I open one last door, and her scent hits me as if I've struck a wall.

Bending down again to walk through the doorway, I stand in her room, realizing this is where she must spend most of her time. The room itself is still a bit sparse. It has more personality than the rest of the house.

There's a long wooden dresser against the wall that seems to be used too. The drawers are worn, and a few don't have handles. There's a crack running down the surface of it, and it's just as worn as the coffee table in the living room.

A mirror is attached to it as well, the edges rusted, and there's a picture slipped into the groove between the wood and glass. It's of an older couple on the beach with emerald-colored waters behind them.

The woman looks similar to Lula except older. Her hair is long and brown with streaks of grey, and she has a few more wrinkles on her face. This couple must be Lula's parents.

"So sorry your daughter is damned to be trapped with a monster like me. I am, quite literally, your worst nightmare for her." I pluck the photo free and turn it around. No one should be allowed to see Lula, not even her parents' memory trapped in a photo.

I analyze her room to try to get to know this woman

who is my mate. She seems to only live off what she needs, not wants, but there is a trickle of what she loves in this room.

Bright, colorful green curtains hang on the window, the bottoms fur-lined in dark green. Her comforter matches, the very bottom lined in fake feathery material.

Two pillows are at the head of the bed, and a deadly rage builds inside me, wondering who the fuck shares her space.

I'll kill him to make her love me. I don't care what I have to do.

A lamp sits on a nightstand, along with a laptop and a bottle of water. A connected bathroom is to the left, where all her toiletries are. The towels are various shades of green.

"Is green your favorite color?" I ask, noticing the way my heart seems to skip a beat in hopes that it is because my entire being matches the glimpse of her personality she's allowed herself to show in her room.

And there is only one toothbrush, which makes me release a breath.

Good. No one else shares her space.

I set her on the bed, carefully placing her head on the pillow. Picking up a fistful of her hair, I bring it to my nose, inhaling deeply, and drift the silky strands over my cheek.

"You smell so good, Little Dream." I crawl on top of her, caging her head in with my hands, and drag my nose down the soft flesh.

Her bed breaks, the slabs underneath snapping in half from my weight, and the entire mattress falls to the ground.

"Oops. I'll fix that for you. You're going to need a stronger bed so I can fuck you properly in it." I cut her shirt from her body with a quick slice of my sharp claw, revealing the sexy light blue lace bra.

Her brows pinch together, and she turns her head, pressing her uninjured side of her face against the pillow. A blue and purple bruise spreads across her cheek from hitting the steering wheel.

A feeling of guilt swims in my veins, irking me with emotions. I do not like that my mate was hurt because of me. I'll have to find ways to apologize. Is there a way I can heal her? I noticed that I heal quickly. The scientists said that's due to the vampire DNA. If I had her drink my blood, would she heal?

I don't bleed normally. When I'm cut, black smoke drifts into the air. I'm assuming it's the nightmare that lives within my skin.

"I'm sorry you hurt yourself trying to save me." I pop the button off her slacks, and it clinks onto the hardware floor. "You should have hit me, Little Dream. I wouldn't have been hurt. You're so sweet to think of me though." Her zipper grinds as I lower it. "No one has ever thought of me before. Not like that. No one has ever cared about my life before."

I grab her hips, fisting the material of her pants in my fists, and tug them down her legs. "Let's get you out of these wet clothes." My claws tear into clothing, and I rake them down, the threads breaking to reveal her body.

Ripping the remaining shredded pieces of pants from her, I drop the scraps to the floor. My eyes slide up and down her body, my cock emerging from the sharpened teeth.

"Tell me, Lula, have you ever been devoured inside and out before?" I straddle her legs, my cock dragging across her stomach, large puddles of precome pooling on her navel as my want for her drips free. "Let me give you a little tease of what the rest of your life is going to be like." Roots begin to snake free from my body, wrapping around her ankles.

Tugging her legs apart, I tie one ankle to the bedpost, then the other. I do the same with her arms, wanting her spread out before me like a meal waiting to be ravaged.

She groans again, turning her head in the other direction on the pillow. Goosebumps arise on her skin as I skim the tip of my claws down her thigh. The flesh gives in warning not to press any harder, or I'll cause her to bleed.

I wonder how much she can take before she screams for me.

"I bet you'll wonder what you did in life to be cursed with a monster like me. The truth is, I don't know what you did to be damned to a twisted, unfortunate soul like me. It's too late to make it right. Whatever wrongs you've made in your life for Fate to deem me your other half, I'm not going to complain one bit."

The roots travel up her body, veining outward by cupping her tits. I'm able to sense everything through my root system. I must have nerves that connect me to them. The glide of her skin strokes the nightshade's lifeline, and my entire body shivers.

Snapping her straps and panties off her, she lies under me completely bare for my monstrous eyes to see.

A growl builds in my throat, the roots retreating so I can take her in fully, only to expose a small tattoo right in the space between her hip and pussy.

Such a delicate area.

I bend down, licking the small tattoo with a smile when I read that it says, 'Thrill Me.'

"I'm starting to see why you were bound to me." Even her skin tastes better than any amount of blood I've ever tasted. A wave of citrus explodes over my tongue as if I've sucked from an orange, and the juice is flowing down my throat.

"I'll do so much more than thrill you, Little Dream." I drag my fang down her inner thigh, wanting nothing more than for her skin to break so she bleeds.

I'm parched, and I know she'd quench my thirst.

"Such a perfect body. It's a shame that I'm going to destroy it every night." Curling over her small, fragile body that I could easily break, I hover my lips above hers. Her exhales puff against my mouth, and my eyes roll back as I breathe her in.

Why do I want to be inside her skin? I want to be swimming in her veins. I want to be her bones, the skeleton that keeps her body intact.

I'm close, but I'm not close enough.

I lie my cock onto her stomach, the tip pressing against her chin, the length the size of her torso. I'd kill her. I'd have to rip through organs for her to take every inch of me.

Licking the shell of her ear, I whisper, "I'm not sure how you'd survive that."

Blood. Give her blood.

A voice in the back of my mind has me pressing my wrist against the anglerfish's mouth, slicing it across the teeth. I moan, my cock jerking from the pain. Black smoke drifts from the cut, and I press my wrist against her mouth, my orgasm crashing through me when she inhales as a piece of me settles into her DNA.

I come over her chest, ropes of black drenching her breasts. There's so much that it drips down her sides and onto the bed, my scent embedding into her pores.

"You smell so good when you're drowning in me." I draw a heart in the come, then write 'Mine' on the inside.

My soul settles a little when I see my mark on her. She's

inhaled my smoke, has my come on her chest, and the last thing I want to do is see what she fears.

I want her to remember me tomorrow. I want her to know she had bad dreams all night and was restless. She'll be so confused, but she's a detective, she'll figure it out.

She'll realize that someone is stalking her.

And I can't wait until she does.

I'll leave her alone for now. I want to start small, igniting her confusion.

"I'll be back for you, Little Dream," I whisper into her ear, hoping she can hear me in her subconscious.

Wanting to give her a taste of what's to come, those roots slip around her neck, and the nightshade berries bloom into beautiful purple flowers. Lula breathes in, the poison sinking into her body. I notice the moment she can't feel a thing.

Her eyes open to the horrid view of me. She tries to scream, but she can't.

I don't say a word. Instead, I reach between her legs and pinch her clit, wondering if she has sensation there or if the nightshade truly takes *all* sensations away.

She lies frozen, her amber-colored eyes watering as they look at me. So round. So wide. They are like moons high in the night sky, and I'm the complete wreckage of a furious sea, a high tide that will drown her.

Her fear is evident. It smells of sunlight, a warmth I crave on my skin.

"Lula-lala-la-la-laaa," I sing, the nightmare darkening the entire room.

And yet, the same scent is paired with her fear, just like it was in the alleyway.

Lust.

My mate loves this.

The roots tighten around her throat, threatening to kill, but I won't. I'll kill everyone in this town before I ever threaten the beat of her own heart.

More of the roots climb up her body, then braid together to create a thicker one. It slips between her pussy lips, dragging itself up and down.

She's so wet.

"My naughty, little dream craves what she doesn't understand. Just as much as I love to taste fear, you love to experience it, don't you?"

Lula tries to scream, doing her best to tug at her restraints. Her eyes drift left, then right, curious about what is holding her.

"You can't get away from me, Lula." I lean in, allowing her to see the monster that belongs to her. A fresh tear drips down her cheek, and I lick it free, gathering the sweet, salty liquid. "You can try." I pat her cheek, squeezing her chin just as the braided root slips into her entrance.

Her eyes roll to the back of her head, the sweet, succulent scent of pleasure sparking the air. The nightmare craves the darkness trapped inside her mind, begging to be set free.

Fucking her with the root, my own desire builds as I feel how tight and wet she is, as if it were my own cock experiencing the soft grip of her soaked cunt.

Lula's eyes land on my cock, widening further if that's possible, when she sees how big and thick I am. She gives a small shake of her head, afraid of what's to come.

"I'm all yours, Detective." I lick her lips. "Every." I suck her bottom lip into my mouth and moan. "Inch." Thrusting into her, the anglerfish light unravels for the first time at the base of my cock, illuminating the dark space.

I still haven't figured out what it's for, but I will.

Lula screams the best she can, but like all the others, it's more like trying to shout while having a nightmare.

You can't.

You're paralyzed.

And that's no different now.

Removing the root, I bring it to my mouth and suck her nectar free.

"Fuck, you taste so good." I release her ankles from their restraints, her skin red and bruised from how tight they were.

Lifting her hips, I watch her cunt swallow the root again, the light wanting to slip inside with it. I allow it, curious as to what it will do.

"Don't fear me, Lula. I'm only here to make all your nightmares come to life." In the next thrust, the light slips in with the root, and her insides are able to be seen.

It travels up, stopping just where her womb is.

It's showing me where I need to be in order to breed her. I growl in appreciation, loving my new abilities even further.

My cock continues to drip onto her bed, wanting nothing more than to bury itself as deep as possible.

To my surprise, Lula begins to rock against me, taking the root deeper. Pinching her clit, she keens, tossing her head back as an orgasm sweeps its way through her.

My thighs become wet with splashes, and as I peer down at her pussy, liquid squirts all over me with each tense of her orgasm.

Marking me.

I slip the root free, lift her hips, and bury my tongue inside her, wanting her to come again to quench my thirst. The longer I'm with her, the more I want, the more I fucking need.

I want her body, blood, bones, and everything in between.

My fangs slice her sensitive skin as I feast, blood trickling into my mouth with every roll of my tongue. She tastes so good that I can't help but groan, drinking her down as if I'm a dying man.

Her body begins to tense, her hips grinding down onto my tongue, wanting to come again.

Just as she is about to come, I pull my mouth free and grip the broken headboard with my hands, leering down at her elegant face. Her eyes are almost neon yellow from the tears brightening her eyes. Her cheeks are decorated in a damp sheen.

"You love terror, Little Dream?" I drag my claw down her cheek, leaving another scratch, and she squeezes her eyes shut, giving the slightest shake of her head since she can't move much more than that.

Gripping the headboard harder, the wood breaks within my grasp, and I lean down, loving to see how she cries for me.

"You ache for the adrenaline of the unknown." I press my nose against her hair again, smelling all the lies she's told herself over the years to justify what she craves.

She shakes her head again, causing another tear to break free.

The roots tighten around her throat again, this time, cutting off all air supply.

"Don't lie to me," I roar so loud, the entire house shakes on its weak foundation. "I smell it on you." I reach down, cupping one of her breasts in my hand.

I engulf her. So small. So delicate. How is such a fragile human capable of handling me?

"I can smell how much you crave more than the boring,

ordinary life you are forced to live." I tweak her nipple, and she moans, her wet lashes reflecting the light. Closing the distance between us until my lips are a ghost against her, I smile. "Can you smell yourself on me?" I breathe into her, pressing my thumb against her bottom lip until the flesh turns a lighter shade.

She nods.

"You smell so fucking good. Imagine how you taste." I press my lips against hers, knowing she is unable to kiss me back.

Not that she would.

Her arousal doesn't lie, though. It spreads into the air with every motion of my lips against hers. I slip my tongue against her, hoping she can taste why I'm so addicted to her.

Pulling back, I stare into her confused eyes, her lips beckoning me for another kiss.

"Tell me what you fear, Lula?" The black smoke drifts into her nose, and the gorgeous yellow tint of her eyes is filled with black raging seas that drip down her face.

A horn blares outside, then voices shout from seeing the accident. I pull out of her mind, sheathe my roots from her wrists, and she falls unconscious again.

"Another time. I'll be seeing you soon." I kiss her forehead, hating to leave her.

I know before I step foot out of this house, I need to do more to claim my territory. This house, this woman, everything inside of it, around it, belongs to me.

Entering her bathroom again because I know there are many things I can defile in here. Taking a peek at her sleeping, I rummage through the medicine cabinet, not finding anything of value that I can ruin with my scent.

Grumbling under my breath, I bend down to open the

cabinet below and smack my head on the counter, growling at the damn thing being in my way.

Rubbing the spot on my forehead, I rummage through the bottles of skincare. How much skincare could one woman have? The entire cabinet is full.

"Perfect," I mumble with a smile, holding a container that is a charcoal face mask. Twisting off the top, I grin, walking over to Lula's bedside, and swipe my come from her chest and into the bottle.

I twist the lid back on, give it a good shake, and place it back where I found it.

Yes, that's exactly what I needed to do. I feel better knowing she will smell of me every time she goes to pamper herself after a long day. I write her a quick note on the mirror before leaving the bathroom.

Grinning, I'm unable to walk by her without giving her a kiss on the forehead. "I'll see you soon, Little Dream." My heart tugs with every step I take away from being by her side.

Dragging myself away from my obsession, I stand in her kitchen, not liking how bare it is. The smell of coffee invades my senses, and it tickles the inside of my nose. I've never been the biggest fan of coffee. If Lula is, then I'll make sure she always has her caffeine.

I follow the scent of coffee, wanting to know what kind she likes. I want to know everything about her. What she loves, what she hates, what she craves, anything, every-thing. I *need* to know.

Opening the cabinet, I pull out a giant fucking bucket of Colombian medium roast. My roots begin to slither down my arm, giving me another idea to infiltrate everything she consumes. Popping the lid off, I break a root from my arm and crush it in my hand, to the point it's just dust, and sprinkle it on top.

Whistling to myself, I snap the lid on, give it another shake, and slide it back into the cabinet as if it never left.

Blurring out of the room, I sit on the couch, the entire piece of furniture threatening to break from how much I weigh. I place all the pieces of paper out on the table to dry, reading each case as if it were my own.

Four cases she's wasting her sweet time on when her time needs to be spent on me. One I've already taken care of.

Standing, the sofa snaps in half, and I roll my eyes at how dramatic her furniture is being about my weight.

"Have sweet dreams," I whisper in the dark to her, as I fade into her home.

Lula-lala-la-la-laaa.

OVE POLI
EPARTMENT

CHAPTER FIVE

LULA

I gasp myself awake when a loud banging on the door manages to find its way into my dreams.

I *think* it was a dream. I'm not so sure anymore. The dream felt so real, but it couldn't have been. What I saw could not be living in the world amongst us. My mind is so jumbled from what happened that I can't remember what was real or what was a dream.

I only remember opening my eyes to see a giant monster hovering over me. His entire body was green with black veins and odd vines with weird flowers and berries on his body. Remembering his eyes causes me to shiver. They were pools of darkness, the color of the deepest part of the ocean that sunlight can't reach. Horns decorated his head in a way I had never seen before.

Depictions of the Devil come to mind with two horns growing out of his forehead, but this monster was very different. One large horn grew out of his forehead, followed by others behind it in a straight line, varying in size. The horns went from largest to smallest, reminding me of a mohawk.

Each ear was pierced, large bones filling the holes. His nose, eyebrow, and nipples were pierced as well, all with pieces of bone. I think it might be my imagination, but I thought I also saw a fish fin on his back.

I can't be sure, but whatever he did to me, I remember the terror I felt.

And I want more.

He's been the only one who has been able to give me what I've always craved. I become lost in thought, forgetting the men banging on my door, when I rub my legs together, and a slight ache twinges inside me. I remember in my dream that I was being fucked. I must have fingered myself to bring relief. That's the only answer.

That's the only realistic answer because the real one is too far-fetched. Dreams can't come to life.

Deepest desires can't be born from the imagination. If they could, my thrills would have been sated a very long time ago.

The loud pounding on the front door pulls me from my thoughts. I swing my legs over the bed and rub my eyes. A tightness stretches across my chest when I raise my arms. Looking down, I gasp when I see the dried black substance on my chest.

My bed is broken too. The mattress is on the floor, and the boards have snapped in half.

What the hell happened here?

"Detective Sanchez! It's Sheriff Holland. If you're here, please come to the door, or I will break it down."

"Fuck," I whisper to myself and stand, snagging my robe from the door. "One minute, Sheriff! I'm just waking up and need to get dressed!" I don't know if he can hear me from here, but I do my best to hurry.

I just bought this house, and on the salary they have given me, I don't want to replace a door.

"What the hell is going on, Lula?" I say to myself, snagging the soft robe from the hook on the back of my bedroom door. "How did I get home? I remember driving and then…" I rack my brain as I slide on my robe and tie the belt as tight as possible, so I'm covered. The last thing I need are questions that I have no answers to.

"Detective! You have ten seconds to open the door before I break it down."

"No! Don't. I'm coming!" I rush to the bathroom, flip on the light to check to see if I'm presentable, when a message on the mirror freezes me in my steps.

Sweet dreams.

"Nine, eight," Sheriff counts down.

I grab a washcloth from the counter, wet it, then scrub the message free. It can't be there. If the Sheriff saw that, he'd want answers, and the only answer I have is that I have no idea what happened.

And automatically, I'd be a suspect. I have no alibi. I only remember driving last night. It was raining.

"Five. Four—"

"—I'm coming!" I sprint from my room, through the kitchen and living room to my front door.

"Three. Two."

With a deep breath, I swing the door open to stare down three police officers.

"What's going on, Sheriff?" I ask, yawning. "Sorry, I'm just waking up. Can I put on some coffee for everyone? Morning Waylon. Zig."

"Detective," they greet me in unison.

"Coffee sounds great, thanks. I've got a few questions

for you, Detective." Jake steps into my house, his boots thudding against the hardwood floors.

"Well, come on in. Sorry it's so bare in here. I just moved in." It's easier to lie than to say this is all I own. I'm not a materialist kind of person, and it's only me who lives here. I don't need anything else, so I don't treat myself with pointless trinkets.

My job is my life. Everything else is secondary.

"Where are all your boxes if you've just moved in?" Waylon asks, standing in the middle of the living room. He studies every inch of the bland walls. "And what the fuck happened to your couch?"

"Just waiting for the rest to be delivered," I lie again, cleaning out the coffee pot and tossing the old grounds away.

"And the couch?" He pushes.
Honestly, I have no clue, but I have to lie. "It's old. I sat down on it last night and it gave out. I need to get a new one."

I don't like people knowing too much about me. The more they know, the more that can be twisted and used against you. Even though I am enjoying this town and Cove Police Department in the little amount of time that I've been here, I keep people at arm's length wherever I go.

Sheriff Holland takes off his hat, setting it on the coffee table where the case files are spread out.

A flash of a memory has me tripping over my own feet, and I catch myself on the counter.

"Lula, are you okay?" Jake asks, running to my side like the savior he is.

"I'm fine. Sorry. I'm not a morning person. Well, not when it is still dark out. What time is it?" I yawn again, my eyes burning for me to go back to sleep.

I dropped those case files in the rain. They were soaked. How the hell did they get in my house, spread out on the table?

"It's around four in the morning," he answers.

He drags one of the dining room chairs out from under the table and takes a seat. Waylon and Zig make themselves at home too, joining Jake around the table. Zig gives me a sad, forced grin while Waylon has his arms crossed, staring at me with narrowed eyes.

Setting mugs down in front of each of them, I fill their cups with steaming hot black coffee. I always keep extra mugs in another cabinet just in case I have company, but I usually keep what I use separate since I don't have many guests over. My new coworkers have already worn out their welcome, and they have no idea.

I fill my mug last, , take a seat, and cross my legs before taking a much-needed sip of the bitter brew.

"Okay, Jake. Come on. What's going on? I'm not liking how secretive this is. I have work to do."

"There's no easy way to say this, Lula, but we found your car at the end of the road in an accident."

I sit my mug down, folding my hands under my chin, then rub my palms up and down my face. "That's impossible. That can't be my car. I'm here. I'm home. I'm unharmed."

Jake leans forward, his eyes taking on a stern shine. "There's a dead body. Another car was in the middle of the road, and the man's spine was ripped from his body."

"Oh my god, that's terrible." I cover my face with my hands, knowing I'm not going to get out of this since there's a dead body in question. I'm going to have to give them answers if I want to clear myself from the suspect list.

Dropping my hands, I notice all three men are staring at me. I rear back, knowing exactly what they are thinking.

"You can't possibly think I had anything to do with that man's murder? I can't rip a spine out of someone, Jake! That's impossible. Do you know how much strength that would take? I'm flattered you think I'm strong enough to do that." I stand, the chair grinding against the floor, and slap my hands on the table. "But don't you fucking dare come into my home and question my integrity. On my badge, I did not kill that man."

Jake shakes his head, then points to my chair. "Sit down, Detective. I don't think you're a cold-blooded killer, but your car is at the crime scene. I need an explanation."

I plop down in the chair, knowing exactly how a suspect feels now when they are the ones being questioned. Zig pats me on the shoulder to comfort me, but something about his touch has me leaning away from him. My entire body felt disgusted by the friendly gesture.

That's new.

"I don't know," I reply in an ashamed whisper. "I really don't know. I remember driving home last night in the rain and swerving to miss something or someone standing in the road. Oh..." I cover my mouth in realization, my hand shaking from the truth. "Jake, did I hit him? Is that what happened? I didn't swerve? Oh god, I think I'm going to be sick."

I barely reach the sink before I'm gagging, the horror of what I've done twisting my gut.

"No! Fuck no, Lula. The victim wasn't hit by a car. We don't know what happened, but when we didn't find you in the vehicle and your house was right here, we figured you might know something."

"I don't know, Sheriff. I really have no fucking clue." I

smash my fist on the table, shaking the mugs so hard, coffee splashes outside the rim. "I don't know how I got home. I don't remember anything from last night until you were knocking on my door. Maybe someone brought me home? I don't know. I'm the suspect, though, right? That's the only answer. You'll need my badge and gun, won't you?"

"Not yet, but I need you to think, Lula. Please, what do you remember about last night?" Jake leans in, placing his hand on my arm, and I pull it away, not wanting his touch in the slightest.

For some reason, his touch isn't the one I want. I crave the touch from last night, whatever it is, whatever it came from, I know that's the touch that is meant to be mine.

"All I know is that someone was in the road. I don't know who. I remember swerving to miss them and then nothing. I might have hit my head on the steering wheel." I press my fingers against the spot on the side of my head. It's sore, but there's no cut. "After that, the next thing I remember is waking up to you knocking on my door."

Jake writes everything I'm saying down in his notepad, the scribbling of the pen louder than usual. Every curve from the letters made with the ballpoint, every dot of the i's and cross of the t's, is like a loud, constant scratch echoing all around me.

"Could you identify this guy? From mugshots? Or give a description to the sketch artist?"

I hold the mug for warmth to bring comfort. "No. It was so dark, and it was raining. I'm sorry, Jake. I'll do whatever you need me to, but I swear, I did not kill that poor man."

"Eh, don't feel too bad for the guy who died," Zig says, sighing after taking a sip of coffee. "Él era un maldito pervertido."

My eyes round in shock, nearly causing me to spit out my coffee. "What do you mean he was a pervert?"

"Our victim is a convicted sexual offender. I don't know if that was the reason for his death. He won't be missed by any means, but we still have to do our jobs."

"Unfortunately," Waylon grumbles.

"Regardless of how he will or won't be missed"—Jake exhales in exasperation—"we still have a job to do. Someone died last night, and one of our officers was there, whether she can remember it or not. It's important we figure out who was in the middle of the road. The facts are on our side. It's clear the body wasn't hit by your car. There's no blood on the front bumper, nothing like that. You hit a tree, but the real question remains. Who was in the middle of the road, and was he the person who killed the victim? If he is, that's dangerous. Any person who is ripping out spines doesn't deserve to be on the street. This could lead to other killings if he is new to town. We have to stay vigilant."

"Yes sir," Waylon says.

"You got it, Boss," Zig mirrors Waylon.

"Whatever you need from me, I'll do the best I can, Sheriff."

Jake nods, closes his notepad, and clicks his pen. "Just do your best to remember everything you can. The more details we have, the better."

"I'll think long and hard. I hope my memory will come back, and I can fill in some of those blanks."

"Great." Jake stands, and his deputies follow.

I don't. I remain seated because if I stand, I think I'll pass out from the shock of it all.

"I'll keep you updated. Don't leave town, Lula," he warns.

I stare at him incredulously. "Seriously, Sheriff? Where am I going to go? Are you sure you don't need my badge until the investigation is closed?"

He places his hat on his head. "No, Lula. I refuse for my only detective to get her badge revoked over something that wasn't her fault."

"I don't want you to get in trouble either," I point out.

"I'm the one who makes the decisions at my department, Detective. No one else. Don't worry about me."

Jake opens the door to see two people standing there in black jackets. A mist of rain collecting on their windbreakers and dribbling down their sleeves. The woman to the right has big, round glasses that are slightly fogged from the weather, and the man beside her is tall and slender, with a balding head.

Both are carrying a kit of some kind.

"Savannah. Bill," Jake greets. "What are you doing here?"

"Well, we heard you were at the suspect's house, and we need to collect evidence from everywhere. The crime scene itself has been taken care of already, but—" she peeks around Jake to stare at me. "But she might have evidence on her too."

Oh, no.

"Shouldn't this be done at the hospital, then? You aren't going to bombard her in her home."

"I don't mind giving them whatever they need. I'd rather have the privacy, Sheriff. If that's okay?" I ask him, clutching the opening of my robe to hide the dried black liquid that's on my chest.

Whatever they do, they can't find that. They will have questions, and I truly don't have the answers.

"I don't think I have anything helpful for you, but I'll try."

"Come on in, then. Make it quick. We've taken enough of the Detective's time."

"It's fine, Sheriff. I really don't mind. I want to know what happened just as much as you do."

Granted, from the small glimpses entering my mind, I have a twisted feeling that I already know what happened —a twisted nightmare can't be proven.

"¿Estás bien?" Zig sits down in the chair next to me, picking up his coffee mug again. He sits back, lifting his brows in concern.

Blowing a breath, I lift a shoulder, tapping my fingernails on the table. "I don't know if I'm okay," I admit, exhaustion hitting me. "I'm telling the truth, Zig. I really don't know what happened last night, but I didn't kill that man. I would never do that. Not unless I was protecting myself."

"Maybe he was the guy in the middle of the road? Maybe he attacked you, and you don't remember. Trauma does that to the brain," he states, bringing up an excellent point.

"Maybe, but I saw a lot of horrible things when I worked in the city. This doesn't even make the top ten. It doesn't make sense for me to forget."

Zig places his hand on top of mine, giving it a reassuring squeeze. Another gut-wrenching urge has me tugging my hand away from his touch, even though I know he means no harm.

Every touch feels wrong when it doesn't belong to the monster I dreamed of.

The forensic team follows behind Jake, and Waylon

trails in behind them, his eyes cold and narrow as if he doesn't trust them.

"Detective, do you have the clothes you were wearing last night by any chance? We'd like to collect them for evidence," Savannah states, placing her kit on the dining room table.

"Um. I think so? I don't remember how I got undressed, so let me go check." Standing, I rush to my room with every single person following me.

My right to privacy is out the window, I guess.

The clothes are on the floor next to the bed, completely shredded into useless scraps of material. Confused, I bend down to pick them up. There's a slight tremble in my hand when I give them to Savannah.

"They are torn to pieces. Do you have any marks on your body? Any wounds?" She lifts what was once my shirt into the air. and I'm able to see her face through the long gashes in the material.

I loved that shirt.

Damn it.

"No, nothing like that. I'm fine. Physically. There isn't a mark on me. Can we make this quick?"

Savannah places my clothes into an evidence bag, sealing it shut, and begins to examine my room. Before she can take another step, my hand is on her chest, stopping her.

"I don't know why you think you are comfortable enough to examine my room without a warrant, but you are mistaken. I am being cooperative. Don't even think for a second you can take advantage of that."

"Detective," Jake warns.

"No, she's right, Sheriff Holland. Apologies, Detective Sanchez. I meant nothing by it. If you could come to the kitchen so I can collect samples from you, that would be very helpful."

"Of course." I stand in the doorway, stretching my arm out to urge them to leave my room.

One by one, they trail out the door. Waylon is the last one out, shooting me a wink of support. Snagging the handle, I take a quick peek around my room to see if there is anything out of place that I need to be worried about.

The picture of my parents is turned around. The aged backside is tinted yellow, and the cursive writing from my mom can be seen, showing the date when the photo was taken.

I *never* have that photo flipped over.

Someone was in my room, and I'm going to make it my mission to find out who. This person invaded me, my home, and my sense of safety.

This is personal now.

Closing my eyes, I gain my composure as I shut the bedroom door, not wanting them to see how worried I am. Taking a seat at the four-person dining room table, Savannah begins to collect her evidence.

From hair, to scraping under my nails, to swabbing the inside of my cheek, I'm certain she has gotten everything she could possibly need.

"If you don't remember anything—"

"—Not if," I correct her, narrowing my eyes at her audacity for calling me a liar. "I *don't* remember anything." Savannah causes my trigger finger to flex.

"Right. Of course. I'm saying maybe there's something in your blood. Maybe you were drugged. It would explain it."

"So would hitting the steering wheel and getting a

concussion." I turn to Jake. "She works for the department?"

I find her incompetent.

"Let her take all the samples she needs so you can officially be off the suspect list, Lula. And then we will be on our way. Stay home today, and I'll call you with any updates."

"This is ridiculous." I shove the robe sleeve up my arm, allowing her to draw the blood she needs.

"Woah, that's interesting." Savannah lifts the vial into the air, the overhead light reflecting off the tube.

The air around me becomes hard to breathe when I see the color of my blood in the small glass tube. Suddenly, my house doesn't seem so cozy with so many people standing around me.

Savannah twists and turns the vial, her eyes laser-focused on my blood inside the glass.

Blood is red.

Mine?

For the first time in my life, it isn't only red, but black swirls have mixed in that remind me of the way smoke drifts.

"You don't remember being drugged?" Savannah questions me again, never taking her attention away from the vial.

I clench my teeth together and dig my nails into the table. "For the thousandth time, I don't remember anything. I only remember swerving off the road because someone or something was standing in the middle of it. That's all I have for you, okay? That's it. I need you all to leave. Now."

"Oh, I'm so sorry. I didn't mean to make you upset. I'm

only trying to understand why your blood would be like this."

"I've never seen anything like that either." Jake leans in closer to get a better look.

"And if I had any answers to give you, I'd give them to you. Instead, you keep asking me if I remember when I've said I don't. Take your vial and your other samples and get off my property. All of you." I drag my eyes from Savannah to Jake. "Please," I add, doing my best not to cry.

I always cry when I get too upset, and the last thing I want to do is cry in front of my new coworkers.

"Of course, Detective Sanchez," Sheriff says in an understanding, yet remorseful tone. "Come on, everyone. Let's respect Lula's privacy. Zig. Waylon. Let's go," Jake orders.

Zig stands, pouring his coffee down the sink and setting his mug on the counter. His hand lands on my shoulder, giving it a supportive squeeze.

"Todo estará bien," he says.

Yeah, well, it doesn't feel like everything is going to be okay.

Waylon is next to pour his coffee down the sink. "Hang in there, Detective. Evidence will be on our side. You're one of us. We have your back." He slaps the same shoulder that Zig squeezed, and I nearly fly out of my chair.

"Thanks, Waylon. I appreciate it."

Savannah and Bill leave without giving me another look. Good. Everything that has happened has been beyond normal. I rub my temples, wondering how the hell I have been in this town for less than three days and somehow now need to prove my innocence.

Jake watches as they leave through the front door. The only person left in the house is him.

He grips the back of a chair with both hands and hangs his head. "I know this is stressful. Usually, stuff like this doesn't happen. Well, that would be a lie, but it has toned down some. I'm sorry you're caught in the middle of what's going on, but I'm on your side, okay? If you need anything, let me know. I've put a rush on your blood samples. I want to know as soon as possible. You'll be okay, Lula."

"It doesn't feel like it, Sheriff."

"Jake. Just call me Jake right now. I'm not here as your boss. I'm here as a friend—even if we barely know each other. You're one of my cops. That means you're family now."

I swipe my fingers under my eyes to gather the tears before they break. "I promise, Jake, I didn't kill that man."

"I know you didn't. Evidence already proves that. It's why I'm not taking your gun and badge."

"Then, why can't I go to work? I have case files I need to work on."

"Because you were in a car accident. You were part of something horrible that happened, and we need to figure out what it is. You'll rest here at home today, okay? I won't hear another word about it."

I sit there, debating if I want to tell him the truth about what I did see. Do I tell him someone was in my house? A flipped photo isn't enough proof for Jake to believe me. He might think I've lost my mind.

"Before I leave, I'm going to ask one more time, do you have anything you want to tell me?" He lifts his eyes, peering at me through the shadows of his eyelashes.

"No. I'm sorry, Jake. I don't have anything. If I do, I'll call you, okay?"

"Okay. Try to relax, okay? And I'm sorry about your car;

it will be a while before I can get a new one with the budget."

"I have a Chevy Impala in the garage. I'll use mine."

"An Impala? Damn, rub it in a man's face, why don't you?"

I manage to smile through all the truths I'm keeping. "Maybe I'll let you drive it one day. If you're good."

He snorts as he walks to the front door. "There go my chances." Jake steps outside, giving me a curt nod before shutting the door.

Flying out of my seat, I sprint to lock the door and press my back against the wall.

"Everything will be fine. Last night was a nightmare, but what you thought you saw was just a bad dream. That's it. Nothing more."

I don't care that I don't know how I got home, or undressed, or my clothes shredded, or the message on my mirror, or the dried substance on my chest—I'm just glad I'm alone.

Growing up, my parents always told me I was a beacon for trouble, as it loved to find me. Granted, I've always loved the thrill of the dangers in life, it's why I became I cop. I wanted to dive into a world where I could protect people and get what I crave.

I never really believed my parents.

Until now.

I should have told Jake the truth, and yet, the thought of speaking against the monster that was in my bed leaves a bad taste in my mouth.

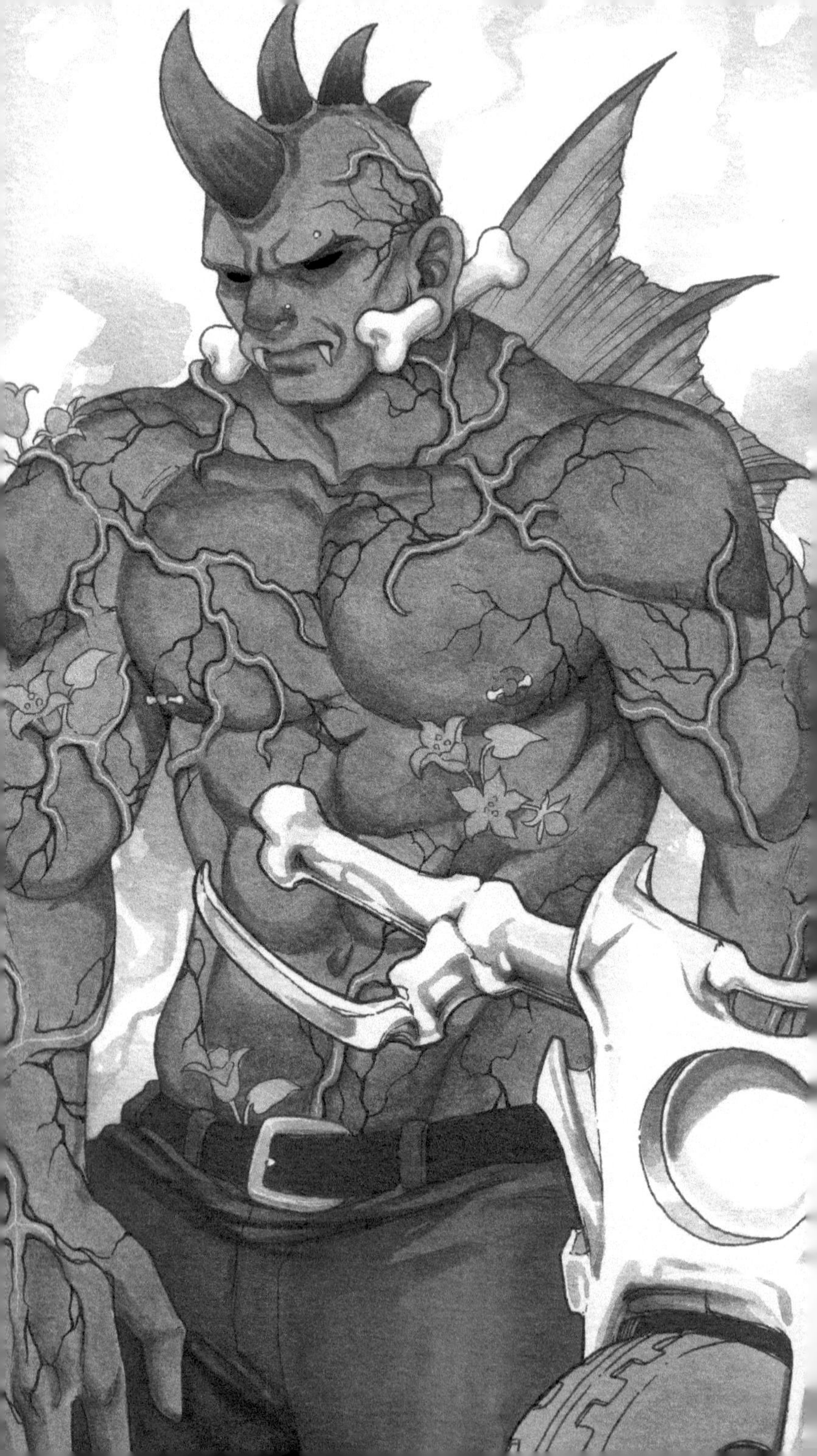

CHAPTER SIX
SHADE

I hated to leave Lula when she needed me most.

I had to leave. She isn't ready to believe in me yet.

That's okay.

She will one day very soon.

I already miss the scent of her fear and the taste of her cunt. I should have done more than feed her my blood. I should have bitten her, so she had no choice but to be bound to me. I've wasted too much time.

Lula needs to be mine.

Lula-la-lala-la-laaa.

I can't help but sing her name, the nightmare inside me desperate for her terror, her lust. Oh, I know she'd have so much desire if her reaction to me was anything like early this morning.

"Please—" The taxidermist begs as my roots wrap around his body. "You can just take the beetles. You don't need to kill me," my victim stammers, wiggling his bone-thin body against the roots that are much more powerful than him.

"Need?" My eyes lock with his, the vampire awakening

inside me to meddle in his mind. "I *want* to kill you." The longer he stares at me, the more he relaxes, his tense shoulder sagging as if he will be free. "Stay still. Don't beg. You won't be able to scream. Your cries for help will not be heard. Accept your fate."

"I accept," he drowses, a slight smile appearing on his thin, wrinkled lips.

It's clear this man doesn't get outside much or eat. By the smell of him, he is dying anyway. I don't know what from, but the scent is rancid. I'm doing him a favor so he won't have to suffer anymore. If he wasn't so hysterical about dying, he would have been able to see the gift I am giving him.

Snagging a box of flesh-eating beetles, the smoky apparatus of my nightmare slips between his lips and slides down his throat. His eyes turn black, filling to the point that it drips down his face. Such a beautiful sight.

I swipe the onyx drop and suck it into my mouth, the taste of Lula's fear still strong, and my cock awakens.

Lula-lala-la-la-laaa.

"Yes, it's her. We will go back to her tonight." The nightshades bloom over my roots, poisoning the taxidermist with every breath he takes. "Show me what you fearrrr," I drag the last word on a growl, needing his death almost as much as I need Lula's cunt filled to the brim with my cock.

I chuckle when he begins to run away from the beetles chasing him in his imagination. "Of course you're afraid to die like this. How painful would it be to be eaten alive?" I bite my teeth together, the promise of violence causing saliva to pool in my mouth. "Perhaps you can tell me. Scream. Scream, and I'll let you live."

His physical body yips like a puppy, doing his best to

follow my instructions, but inside his mind? He's screaming as the beetles crawl over him in a massive, hungry wave.

"You said you would save me!" His arm punches through the beetles, stretching to reach for me in hopes I'll save him from his impending death.

Bites on his arms begin to appear, showing that the nightmare is in full effect.

"I lied."

His final screams are music to my ears, sending a shiver of arousal down my spine. The high from killing him only has me craving Lula more.

The bites begin to show bone across his entire body. Blood begins to drip onto the floor, and I curl my lip in disgust, wanting Lula's over his.

Again.

"You're lucky I can't eat you, or I'd drain you dry before another drop got wasted on the floor." The nightmare adds a harsh whisper to the end of my sentences, empowering me more with how much stronger that side of me becomes.

Fear doesn't kill this man as he is being eaten alive. Pain doesn't make him pass out. The blood loss is what kills him.

Taking a step back, I admire my work. The roots unwrap from around him, his bite-ridden body falling back into his chair.

"Thank you for the beetles." I gather the beetles into the bag with the bones, wanting them to get an early start, then zip the duffle shut, hoping the bones will be clean by tonight.

Without a care in the world about his death, I flip the sign on the door to say 'open' since I made sure the entire business was shut down while I got what I wanted.

The next customer who walks into this shop will have

the shock of their life. If only they would be like me, uncaring if the world lost another human.

With the bag of bones in one hand, I swing the door open, the bell jingling to signal my exit. I step outside in a light mist of rain, tilting my head back to enjoy a few seconds of peace before I start wreaking havoc.

Taking a right, I walk down the sidewalk, passing a few people carrying umbrellas to protect themselves from a little rain. Everyone who looks at me takes a step away to put more space between us. They don't smell afraid of me, wary yes, but not the fear I love to entice.

That's not normal.

I need to find out why.

I'm about to cross the street when I see a face that belongs to someone in Lula's case files. She's running out of Demi's Diner with a satchel on her shoulder, a red beanie on, and she looks both ways before crossing the street.

Fireopal.

According to her file, she's a hacker. She's done a few stints in prison too, for hacking into government websites. Her record is long and dates all the way back to middle school when she was caught changing her grades in the computer system.

Fireopal was also accused of stealing three million dollars, but it couldn't be traced. She covered her tracks, and the money was never found.

"Two in one day? How lucky am I?" Crossing the street to follow her, a car blares its horn and slams on its brakes, stopping inches away.

I slam my fists on the car, denting the hood. White smoke drifts from the engine, a clicking noise sounding from the vehicle before it shuts off. The driver lifts his hands, slamming them on the wheel, and even goes as far as to step out of the car.

"What the fuck is wrong with you? You're going to pay for this to get fixed. I had the right of way."

He hasn't looked up yet from his car as he spews his anger. I step in his way, and he slams himself against my chest.

"The light was green! And you"—he tilts his head all the way back in order to see my face—"holy fuck."

I bend down, hating that I am making myself smaller for someone who doesn't matter.

I don't say a word. I take a step closer, which causes him to take a step back, naturally.

"I'm going to go. It's fine. The car is fine. No big deal. We're both unharmed, right?" He opens the driver's side door and slips in, pressing the button to lock the doors.

I'd kill him too if I weren't in such a hurry to deal with Fireopal. She's a threat to Lula, and the only threat Lula is allowed to have is me.

Pressing my hands against the side of the car, I push it out of my way, leaving the driver who tested me to live another day.

Using my vampire speed, I disappear, leaving him with more questions than before.

Fireopal is walking through the park with her headphones on, her hands shoved in her pockets.

The park is nice. Plenty of humans are around, so I can't do anything drastic just yet without bringing attention to myself. I hate attention.

Kids are playing on the playground, screaming and

laughing as they have fun. Parents are sitting to the side, watching their spawns so they are safe.

As the children play, I begin to wonder if being a father is something I'd want with Lula. I don't know if I could share her. The thought alone has violence awakening inside me.

But then, if she did have my child, she'd be bound to me in every way possible, and even my nightmare loves the idea of that.

Yessssss.

But then I hear a little human scream when he sees me. His scream turns into a full, out-of-control sob that has me clutching the bag tighter.

That high-pitched cry is annoying. I don't like it.

Flashing a fang at the annoying little boy, I continue to follow Fireopal, wondering what scheme she is up to next. I only want to focus on Lula, but I can't do that if all these outside threats take her attention away from me.

Every aspect of her life belongs to me. Her body. Her mind. Her time. Even the breaths she takes belong to me. No one deserves Lula's energy. The more distractions I take from her, the more of her I'll be able to get.

The problem is that her world doesn't revolve around me. There are people taking her attention, like Fireopal, when Lula's attention needs to be on me.

The only way her world can rotate on its axis is if I'm the one spinning it. Her universe will become mine, and the only stars she sees will be the light I provide.

Fireopal stops in her tracks, looking left, then right. I bet the hairs on the back of her neck stand up. Her instincts are telling her something bad is about to happen.

It's me.

I'm that something bad.

I sit on a nearby bench, the iron rods bending from my weight, and open the bag to pretend I'm busy. The beetles are doing an amazing job. They have already taken so much flesh off in such a short amount of time.

Lifting my head, Fireopal is on the move again. This time, she's walking faster.

I zip the duffel bag, and a beetle manages to get in the way, the guts spewing everywhere. Uncaring, I sling the bag on my shoulder and continue on to satisfy my kill list.

My boots thud against the pavement. Fireopal must sense me again because she starts to walk even faster, clasping her bag to keep it still.

She'll never be able to outrun me. Her time in this town and wasting my mate's time has expired.

I pick up the pace, not calling on my vampire side just yet. I want to scare her first. I want to be able to smell the fear I instill inside her. I want to be able to hear the tremor of terror tremble her bones.

And I always get what I want—regardless of the methods used.

She looks over her shoulder, eyes widening when she spots me, and stops in her tracks.

I do the same, tilting my head as I wait for her to decide what to do.

I love playing with my meal. She's so sweet to think there will be a tomorrow when there won't even be a tonight.

There it is.

Fear.

The bitter-sweet aroma plays a symphony in my head, the chorus of untuned strings paired with the wrong tempo.

It's the sound of chaos.

She swallows, taking a step back, then another, and another, doing her best to put as much space between us without me noticing. With every step she takes, I step forward, showing her that no matter what she does, there's no escape.

Fireopal darts her eyes across the street to an old, rundown building.

Killlllll. The shadow within me hisses, spit filling my mouth in response to its hunger.

Every few seconds, a car passes by on the street, the hum of the tires cutting through the children's laughter from the playground. The beetles in the bag skitter together, feasting on what's left of Greta's flesh.

"Listen, asshole. I don't know what you want, but you have no idea who the fuck you're messing with. I can take everything from you in the blink of an eye. I can target anyone you care about. I'll take from you, from them, and then anyone they love too. Fuck with me, and so many lives connected to you will be ruined. Is that what you really want?" She smirks with so much confidence while not knowing that all the confidence in the world couldn't save her from a killer like me.

I'm so curious as to how she isn't running away from me. I know what I look like, and I don't understand why everyone here doesn't run away from me.

I don't like that.

I need them to run away. I want to chase. My victims running for their lives. The taste of fear is so much sweeter then. I wonder if Lula would run and let me chase her. She seems to like being afraid, which is perfect for me. The nightmare that lives inside me always needs to feed, and with my mate by my side, I'll be able to get my fill whenever I want.

"What the fuck do you want, freak?" she spits, digging into her satchel and pulling out a gun.

I chuckle, spreading my arms wide. "Go ahead, Fireopal. Let's see what you can do before I catch you," I threaten, hoping she pulls the trigger because nothing makes me harder than pain.

"Mommy, she has a gun."

I turn to see a kid pointing his finger at Fireopal. He isn't afraid. I can't smell his fear until his mom screams. Her panic causes a domino effect. Children and parents everywhere begin to panic, sweeping their children in their arms to run as far away as possible. The massive crowd being afraid fills the air with so much fear, the worst part of me chitters in approval.

Taking a massive, deep breath, I let the fear of children and parents seep into my lungs. There's so much. I'm drowning in terror, and it feels so fucking good.

"It doesn't matter what I want from you. It's what I need from you. And you have the attention of someone who is mine. I can't have that," I growl, taking a step forward to entice her violence.

When I was human, not many had enough hate within themselves to pull the trigger.

"Do it," I beg her. "Fucking do it and then? It's my turn." My voice deepens, the monsters inside me trying to break free.

"La-lala-la-la-laa."

"What the hell was that?" she shouts, waving the gun at me. "Stop messing with my head."

"I can't help it. Heads are my favorite place to be." I take another step, and Fireopal pulls the trigger. The loud crack of the bullet leaving the chamber has the black veins all over my body rippling in pleasure as if I've been stroked.

The first bullet rips into my chest, piercing my heart. I'm impressed with her aim. Black blood oozes from the wound, sliding down the front of my chest. Fireopal gasps in shock, firing the gun again.

Again.

Again.

I take the bullets in my chest, the piercing, stinging pain ripping my flesh has my cock leaking, forming a wet spot on my jeans.

One last bullet lands between my eyes, my head jerking back from the force.

"Why won't you die?" I'm able to hear whispered from her small, shaking frame.

I roll my head over my shoulders, the wounds healing as I pull the bullets from my chest and head, guiding them to my mouth. The gunpowder is still warm in my stomach while the gun smoke drifts in my lungs. I blow the gun smoke out through my nose, the bullets clinking between my teeth.

"What the fuck are you?" She drops the gun onto the sidewalk just as I hear sirens in the distance.

The cops are on their way.

"I'm your worst fucking nightmare, Fireopal." Inhaling as deeply as I can, I lean back and launch a bullet from my mouth.

The ammo rips through her thigh, blood shooting from the wound and painting the pavement. I remember the time when I'd want to drink her until her body would be withered to nothing, but her blood smells rotten—something I couldn't dare possibly stomach.

No one's blood compares to my mate's.

"You're insane." Fireopal grabs her thigh and runs

across the street to the house she has been eyeing since I confronted her.

I chew the metal projectiles and swallow. "You have no fucking clue," I growl.

She runs the best she can, crossing the road with a limp as she does her best to keep herself from bleeding out.

"I can't wait to see what you fear. I can almost tasttte it," the nightmare grips hold of my words again, a slight hiss escaping.

I cross my arms in boredom as I wait for her to get to the house she thinks she will find solitude in. A car skids to a stop to avoid hitting her, and Fireopal slaps her bloody hands on the hood, staring at the driver in panic.

"Help me! Please, help me! He's coming after me. He's trying to kill me. Call for help! What are you doing? Why are you just staring at me!" she screams, slamming her palms on the hood of the car so hard, the metal dents.

The driver rolls down the window, stretching his arm outside. "What the fuck are you doing? Get out of the road!"

Fireopal's blood oozes from her wound in thick rivulets over her fingers and drips onto her shoe. She whimpers, pushing herself off the red sedan, hobbling to the other side of the road at last.

Frantic, she bangs on the door, turning to see if I've followed her.

I haven't.

I'm having too much fun watching her panic.

"What are you waiting for!" she shouts, tears running down her face. "Come and get me!"

The door swings open, someone grabs her by her hoodie and yanks her inside. Blurring across the street so no one can see me, I urge my nightmare forward, slipping into the keyhole to unlock the door. The coal-ridden entity clicks, the chitter of excitement ringing in my head.

"La-lala-la-la-laa."

"I know. I'm excited too. Don't worry"—I inhale, scenting four other people in the house—"there's so much to eat inside." Backing away, I fall onto all fours and lower my head. Using my vampire speed, I use my entire strength and ram my horn against the door, snapping it right off its hinges.

Splinters fly, chunks of wood smash against the wall and land on the staircase. I straighten to my full height, kicking the debris out of the way.

"Come out, come out, wherever you are," I snarl, scratching my nails across the walls as I walk down the hallway. The drywall crumbles to the ground, exposing the frame of the house.

I could find her easily if I wanted to. Even without my senses, there's a trail of blood on the floor. All I need to do is follow it.

But where's the fun in that?

"La-lala-la-la-laaa," I sing, continuing to drag my claws across every surface I can find.

A creak of the floorboards from the right signals someone's presence. I pause at the edge of the wall before it opens to another space. The person in question steps out with a wooden bat in his hand. He's young. He can't be over twenty-five.

What a shame to have so much life left to live and not be able to live it.

He swings, the air whooshing from the momentum. He's using every part of his body to put in as much energy and strength as he can muster. The bat connects with my chest, and I don't move an inch. One half of the bat flies over his head while he is left holding the handle.

I look down at the man who dared to swing. He licks his lips, visibly shaken.

Wrapping a hand around his throat, I lift him into the air until we are eye level. I see my reflection in his eyes, and it's the same monster I see in the mirror.

"What do you see when you look at me?" I'm too curious as to why people don't run away when they are met with the sight of me.

His hands grip my wrist as his feet dangle off the floor. "What? I'm not telling you anything! Put me down!"

I lift him higher, the roots slithering down my body. "If you want to live, you'll tell me."

He swallows the best he can, his face turning red from the lack of oxygen.

"You—" he gasps. "You have a shaved head. You're tattooed all over. Your eyes are black. You have piercings. What the fuck, man?"

I choke him harder, squeezing until the whites of his eyes turn red. He sees me as I was in my human form. How is that possible?

"You couldn't be more wrong."

"I thought you said you would let me live?" He kicks his feet, a pathetic attempt to rescue himself.

"I lied." I pull him closer, hoping he can see the evil swimming in my eyes. "Monsters never tell the truth," I whisper.

Grabbing his legs, I lift him horizontally in the air, raise my knee, and slam his back down on it. His spine snaps in two, blood pooling out of his mouth while his lifeless eyes stare up at me.

Tossing his body to the side, he slams against the staircase, breaking the rails. I begin to whistle, making my way through the rest of the house for the rest of the people here. I have to kill them all before the cops get here. They were probably at the taxidermist when they got called about the gun, so it will only be a matter of time before they show up here.

I turn left down another hallway, meeting another stranger who is holding a shotgun.

"Who the hell do you think you are coming into my house? Coming after my girl?"

"Don't forget." I blur until I'm standing close enough for the barrel of the shotgun to dig into my chest. "I killed your friend too."

His bright blue eyes are round and fill with tears. "What? What did you do? What did you do, you mother fucker!" he shouts so loud, spit flies from his mouth and onto my face.

He dares to fire his shotgun three times, blasting holes into my chest. Black smoke drifts free, the blood almost evaporating into thin air. My chest stitches itself together, followed by the stench of piss.

He's wet his pants.

Coward.

I frown, wiping this stranger's spit off my cheek. "The only person allowed to spit on me is my—fucking—mate," I sneer, gripping the barrel of the shotgun and bending it backwards.

The barrel is in his face.

His fear is palpable, cloaking me like a cold night promising a warm meal.

He's delicious.

We lock eyes, and the moment my vampire influence grabs onto his mind, his entire body relaxes, his eyes hood with drowsiness, and a hint of a smile stretches across his lips.

"Pull the trigger."

"Okay."

His index finger moves, and in the next second, a loud bang reverberates off the walls. My new friend's head is gone, splattered across the floors, walls, and ceiling. His body is still standing somehow, and with one finger, I poke his chest.

"Timber," I sing, watching as his body thuds against the ground.

Stepping on him, blood squirts from his neck. I step into a puddle of it on the floor, following the scent of terror from the last two heartbeats I hear in the house.

"Might as well come out," I urge. "I promise to make your death quick." It's a little lie, but they don't need to know that.

I curl my fingers on the edge of the wall, the long claws tapping as they make contact with a hard surface. They aren't in the room. Their heartbeats are faint and coming from upstairs. Their pulses are so fast, adrenaline binds with their blood to pump it harder and faster in their veins.

Footsteps from up above have me look up at the ceiling. They think they are being quiet. Every step they take creates a small creak on the floor as they try to find a safe place to hide.

Don't they know?

They can never hide from me. I will always find them, hear them, and smell them. I'll give them a little hope just so I can feel the excitement of when I take it away.

I step on the headless body, my boots squelch on the ground from the blood as I walk to the staircase.

"Is anyone home?" I chuckle to myself, climbing the

first step, then slam my claws into the wall again. With every step I take, I engrain grooves in the walls so this house is cursed by my presence. "I have a joke for you." The staircase groans, threatening to give under my massive weight. "Knock. Knock." I pound on the wall with my fist.

I wait for someone to answer, even though I know they won't.

"Who's thereeeee?" The nightmare asks, dragging his breath across every word.

"Your worst dream." The grind of my claws is the only sound in the quiet space.

"Your worst dream, who?" Nightmare hisses.

I stop at the top of the stairs, skimming my gaze down the darkened hallway. Left, then right.

"Me." I slam my fist into the family photo hanging on the wall. The glass shatters, but the sharp pieces don't penetrate the thick rhino skin.

Roots stretch from me, swimming on the ground, overtaking the ceiling, the floors, and walls. They creep further down the hallway, looking for someone to render motionless.

"La-lala-la-la-laaa."

I stop mid-step, listening to the loud pounding of their frightened hearts. I'm getting closer.

Actually.

I turn my head left, staring at the wall covered in roots, pressing my ear against the impatient plant.

My next victims are whispering to one another.

"What do we do? What do we do? Oh my god, he is a monster. He did this to me. He—he—"

"Shhh, stop, he will hear us. You have to calm down."

"Don't tell me to calm down. You didn't get shot in the leg by

him spitting a fucking bullet at you!" Fireopal whispers harshly in panic.

I grin, loving that they find me important enough to talk about me in 'private.'

How sweet.

I don't do sweet.

Following the sound of her friend's voice, I readjust my position, pointing my feet forward, and then take a small step to the left. Flexing my hand, I punch through the wall, wrap my hand around the back of his nape, and pull him through. Letting him go, so he slams into the wall.

Screams ring out, somehow harmonic and soul-easing.

"Don't! Don't! Please," Fireopal begs through broken breaths and heavy tears. "I'll do whatever you want. Do you...do you want money? I can get you all the money you want." She crawls out of the hole in the wall, a belt tied around her thigh to slow the bleeding.

Her pants are soaked in red, and the color in her face is gone—pale and lifeless.

The man I ripped from the other side of the wall yells, charging at me with a sharp piece of wood that broke from the staircase. I don't move. I don't flinch. I stand my ground, tilting my head in curiosity.

He rams the sharp point through my chest and steps backwards, smiling in triumph.

"I got you, you sick son of a bitch," he spits, literally, onto my boot. "Cops will be here any minute. You're done. You'll answer for all your crimes."

Without saying a word, I wrap my hand around the spike, then tug it free from my chest—without blinking, without breaking eye contact—and his grin of accomplishment fades little by little.

Blood pours from my chest, the hole healing within

seconds. My flesh stitches back together as if his attempt at murder didn't happen.

That's the thing about attempts—you always need to make sure you do it right the first time.

Twirling it in my hand quicker than he can possibly see, I launch the wooden spike in the air, and it lands in the middle of his chest, pinning him against a wall.

"No!" Fireopal cries, limping her way over to her friend, maybe even another mate.

I don't care enough to find out.

He gurgles blood, red waterfalls spilling down his chin. Such a lovely sight to see. I couldn't have painted a more picture-perfect moment. If this could be turned into a canvas, I would hang it above Lula's fireplace so she could see the lengths I would go for her.

"Save him! Please. Save him!" Fireopal begs of me, going as far as dragging herself over to my feet. "I'll do anything. He doesn't deserve this. I'm who you want."

"He doesn't?" Gripping her by the roots of her hair, I drag her across the floor and toss her at his feet, where his blood is collecting. Clutching his chin, I force him to lift his head so his eyes can lock onto mine.

He's barely breathing. He only has a few moments left before he dies.

His mind and body are so weak, he is easily locked into my influence. "Tell me, what's the worst thing you have ever done? I'll save your life if it isn't bad."

"Fuck you," he spits.

I rip the spear from his chest, and he falls onto the floor, gasping for breath as the hole in his chest floods with blood. Gripping him by his shirt, I lift him to his feet that aren't strong enough to hold him up and shove the wooden spike up his ass, through his body, and out of the top of his head.

"I do the fucking," I growl.

His eyes move left and right before death finally takes him, gravity bringing his body to the ground.

"Why! Why would you do that? No. Bring him back. Please, bring him back," she sobs, touching his face with shaky hands. "I'm sorry. I'm sorry for shooting you. I'm sorry. Please."

"La-lala-la-la-laaa."

She sniffles, rubbing her nose on her sleeve. "What is that?"

"Your worst nightmare." The roots blur with speed, wrapping around her, then sling her against the wall, trapping her for me.

"I'll give you all the money I have. I have millions stashed away in foreign bank accounts. You can have it. You can take it. Don't kill me. Please," she shouts. "Help! Someone help me!" she screams.

The nightshade flower blooms, releasing the invisible poison, and her screams for someone to come save her become silenced. Fireopal coughs and chokes, struggling to even say one word.

"No one is coming for you." I scratch a claw down her cheek. "No one is saving you." I press my finger against her gunshot wound, and her mouth parts, a silent scream leaving her. "I'm not in the business of saving lives, Fireopal. I take them."

The nightmare leaves me as smoke, entering through her mouth. Her big, fearful eyes release one last tear before sin possesses her, melted coal dripping down her cheeks in replacement of her sadness.

"What do you fear, Fireopal?" Nightmare asks in a breathless haze. "Let. Us. See."

I drift into her mind, chasing her subconscious.

In the depths of her mind, we've found ourselves in a very dark, cold fog. I look up to see snow has started to fall, gentle like Lula's hand when it will one day caress my face.

My boots crunch over rocks, and I look down, noticing I'm standing on a cliff or a mountain of some sort.

"Help me, please, help me!"

Her voice echoes through the empty space, bouncing off the stone walls. Rocks crunch under my boots as I follow the sound of the desperation hitching in her voice.

"Someone! Please, don't let me fall. Please! Oh, god!"

I haunt her through the dark, my breath the only cloud my eyes can see. Snow begins to gather in the cracks, showing that time is passing by. A brisk chill howls, a frigid storm—another threat to her life.

Making my presence known, I kick a rock hard enough that it rolls to the edge of the cliff. It falls. Seconds pass until I finally hear it hit the ground. The impact bounces between the cliffs, taunting Fireopal with just how loud her death will be.

"Is someone there? Hello? I'm going to fall. Please, I'm afraid of heights. I'm afraid of falling to my death. Help me!" Her cries echo pathetically in the fake scenario of her mind.

Her fear feels so real because I make it reality, but if she wanted to, she could fight me. She could fight her way out of this nightmare. It would be the only way she could survive me.

No one has been that smart.

And I hope they aren't. Feeding would truly be a nightmare if someone figured that out.

Falling to all fours, my nails click against the rocks. My movement is slow, creeping, and methodical. I crawl up the side of a mountain, using the sharp, strong points to pull me up to higher ground.

As I play with my food, the tall, slender mountains become taller, heights that remind me of Gothic cathedrals. Only this isn't a sanctuary. Prayers can't be reached here. She's trapped in the torment of the Hell she has created for herself.

Unholy darkness for an unholy soul.

I climb high enough to find a plateau, crawling to the edge on all fours. I perch on the very tip, sitting on a throne of death. Looking down hundreds of feet, I fixate on Fireopal gripping the edge of the cliff with her fingers.

From here, I can smell the strong stench of her fear. I twist my bone nipple rings, growling at how good it feels to be so close to inhaling another's will to live.

It's all mine.

"Someone please!" she calls out, her isolated shouts all alone in the cavern of her mind.

Such a pitiful thing. It's a good thing I'm here to put her out of her misery.

One hand drops from the edge, exhaustion mixing with the bitter tinge of terror snowing down on us. A beautiful scenery for such an ugly death. Cue the violins and sad symphonies for her to rest in pieces.

"I'm getting so tired, please!" she sobs.

So. Much. Crying.

If the ocean were empty, she could fill the basin with endless salt water.

After giving her arm a break, she switches limbs, allowing her other side to get much-needed rest.

Rest that is about to last forever. A sleep she will never revive herself from. A nightmare she can finally escape.

"Fireopal," I hiss, her name ricocheting off the dark.

She gasps, turning her head in every way she can to see where I am. "No! No, please. Get me out! Get me out of here! Please. Please, I'm begging. I hate heights. Kill me any other way." She grabs onto the ledge again with both hands, her knuckles turning white from the pressure.

Her nails are broken from digging into the solid foundation. A few fingers are bleeding, the flesh torn open, and one nail is missing completely.

That has to be so painful.

I jump from my perch, piercing her night with my body. Landing on all fours, the stone under me cracks and moves, threatening to crash into the abyss below.

"Why would I do that?" I ask, tracing her fingers with my claw. "I love that you're dangling here and holding on for dear life. Eventually, you'll be too tired to hold on anymore, and you will fall, Fireopal. You'll be so afraid, and it will be"—my eyes roll to the back of my head, thinking how potent her fear will become—"delicious."

"What are you?" She looks up at me, her eyes showing how full of life she is.

I slice one of her fingers off, causing her to cry out, but to my surprise, she doesn't let go.

Oh, what a fun game this will be!

She rests her head against the cliff, trying to catch her breath between the crying and hysteria of knowing she's going to die.

"I'm what you fear most. I'm what hides in the dark. Under your bed. In the closet." I cock my head to the left, slicing another finger off.

She screams so loud, her voice becomes hoarse.

"I'm why you can't walk home alone at night. The reason you carry your car key between your fingers. I am the wrong place at the wrong time."

"I don't understand." Blood coats the cliff, causing it to

become slick and hard to hold onto. "Why me? Why are you doing this?" Fireopal continues to wet her cheeks with frivolous nonsense.

I bend down, the scent of iron potent as it continues to pour from her fingers. "Because no one takes the attention of my mate away from me. Because you do terrible things to others."

Her eyes harden, narrowing at me with the first sign of fight I've seen from her. "You are no better. You should kill yourself then if you want to practice what you preach."

A sardonic chuckle pulsates into the space, sparks fly above, her neurons firing so fast, they decide to give us a lightning show.

I slice another finger off, and she rears her head back, yelling in agony. Two fingers are left, and they curl against the edge for dear life, her nails bending until they break.

"The difference between you and me is that I know what I am. I am a fucking monster, and I don't pretend to be anything or anyone else. I don't cloak who I am for the masses. I know who I am. If I don't kill people like you, the world would continue to worsen."

The fireworks become brighter, and when she looks at me again, her eyes widen to the size of moons, her face losing color.

"What are you? You aren't human."

I lean forward, and the bright lights of the electricity cracking above us illuminate my face. She can finally see who I am. I don't know why, but I'll find out. I'm too curious.

"I told you," I whisper into her ear. "I'm a monster." Using both hands, I swipe them across hers, cutting her hands from her wrists so she has no choice but to let go.

She screams, blood leaking into the air. Gravity pulls it down on her, her own blood splashing against her face.

Freeing my cock, the jaws of teeth spread open, and I stroke myself to the scent of her fear that fills every crack in the cliffs she created with her mind.

Using both hands, I twist and stroke myself, inhaling every fucking drop of her I can before she dies. Once her heart stops, so will her fear, and I'll be pulled into reality again.

A thunderous growl reverberates when she falls so far, I'm unable to see her through the onyx depths. Her scream fades, traveling so far down, her noise is muted.

I imagine Lula screaming for me like that, begging me to set her free, to let her live. Not that I would ever kill my mate, but perhaps she would like it if I tried.

The thought alone has me coming, my orgasm mixing with Fireopal's blood.

Bones breaking, a body becoming demolished, has fear ceasing to exist.

Opening my eyes, I stare at the broken, bleeding body of Fireopal. Her neck is snapped, her brain scattered along the wall, and her blood drips from nearly every orifice.

My black come paints her shirt, and I frown, not liking that my come was wasted on someone who wasn't my mate.

It wasn't her that got me off, Lula. It was her fear.

I hope Lula understands.

"CPD!" is yelled through the front door.

Using Fireopal's blood, I speed write a message for her.

She will know it's from me.

Smirking at my destruction, I blur out of the window.

Lula-lala-la-la-laaa.

OVE POLI
EPARTMENT

CHAPTER SEVEN

LULA

"Feels good to be out in the field again, doesn't it?" Jake asks as I stand in the only taxidermist shop in town.

I pat my badge proudly. I know it's only been a day, but being cooped up in the house always puts me on edge. It felt more like a month. "It does. Thanks for believing that I had nothing to do with that man's death. Did they ever figure out what was wrong with my blood?"

"No. It didn't even show up in testing."

Then, I'm not going to worry about it.

I walk around the body, wondering what the hell happened to him. "This is disgusting. Do we know the cause of death?"

"You're looking at it." A woman's voice comes from behind me.

I spin around to see a woman I've never met before. She has short, brown hair and big glasses that take up the majority of her face.

"I'm Devi. Forensic Pathologist." She grabs the tweez- ers, collecting evidence from the body.

"I'm not following, Devi."

"He was killed by flesh-eating beetles. I don't know where the beetles are. It was like the murderer collected them all, but that would take hours, and by how warm the body still is, that's impossible. This is recent."

"But how?" I ask more to myself than anyone else.

"That's for you to figure out. I'm only here for the cause of death. See these tiny markings along his body? His organs?" She points with tweezers, showing me how the beetles took small bites out of him. "This wasn't instant, but the cause of death was when the beetles bit into his aorta. He bled to death. Horrible way to go." She clicks her tongue as if this is just another day at the office.

"And no beetles were found on his body?"

"Not a one, but I only know one kind of beetle that can do this. It's the flesh-eating beetle. A taxidermist would have access to insects like that to help him clean bones if needed."

I inspect the shelves, a light layer of dust sticking to the wood. He only replaced the boxes from the looks of the dust gathering between them. The shelves line the entire wall, and by the tags on the side of the box, this is where the insects were.

My brow lifts when I see an empty space. "Hey, Sheriff?"

Jake turns around, hands hooked on his belt buckle. "Detective."

"I'm going to go out on a wild limb and say our flesh-eating beetles were here, but they aren't now."

"You find the person with the beetles, you'll find the killer. There's only one reason he would want those beetles," Devi informs. "And the reason isn't a good one."

The slickness of the body causes it to slip from the chair and fall onto the floor, along with what's left of his intestines slipping free.

"I'm going to step outside for a little bit of fresh air." I cover my mouth with my hand, closing my eyes so I'm not forced to look at the victim.

Plus, the smell. The space reeks of death and the pungent aroma of blood.

A decaying corpse is a scent that can never be forgotten, and it takes forever to fade. Now, the scent of death will follow me around all day.

Pushing the door open, the humid afternoon is a breath of relief when it hits me in the face. I lean against the wall, staring at the afternoon traffic, when children and parents begin to run towards me.

"What the hell is going on?" I whisper, pushing myself off the wall with my foot.

"Are they coming in hot, to you?" Waylon asks, taking a stance next to me.

The crowd of panicked parents gets closer, and we're finally able to hear what they are yelling.

"She has a gun!"

"Someone's been shot!"

Waylon and I straighten at the same time.

"Where? Is everyone okay? Did any of you get hurt or shot?" I ask, trying to eye them all for any bleeding.

One parent shakes his head, pulling his daughter close to him to keep her safe. "No. We left. They weren't bothering us, but they looked like they were going to kill one another."

Waylon steps forward, his wide shoulders surpassing the width of the man in front of us. "Who? Can you describe them?"

"Yes, the woman was small. She had a satchel where she kept the gun. She wore a beanie, so I don't know what color her hair was. She was short, with long sleeves," the parent explains.

His daughter peers up at him. "And she had pretty eye makeup. It was so colorful!"

"It was. You're right. Good catch, baby." He smiles down at her, rubbing her back.

Fireopal. That has to be who they are talking about. She fits the description.

Waylon scribbles the details down. "And the other person? Who was that?"

"I have never seen him before. He is huge though. His entire body is tattooed, his eyes are blacked out, and he has a nose and eyebrow piercing. You can't miss him. He sticks out."

"And where did this happen?" I question just as more shots are fired.

Waylon and I share a quick glance before leaping into action. Opening the door to the taxidermist's office, I yell to the Sheriff, "Shots fired across the park!"

"Go. I'll call you if I need you," Devi states. "I'm still collecting evidence from the body. It will take time."

Jenkins, Jake, and Zig sprint into action, following the path that cuts through the park.

The playground is on the left. It's so odd to see it deserted at this time of day. The wind blows the swings, the chains screeching from age and rust. I pump my arms, focus on my breathing, and wonder who the hell made this park so damn big?

The thuds of everyone's footsteps sound like a stampede of wild animals as we try to locate the suspects. We finally arrive at the other side of the park, looking for any sign of them.

"They aren't here!" Waylon shouts, looking all around the park to see if we missed them.

I hang my head, defeated that we were so close to catching a murderer. I don't know if Fireopal has it in her to kill anyone. That isn't what she does. She likes to steal money. That's all she ever cared about.

Taking off my sunglasses, the sun barely shines through the clouds, but it's enough to have me squint at the ground. Twisting, I follow the red drops, connecting the dots that shots were fired.

"I have blood!" I yell, slowly standing so I can get a better view of the trail.

Waylon, Zig, Jenkins, and Jake come closer, their shadows swallowing me.

"Looks like it goes across the street." Zig points his finger at the street, and we all follow.

I'm the first in line, lifting my badge at traffic during the red light so drivers know not to go on green. The blood trail becomes more visible on the sidewalk; the bright red droplets are still wet, meaning it's fresh.

And it leads to an older, rundown house. A small puddle collects at the stoop of what used to be a door that's smashed to pieces.

"Leads into the house," I whisper, unholstering my weapon.

"I got your back," Waylon says, lifting his gun into the air and pointing it forward. "Ready?"

I nod, taking the first step into a war zone.

"CPD!" I announce, out of breath from running across the park.

Gun drawn, I aim it in the direction in front of me.

"Body!" I announce to Waylon and Zig, who are behind me, wondering how the victim ended up bent in half.

I continue my sweep, careful not to step on any broken pieces of wood or glass. I don't want to fuck up a crime scene. I'll never hear the end of it.

Turning left, I nearly lose my lunch when I see what is in front of me. "Jesus." Not much makes me gag. I've seen a lot in this career, but this is beyond anything I have ever seen before. "Another body!" I shout, covering my mouth when bile threatens to creep up my throat.

"Two bodies up here!" Waylon yells from upstairs.

"I've never seen anything like this before," Zig says, clearing the living room for any other suspects. "¿Quién podría hacer algo así?"

"In this small town? I have no idea who could do something like this, Zig. I have never seen anything like this before," I say, stunned to my soul.

The body lying on the floor has a gun in its hand. I would say suicide, but the barrel is bent backwards towards the direction of where his head used to be.

"Upstairs is clear!" Waylon announces.

"Clear down here too!" I reply, squatting next to the body.

Pulling out a pair of gloves from my pocket, I slip them on, not wanting to contaminate evidence. I wrap my hand around the barrel, and it's still warm, as in, it was recently fired.

"We need a three-block sweep! The gun is still hot. He can't be far."

"I'll get Jenkins. We will do it." Zig walks away and radios them with the information.

Standing, I make my way to the man bent in half near what used to be a staircase. His head is touching his feet. His back is completely broken, his entire body snapped in half as if it were a toothpick. His eyes are still open, his mouth stained with his blood, and even though he is dead, one expression is permanent on his face.

Fear.

His mouth is parted on a scream, and his eyes are as round as possible.

"What happened to you?" I ask him, knowing damn well he can't talk. "What happened here?" Brainstorming, I think about what can cause this amount of damage.

There's no way kicking the door in would explode the wood like this.

"You are going to want to come see this," Waylon announces from upstairs. "I think there's a message for you."

I whip my head around, looking up at Waylon. "What?"

"You have a message here, Detective. And I think it's from our killer."

Keeping my gun in my hand, I climb up the staircase, dragging my gloved hand over the grooves in the wall. I pause when I see something long and curved sticking out of one of the marks. Glancing up, Waylon's attention is glued to one of the victims.

Plucking the foreign object out of the wall, I place it in my palm to get a better look. It's black, curved, and thick. It reminds me of a nail or a claw. That would be impossible. A nail like this could only come from an animal of some sort.

And what animal has the ability to kill like this?

"You coming?"

I curl my fingers around my find. It's evidence. I should place it in an evidence bag. That would be the right thing to do. This probably has plenty of DNA on it to run matches.

As if any matches would appear for an animal.

"Yeah, I'm coming. We need to dust every inch of this place for fingerprints. The killer doesn't seem that organized. I bet prints are all over." I slip the giant claw into my jacket pocket and hope it isn't too noticeable.

"Oh, this place will get turned inside out. There's evidence here. We just have to find it."

My jacket pocket begins to burn from his words alone. The cop inside me is screaming to do the right thing. Another part of me is louder, convincing me to protect this claw with my life.

I've never ignored my instincts, and I'm not going to now. This claw is important to me. I have to figure out why.

The scenery before me has me gagging again. The taxidermist doesn't even compare to the violence this crime scene holds. To the right, we have a young male, probably in his twenties, and he is staked through his entire body, the spear piercing his skull.

Then, my attention lands on the woman who looks as if she has been flattened.

"That's her," I sigh. "That's Fireopal. She was one of the case files I brought home. I wanted to look into her more. I know there have been a few sites that have been hacked lately, and I wanted to know if it was possible that it was her."

"I think you might know the killer, Detective."

"There's no way I know a monster like this, Waylon. I know I'm new, but that's one hell of an accusation."

Waylon steps to the side and points to the wall. "It isn't an accusation."

"What are you"—I'm silenced by the message written on the wall—"talking about." The words fall flat.

"Lula-lala-la-la-laa,
Sweet dreams."

It's written in Fireopal's blood, specks of her brain sticking against the wall.

The familiar chill that someone knows me well enough to break into my home, kill anyone in my case files, and leave me a message written in blood, has me pressing my thighs together.

I know it's wrong that my panties are wet with need and there's a throb in my clit, pulsating with every wild thump of my heart. I can't help what the unknown mystery does to me. It's out of my control.

"Are you okay?" Waylon questions, pulling me from my inappropriate thoughts.

The image of the monster I saw hovering over me in bed, wondering if my imagination would be able to conjure him again. Unless he is real, and he is the one causing all of this commotion.

"I'm fine. Rattled. No one has ever left me a message at a crime scene before. I don't know anyone here, Waylon. Except for who I work with, I haven't had time to make friends, especially friends with a murderer."

"Maybe it's someone from New York? You worked there for a while, right? Maybe you pissed off too many people that you arrested and sent to prison."

I didn't think of that. I should have. There have been a handful of threats over the years. One guy promised that when he got out, he would cut my throat for ruining a sculpture he was making out of human bodies. Another threatened to kill me by sinking me to the bottom of the ocean by tying cement blocks to my feet. It was a mafia tactic, one of the biggest syndicates used to get rid of bodies. My partner and I, at the time, arrested the second-hand man of the O'Byrne family. It was a giant bust for me —in a good way. That was the arrest that set me up to be a detective.

"You're thinking about that a little too long," Waylon says with a quirked eyebrow.

"Well, I have years of arrests to remember. There are a few, but they are still in prison, Waylon. They won't be getting out for a very long time."

"What if they didn't? What if they are calling the shots from prison?"

"Maybe. I don't know how they would know where I am. I suppose anything is possible. Usually, there are other threats though. Threats that are more personal. This isn't personal. Someone knows I took her file. That's the only connection. I wasn't friends with Fireopal. She was on my list to open an investigation on."

"I want you to walk this off. Go to Demi's," Sheriff says from behind me.

I spin around, groaning when he has his arms crossed with a 'don't argue with me' expression on his face.

"Come on, Sheriff. You can't be serious? I'm fine. I don't know this person."

"That you know of," he adds. "We have the crime scene. Your expertise is welcome at the station later when we are done here. If the killer knows you, we will need to dig into your past. Do you have anything that you need to tell me now? Ever since you got to town, there have been deaths. There's a connection there we can't ignore, and you know it. I know you want to argue with me about it." He holds up his hand to stop me from speaking. "But you know I'm right. Get out of here, Sanchez. I'll call you if we need you."

"This is bullshit, Sheriff. I'm the only detective in this town. You need me."

"And we plan on using you. I'm asking that you separate yourself for a few hours. Think about everyone you've ever met in your life and come to the station with a list."

I grit my teeth together, fury welling up inside me like the sea during a catastrophic storm. Holstering my firearm, and without saying another word, I leave.

"¡Qué maricada!" I hiss to myself, stepping over the destruction of the door to walk outside.

Zig runs up to me, sweating from canvassing the neighborhood. "What's fucking ridiculous?" he asks, bending over to place his hands on his thighs.

"Jake kicked me off the case for now since the killer left me a message."

Zig straightens, brows raise, and he wipes the sweat from his forehead with his forearm. "Come on, Sanchez. You know that's the right call. You would have made the same one if you were calling the shots and you know it."

"That's what is more frustrating. I know he is right, but I'm pissed, Zig. I feel like this person is coming after me somehow, and I don't know why. It's my fault all these murders are happening. Ever since I came here, this department has been slammed with chaos. Maybe..." I exhale at the thought, but it needs to be said. "Maybe I need to go back to New York. They have more manpower to handle something like that. You, Waylon, Jenkins, even the Sheriff, you're exhausted."

"We're doing our jobs. We're happy to have you here, and if someone is messing with you, taunting you, or if you're their next target, we want to be the ones protecting you. You are one of us now, Lula. You're Cove Police Department family. We won't risk your life just because this happened. We've had serial killers before. Hell, that's the reason the old sheriff quit, and Jake took over. Granted, they were never caught, so maybe it's the same guy."

I slap his arm and walk away, deciding to use the stroll

home to clear my head. "You're sweet, Zig. You and I know that isn't the case, but thanks for making me feel better."

"Sure, no problem. If you need me, call me."

I turn, giving a small, forced smile and half salute, half wave. A light mist of rain begins to fall, and the clouds churn a darker shade of grey, a storm brewing like it does every day.

I'm starting to wonder if I made the right choice transferring here. All I have brought is trouble.

I've seen these types of cases before. The endings are all the same.

I'm going to be this man's last victim.

He's going to kill me.

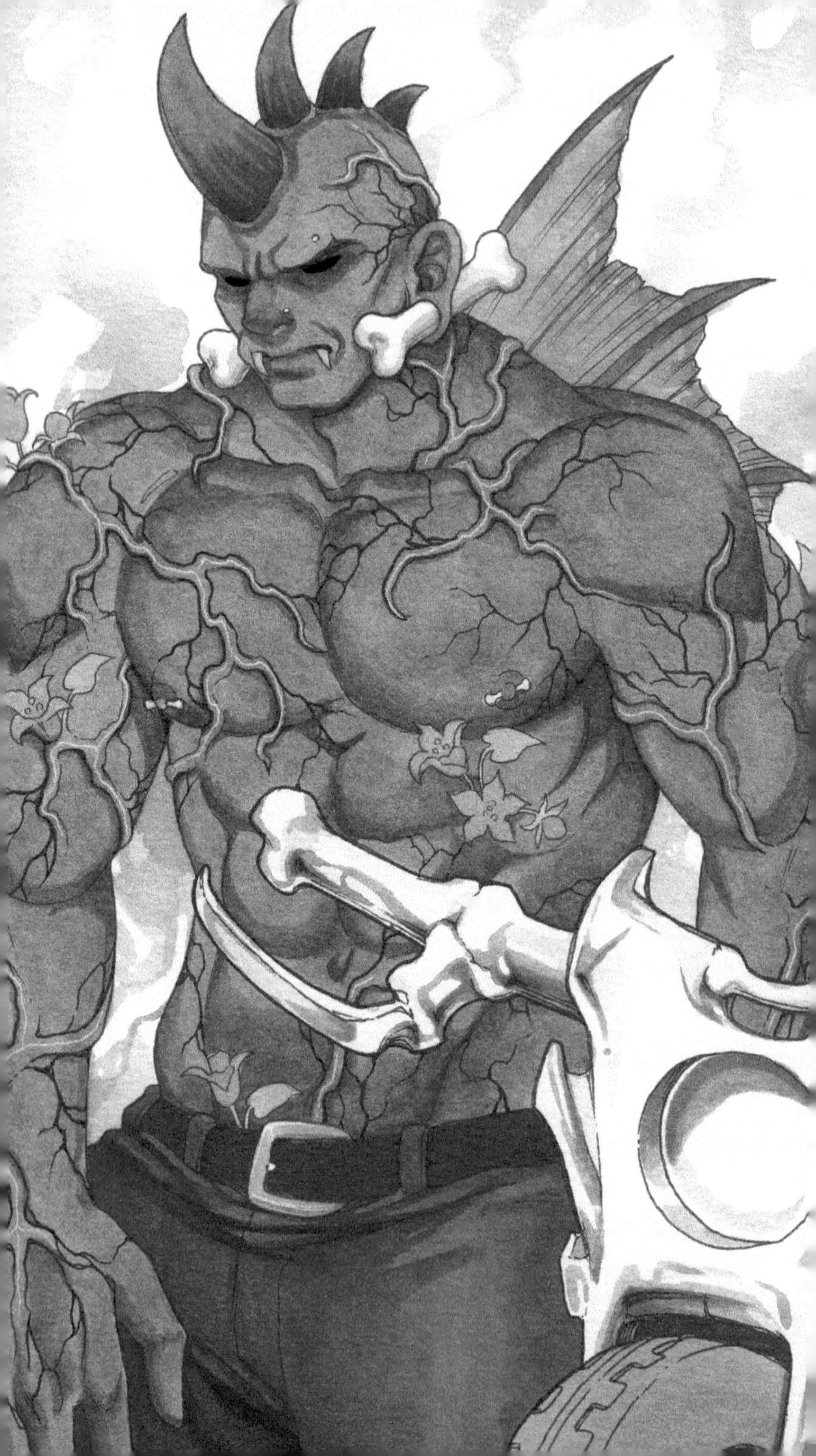

CHAPTER EIGHT
SHADE

I follow Lula, keeping myself in the shadow of the trees so she can't see me.

The wind blows her aromatic perfume in my direction, sweet and tempting, unknowingly feeding me enough not to kill another. I have a lot of blood on my hands, and because of that, her cop friends seem to think I'm putting Lula in danger.

I'd *never* do that.

Okay, I'm lying.

I would, but that would be for her as well. I've smelled and seen how wet she becomes when she is afraid. I'd use that to our advantage, but I'd never kill her.

Her blood is the last I ever want drenching my palms. Her life is too important to me. Her existence is vital to mine. If she ever did allow me to bleed her dry, I wouldn't let any drop go to waste. I'd lick her from my hands and suck my fingers in my mouth, relishing the flavor that was made for me.

And only me.

Then, I'd have her feed from me. I'd cut myself open and allow my smoke to fill her veins, to bring her to life again.

She stops in the middle of the sidewalk, and I do my best to hide my big body behind a tree. Lula feels me watching. She's a good detective and knows when someone is following her. What a fun challenge it will be to stalk her when she has no idea.

"I know you're here," she whispers to herself, not knowing I can hear the words breezing from her lips.

Her gaze surveys her surroundings, curious and accusatory, waiting to find the reason for her unease. The wind blows her hair, a few pieces framing her face.

I'm jealous of the way the strands glide across her lips, caressing her cheek in all the gentle ways I'll never be able to.

I'm not capable of being gentle.

I was created to break and kill.

Not cherish and cuddle.

It's too bad her soul is tethered to mine. Another man would nurture the good in her, so she becomes the best version of herself. I'll protect the good she has because it's the only time I'll ever get to touch such greatness.

But cherish? I'm not capable.

Her soul is twisted within mine, and the rotten core that pumps my heart will taint hers somehow. All the bad that lives within me will live within her. I won't let it get to the point where it consumes her.

Pure good deserves to be protected—even from nightmares like me.

"Lula-lala-la-la-laaa."

She tucks her hair behind her ear, pulling her gun free and aiming it in the direction she thought she heard my song. "Who's there? Who are you? What do you want?"

What do I want? That's such a difficult question.

I want her in bed, legs spread, body laid out for me to ravage.

I want her eyes to bleed black while I search for what she fears most.

I want her to scream.

Beg.

Cry.

And then come all over my massive cock while it splits her body in two.

There are so many wants that I'm unsure how to answer her question.

"Lula-lala-la-la-laaa."

She swings her arms in my direction, another barrel threatening my life again. Fear pours off her in waves, and I inhale, drinking her in, wishing my lungs could taste her the way my tongue can.

"I will shoot you. I have no problem pulling this trigger. I've done it before, and I'll do it again!" She shouts over the howling gusts that rustle the long branches of the trees.

Holding myself back to stop myself from standing in front of her is difficult. I dig my claws into the trunk of the tree to keep myself in place. I so badly want to taunt her, to beg her to shoot me so she can see that she can do all the bad things she's ever thought about and inflict them on me.

And I'll be just fine.

Underneath the perfume of her bravery and fear, there's that electrifying and shocking scent of lust.

My mate loves to be afraid.

"You're losing it, Lula. You're fucking losing it." She holsters her gun, tucks a few more loose hairs behind her ears, and covers her face. "It's just the wind. Nothing more."

"Oh, Lula." I stare at her, clawing the bark so my control

is forever carved into the trunk. "I'm so much more, and that should terrify you."

Lula studies the bushes beside her, then the crowd of trees I'm hiding in, finding comfort in the shadows they cast. A couple passes on the other side of the street, and she watches them as if they are suspects waiting to be interrogated.

Thunder shakes the ground from its anger, the skies darkening with the same fury that I feel with every breath I take. Staring at Lula helps soothe the rage that constantly lives within me. Even with all the beasts that make me, the strongest one was never a DNA strand that was forced into my veins.

I was born with lividity—an anger that demolishes any rationale.

Lula gives up, blowing out a breath that has me closing my eyes and pretending the breeze is the air leaving her lungs. I'll get to feel her tonight.

Turning around, she blesses me with her backside, her wide hips swaying to the beat of my everlasting want.

Cruel intentions are all I can promise her. If that isn't enough, that's too bad.

Stepping out from behind the tree, I stay within the shadows, never taking my eyes off her. As if I could. My thoughts are consumed by her existence. Given the choice to save her or the world, I'd save her, so the world could be ours and ours alone.

She collides with another man, causing her to drop her phone on the sidewalk.

"Oh, shoot!" he says, bending down to pick up her phone that fell from their collision.

He takes a peek at her badge. "You're the new detective, right?" Flipping the phone over, he groans. "Crap. The screen is cracked. I'm so sorry. That's my fault. I'll pay for it."

"It's fine. Don't even worry about it," she says with a smile on her face.

A smile that belongs to me. This man is as good as dead. I hope he felt the wet heat of a woman's pussy lately because it will be the last time he will ever feel such heaven.

"And yes, I'm the new Detective in town."

He jerks his neck, pushing his hair from his eyes. That's a fucking sign your hair is too long.

I'm going to rip his scalp from his skull and stuff it down his throat.

He grins, his eyes wandering a little too much for any of me to be okay with. Growling, I fall to all fours, digging my claws in the damp earth to stop myself from killing the stranger flirting with my mate.

"So maybe to make it up to you, I can take you for dinner? Or coffee? Whatever you're comfortable with. In exchange for ruining your phone."

I listen to her heart, the beat becoming fast with anxiety.

"I appreciate it, but really, it's okay. I've broken a hundred screens. I'll get it replaced. It's insured."

"Okay," he chuckles, scratching the back of his head. "Would you want to go out anyway? Nothing to do with the phone, but I'd love to get to know you better."

Her eyes slide to the side where I'm hiding in the trees. I swear our gazes lock, and for the first time in my life, I hold my breath, hoping she can't see me.

I'm not sure I want her to. For the first time, insecurity manifests, which is completely new for me. I'm not an insecure man. I've never cared what anyone thinks of me.

But I care what *she* thinks about me.

"Go to her. Mine. Mate. Beloved." Nightmare hisses, pushing the inside of my skin to go to her.

I can't.

"Lo siento," she says in her native tongue, and a purr rattles my chest when I think of her whispering her language into my ear.

She realizes he can't understand what she said by the confused wrinkle between his brows.

"I'm sorry. I'm not really looking to date," she says. "I just got to town, and I'm focused on my job right now."

Lies.

Deceit radiates from her pores. She does want to date, but she doesn't want to date *him*.

"It's just a coffee. I promise it won't take much of your time."

I snarl in my chest, and this time, the thunderous growl is louder than I intend it to be. They both look around, wanting to know where the sound came from.

Her eyes lock onto mine again, staring straight into the pit of my soul.

"What was that?" he asks, jerking his head to the left and right.

I curl a lip in disgust when I smell his fear. Not even Lula is afraid. Cautious, yes, but I think that has more to do with him than me.

"Probably just the storm coming in. Listen, I'm not interested. I only want to focus on my job. I hope you understand. I need to go. I'm on an assignment for work. I hope you have a good day." She takes a step to walk away from him, giving him a slight wave of her delicate fingers that I'm dying to feel wrapped around my cock.

He snags her wrist, tugging her back. "Listen, bitch—"

In a move I don't expect, she twists around, locks an

arm around his throat, and applies pressure to the point he can't breathe.

"No, you listen, *puta,*" she states, adding more pressure when he begins to struggle.

I growl, giving myself a firm stroke at the sight of Lula putting this man in his place.

"I could arrest you for assaulting a police officer if I wanted to. You need to learn when someone says no. It means no. Period. I said no, and you know what, it's not because I don't want to date. I just don't want to date a man like you. Pushy, cowardly, and stupid. I have standards." She hits him in the gut, and he doubles over, spit dripping from his mouth.

Desire burns in my veins like a river of molten lava, heated to my core for Lula and her violence.

"I don't want to be able to take down a man I'm interested in so easily." She shoves him away, his feet tripping over one another as they catch a loose lace from his shoe, and he stumbles until he finally falls.

He smashes his jaw against the pavement, and the scent of his blood has my stomach turning. I'm starved for blood. My fangs lengthen, my vision zeroing in on the vein at the side of Lula's neck.

With every pulse, my mouth waters. The need to claim, bite, mark, fuck, own, and ruin her for anyone else is all I can think about. I'm starved for her blood. I'm going to have to steal it for myself tonight.

She'll understand.

"I'm going to sue you and the department."

Lula points down the empty street. "If you take this street another block down, you'll see the department. Have a great day." She gives him a big, bright smile— another item of hers that belongs to me—and walks away, her ponytail swaying from the saunter of her hips.

"That bitch." He pushes himself to his feet, brushing off his jeans of any dirt.

I'm torn about what to do. Do I follow Lula? Or do I follow the man who just threatened my mate and touched her?

Growing more irritated by the second, I decide to follow him. From the looks of it, Lula can protect herself, which has me puffing out my chest with pride. I know I can protect her in every way, and that's what I have been doing for us. I hope she will understand when she learns the truth.

But watching her handle herself like she just did makes me wonder how she will handle me—if she dares to try.

I come out of the tree line, holding my bag of bones in one hand and clenching my fist with the other. So many different ways to kill him are coming to mind.

Do I kill him with my bare hands? Torture him? Kill him by his greatest fear? Do I make it last? Or do I make it quick? The faster I'm done, the sooner I can go see Lula or kill another suspect from her case files.

I've been dying to make myself at home in the spare bedroom.

I wonder if she's caught on to my plan that everyone in her life is a target.

Stepping out from the tree line, I follow behind him, my shadow growing next to me, waiting to engulf him in nightmares. I am curious what a man like him fears. His scent tells me he puts on a brave face, but really, he's scared of everything.

Which only makes my mouth water for the taste of how

strong his fear will be. I bet I'll get drunk off his false bravado, swaying to the screams I'll force from him.

The overcast of the clouds begins to rumble, the promise of more rain. I don't know what it is about this little mountain town, but it rains more than usual.

I unzip the bag carrying Greta's bones, wishing I had added part of Fireopal to my treasure chest. Maybe next time. I flick a few flesh-eating beetles from what used to be Greta's award-winning smile and pry her mouth open to grab my pack of cigarettes.

Flipping open the top, I peel a smoke free by wrapping my lips around the orange filter. Tossing the pack into the bag, the beetles swarm it and tug the zipper to enclose Greta's skull.

"Hey, man!" I shout at the guy who dared to put his hands on Lula. "Hey!"

The guy stops in his tracks, the fragrant scent of annoyance trickling in the air between the drops of rain.

"Yeah?" He turns his head, tucking his hands into his jeans pockets.

"Do you have a light? I forgot mine."

He pulls his hands free, and my gaze zeroes in on the one he touched my mate with. All I can think about is ripping his entire arm from his body. I roll my head over my shoulders, the deep huffs sound from my rhino, not liking that this man is still standing. He should be bleeding on the horns of my head, begging to live another day.

"Actually, yeah. I do." He pats his pockets, finally pulling a red lighter free. "Here you go, man."

I snag the lighter and flick it, covering the flicker of fire from the rain as it burns the tobacco until the ash begins to show itself.

"Thanks." I toss it back to him. "I appreciate it."

"No problem." He begins to walk away, and I grab the back of his neck, forcing him to turn around and look me in the eye.

I deepen my voice. "It is a problem. *You* are a problem."

"Fuck you. Let me go, or I'll call the cops."

I lift him off his feet, then tilt him back, his head resting on my shoulder. "What do you think the cops will do? I could bring that pretty detective back. Let's see what she would think about me dragging you into an empty room to make sure you can't demand anything from a woman ever again."

I flip him around, catching him by his neck so he is forced to look into my eyes. "I want you to fight me, so you know what it's like to be overpowered."

"I don't know what game you're playing at." He punches my wrist, so I let him go, but I can barely feel a thing. His strength is a show of weakness in itself. "But I have money. I can get you money. Any amount you want."

A man can only be measured by how he treats a woman. "I don't give a fuck about your money." His eyes meet mine long enough to fall into my influence, his body going lax in my hold. "You'll come with me."

"Sure," he agrees. "Whatever you want, man."

I place him on his unsteady feet, his body swaying from the lack of control he has in his body now that I'm in charge of it.

"Follow me." I walk across the street, taking a long drag of the cigarette and flicking the ash free.

My new friend drags his feet behind me, following my every step as he was told. There's an empty building nestled between an ice cream shop and a restaurant. The windows are boarded up with plywood, and there's a massive lock on the door handle. I've seen these before. I'd have to enter a code to get the key to unlock the door.

Good thing I don't give a fuck.

I ram the door with my shoulder, and it swings open easily enough. Closing it is another story, and I don't give a fuck about that either. Let people come inside. Let them wander into the unknown.

I'll kill them.

The natural sunlight peeks its way in. A few windows aren't covered completely. Probably from others trying to break in. There's the sound of dripping water in the distance, a large crack in the ceiling, and drywall crumbled onto the floor.

An old weather-ridden couch sits lopsided in the room to the left of us. Frames that hang on the wall are crooked, the art ruined by the dampness in the air or a thick grime covering the canvas. Whatever this place used to be, I bet it was lavish.

The floors are hardwood and beyond saving, which is a shame. There's too much damage from years of being forgotten. This place went from being the first in someone's life to nothing but a fleeting thought to a rundown building.

Oh, the stories this place could tell. I bet the walls themselves are haunted.

I scratch my claw along the mantle, engraving my own presence into the shambles of its history.

"Farington Place."

Oh.

I forgot he was here.

"What?" I sneer, annoyed that he interrupted me.

I'm fascinated by this house. I like that it isn't perfect. I like that it needs work. To be forgotten doesn't necessarily mean it lasts forever; only until someone notices how special it is, and can breathe life into it again.

"This is Farington Place," he says again, as if I am supposed to know what it means.

"And?"

"A brutal murder happened here. It was about fifty years ago, and the house has been empty ever since."

"Murdered?" I chuckle at the irony. "What happened?"

"No one knows. It's a cold case. They say it was murder suicide, and the only survivor was the son. He owns this house."

I'll have to visit this son. I want this house for me and Lula. I have enough money if I can figure out how to get it from my bank account. My assets might be frozen because of my being gone for so long.

Lula will love trying to solve the cold case, and I can feel right at home being in a house that has tasted blood.

It's a match made in Hell.

"What's your name?" I ask him, pointing to the ruined couch. "Sit."

"Ricky." He sits on the end that isn't broken, the springs creaking from years of being unused. The color of the material that makes up the couch is hidden under dark brown stains.

Mildew hangs in the air, and the hardwood under my feet cracks from my weight, threatening to give way.

"Ricky." In the blink of an eye, I'm in front of him, his eyes glazed by my will. "How many women have you abused in your life? Do you know off the top of your head? And be honest." I poke him in the middle of his forehead.

"Because I can scent your lies. And with every lie you tell, I'm breaking a finger."

He settles deeper into the couch, spreading his legs as if he doesn't have a care in the world. "I don't know, man. A couple dozen? Maybe. I don't like it when they tell me no."

I wish I could see inside his head. I wonder if his mind is rotten, coated in darkness like mine. I suppose I'm similar to him in a lot of ways, especially when it comes to Lula.

In the rancid unknown of pitch-black night, where wrongs live, Lula cannot be found. She's better than the abyss of an empty, damned core. She is the light that has somehow penetrated the deepest depths of the broad ocean in my chest, in my mind.

Reaching for her light is what I fear.

I realize that now, while staring at Ricky, a man who didn't appreciate the sun radiating from her skin.

I'm so damaged. I'm beyond repair. My humanity is gone. I do not care who I harm, who I kill, who I torture in the name of protecting what is mine.

And yet, what if all the reaching, all the craving for her light, what if I'm not strong enough to hold it? What if her light burns away the sin that made me? What would I be then?

I lean down, placing one hand on either side of his shoulders, caging him in. The green skin is bright against the discolored sofa. I don't like that he can't see the real me, the monster he should be afraid of. He will once I enter his mind, and I can't wait much longer.

The terror he instills in women will finally be felt in him the moment his eyes land on my true form.

"I told you everything. Just let me go, and I promise, I won't tell a soul—"

A root slithers down my arm, forcing his lips apart, and filling his mouth so he can no longer speak.

"Silence," I hiss, flashing my long, sharp fangs that have been aching to slice into Lula's neck. "Hearing you speak is like nails against my bones."

His eyes are broad, so round that I can see the bright whites and red blood vessels. He doesn't blink. He doesn't move. Tears gather, knowing his life is over, and the mourning drips down his cheeks.

"Let me see what you fear, Ricky."

He shakes his head, his subconscious begging to be freed. He is now in the shackles of my evil, and he will never have the privilege to feel a woman's softness again.

Even a monster like me, brutal and unrelenting, appreciates the delicate skin of a woman.

The room darkens with the nightmare leaving my body, eating away all traces of light that slip through any nooks and crannies of the house, sinking us into a void he will never escape from.

The only brightness left to see is the whites of those eyes I'm about to invade. Prying his mouth open with a root, the shadow slips down his throat as if he is about to be possessed by a demon.

For all I know, he is. I don't know what I am. I can only define myself by what I see in the mirror and how I feel. I don't know what actually created me. Yes, DNA, but where was this DNA taken?

I don't know, and I don't care to know.

I am who I am, regardless of the origin where I was created.

The moons of his eyes drift to an endless, empty galaxy, one where stars can't be born or seen. Ill intent begins to drip down his cheeks, unknowingly getting lost in the part of his mind that will lead to his death.

Falling into his mind, the roots crack and crinkle around me from reality, sinking their way into the nightmare.

I land in the middle of an old home, one that reeks of nostalgia paired with bad memories and infrequent laughter. Everything seems still. No one is home. Dust drifts in the air, swaying through the rays of light pouring in the windows. I drag my finger across the old box TV, layers of embedded memories sticking to my skin.

I can almost taste the hatred that was born in this house.

Taking a step forward, something crunches under my boot, shattering easily under my weight. Grunting, I bend down and pick up a broken picture frame. Ricky is in this photo, surrounded by two people who should have loved him more than anything in the world.

They didn't.

And neither parent is smiling. I know all too well what life with abusive parents is like—was like.

Staring at the photo again, I analyze it like a story. I've never been too smart. I dropped out of community college, uncaring about the words in books, but I've always been great at reading a room or a person.

The mother looks tired and afraid with dark circles under her eyes. The father is stern, eyes tightened into slits with anger and annoyance. One of his hands is clutched on his wife's shoulder while the other is on the child—Ricky. The man's knuckles are white from the grip.

I can sense the evil, nearly tasting it from how it births itself from the walls. My veins awaken, the roots swirling along my limbs as if they recognize the sinister being that was once here.

Likeness knows likeness.

This house has been frozen in time, an icy tundra aban-

doned and left to be forgotten, like bad memories that taint the soul.

Two mugs sit on the coffee table, more dust building around them. One has a light pink shade of lipstick on the rim, while the other is nestled by a newspaper.

Whimpers come from down the hall that has me turning my head, my eyes narrowing down the darkened tunnel. My claws lengthen, dragging across the leather of the recliner.

Peeking into the kitchen, dishes fill the sink while drops of blood are on the floor. Falling to all fours, I scurry to the red dots, close my eyes, and inhale the scent. Evil lives within these blood drops.

I growl, loving how good it smells. My nightmare is happy being surrounded by darkness and pure violence.

Opening my eyes, there's a larger puddle of blood under the dining room chair. A man sits in that chair. I can tell by the loose fit of his pants and the laced boots on his feet. Pushing myself onto my feet, I cock my head, trying to understand what I'm seeing.

It's the same man from the photo. His head is jerked back, his hands on either side of an empty plate. Blurring to him, my fingers trace the bullet wound between his eyes.

The sound of whimpers catches my attention again, and I follow them out of the kitchen. I stand at the beginning of the hallway, eyeing four doors that are closed.

"Ricky, Ricky, Ricky," I tsk with annoyance.

I dislike it when nightmares get too complicated. They are supposed to be simple. A simple tactic to instill fear, but it seems Ricky is a complicated case.

Sighing in boredom, I swing the first door on the left open, seeing a woman sobbing in a rocking chair in the corner. She's holding a shotgun. in her hands, her mascara stains black lines down her face as she sobs.

Ricky can't be more than fifteen as he screams at her, sobbing to the point that drool drips down his chin as he is handcuffed to the radiator. He's too skinny, and he has two black eyes with handprint bruises on his throat.

"I'm sorry, Ricky."

It's the last thing she says before placing the barrel under her chin and pulling the trigger. Her brains splatter against the wall, painting it as if it were an empty canvas.

Closing the door, I eye the room across the hall, excited to see what waits for me. The nightmare within me screeches with joy, soaking in all the pain and suffering that is held within this home.

Such a sweet little treat for a wicked monster.

Grabbing the doorknob, I swing the door open to see Ricky being suffocated by his father. Two hands are wrapped around his throat while his father screams and yells at him.

"I'll skin you! Do you hear me? I'll skin you and hang you up like a piece of fucking meat if you ever talk back to me again. Your mother is mine to do with as I please. She's my wife. Do you understand me?"

I close the door, getting bored with how long it is taking to get to adult Ricky. I have a mate to be infinitely curious about, following her, learning all of her moves, the way she walks and talks.

My everlasting obsession starts and begins with her.

Speeding to another door, I pause when it begins to snow again, something I find curious. Opening my palm, I'm mesmerized by how softly it drifts into my massive palm. It stays for a moment, the chill momentary before it melts into a droplet of water.

Another falls, then another, cascading to the floor until it begins to stick. With each caress of a snowflake upon my skin, split seconds of laughter, sobs, screams, pain, and glass shattering, tease my ears.

Reaching for the third doorknob, snow is piled on the curve of the metal. Curling my lip in annoyance, I bend my head down and ram my horn through the door.

Adult Ricky is hanging by his shirt, lifted onto a hook just like his father promised. Ricky, the rapist, is crying, hands and feet bound, and the ghost of his father stands in front of him.

I step in, the man who caused Ricky to turn into a monster of his own, turns to look at me before vanishing into thin air.

A blade is left on the top of the dresser, a hint of blood on the silver. Staring at Ricky's arms, I see his father has already started to deliver on the promise he made.

Pieces of skin are on the floor, blood running down his slender arms.

"Please," Ricky begs like the others I've killed.

I bet he hopes to reach compassion or the humanity inside me, not knowing that the only humanity I hold is for Lula.

Everyone else can be damned for all I care. The world could burn, and souls could scream, people could reach for me to save them, but I'd step on their hands and break their bones to save Lula. Every person is a stepping stone to get to her, nothing more.

Their lives are useless to me. Nothing but an annoyance for me to scare so I can feed myself. They are food, and Lula is water, the liquid I need to wash them down with.

"Please, get me down. He'll be back."

Turning my head, I look at him like a confused animal, trying my best to understand why he thinks I care, when I remember he thinks there are others out there who do care to save his life.

He doesn't remember that I am in control of his next heartbeat, and he will hang on the hook his father placed him on until his body rots and his bones clatter to the floor.

"He won't be back," I state, ignoring the blade that only a weaker man has to use.

I drag my claws across the dresser as I step closer to Ricky, his shirt soaked in sweat and tears.

His gaze finally looks up at me from focusing on the floor, eyes widening when he sees the monster that I am.

"No. No. Get me down! Get me down! Oh, god. I'm sorry. Please, don't kill me."

Digging all five nails into his chest, I rip his skin, growling in pleasure when his screams cause my ears to ring.

"Being skinned alive is your worst fear because your daddy threatened you?"

He continues to scream at the top of his lungs as I use his body like pottery being sculpted. Digging my claw under his skin, I cut away at the tissue between the muscle and flesh.

I peel away the first layer of skin, dropping it onto the floor by my feet, and it lands with a splat.

"You have no idea what I went through in this house!" he roars, struggling against his restraints.

Wrapping a hand around his throat to keep him still, I lean forward until our noses touch.

"I don't care what you went through in this house. Your memories of being a disappointed and hurt boy do not hurt me. I do not feel sympathy for you. I might be a monster, but you are an untamed animal who needs to be put down. My violence"—I roar, slashing my claws across his stomach, then begin to cut away at his body again—"has rules."

His eyes burn with malice, even in the hands of death, his father shines in his irises.

"I'd do it all over again," he seethes. "I regret nothing. They deserved every bit of what I gave them."

I know I'm a beast built to spill blood. I know what I do to Lula people would question, but they need to mind their fucking business because they don't know that she fucking loves what I do to her—what I will do.

"And you deserve every moment of your skin being cut from your body." I slice him again, peeling the biggest piece of flesh off his stomach.

He lurches, puking all over my boots.

I liked these boots.

Locking eyes with him before they roll to the back of his head in unconsciousness, I demand, "No matter the pain, you are not allowed to pass out."

"What are you doing to me?"

A dark chuckle echoes in the chamber of his mind.

"I think the question is, what won't I do to you?" I toss another flap of flesh by my feet, relishing in the beauty of the muscular skeletal system peeking through the vulnerable raw spots on his body.

Sinking my claws into high thigh, I snarl, "Scream for me."

The pitches range from high to low, an orchestra of pain just for me.

So beautiful.

So terrible.

So remarkable how death can have a song of its own.

And it's all my doing.

OVE POLI
EPARTMEN

CHAPTER NINE
LULA

I'm starting to wonder if bad energy follows me everywhere I go.

It doesn't matter where I move, what I do, or what job I take. Horrible things always happen, and I can't escape them. They all have the same thing in common.

Monsters.

I know not all creatures are bad, just like I know all humans aren't bad. There is a part of me that hates that I can see them for what they really are. It's damned me in a way. I view the world so differently than others. They don't know what truly exists, what hides in plain sight, in light, in dark; creatures beyond the imagination live among us.

It's a well-kept secret—these creatures.

My mamita taught me everything I know about them. It's not much, but I know that creatures can disguise themselves either with their own abilities or magic of some type from a witch.

The monsters who want to exist in peace usually hide themselves, but of course, there are the ones who keep themselves a secret for nefarious reasons. Ones who show themselves to the world without any type of protection do not want to coexist.

They want to rule.

I rub my eyes when my vision becomes blurry from staring at these case files. Leaning against the broken couch, I stare up at the ceiling as the light from the TV changes from bright to dark with every passing scene in the movie that's on.

The brief thought of calling my mamita again to get more answers crosses my mind. She seems to know everything about everything, but the more I think about it, the more I know she would only be repeating herself from my past experiences.

Until I have more information to give her, I'm on my own trying to figure out what the hell is happening in this town.

Sighing, I stand from the floor and stare at my detective's badge on the table next to the files, second-guessing if I made the right choice coming to this sleepy town that isn't as asleep as I thought.

Heading to the fridge, I swing the door open, still wondering how someone filled it with groceries without my knowledge. I should be more concerned for my safety. A stranger broke into my home and filled my fridge and freezer full of food.

I have much bigger things to worry about, which is why I don't fucking care. If someone wants to test me, I have a nine-millimeter that I'm happy to pull the trigger on.

Snagging a beer from the fridge, I slam the top down on the edge of the counter, ripping the cap off. It clatters somewhere, the metal rolling across the floor until it hits the wall.

In my tired, uncaring mood, I leave it. Let it stay there forever for all I care.

Taking a long swig of beer, I stroll to the couch again, spreading out the files on the table.

My phone rings...from...somewhere.

"Where the hell did I put that thing? Hay, Dios Mío." I hear it vibrate, and I check between the cushions of the couch before finally grabbing it.

It's Zig.

"Hey, Zig. What's up? Do you guys need me? Am I finally not benched?"

"'fraid not," he says, the hush of rain a whisper wherever he is.

I frown, not liking that. "I'm not the reason why these people are dying, Zig. I didn't bring this here. This didn't happen in New York. I swear. You can call—"

"—Sanchez. Cool it. Take a breather. I'm only calling to keep you in the loop. We found three bodies in the Wayward Forest."

I sit up, snagging my badge off the counter. "What? I'm on my way. Send me the location, and I'll be there as soon as I can."

"You can't come here. The sheriff doesn't know I'm calling you. I agree with Jake. For your safety, you have to be home tonight. Jenkins is parked outside your house as well."

"Oh, come on, Zig. No offense to Jenkins, he's a great guy, but you know I can protect myself more than he can protect a fly."

"I know, but he was the only officer available for surveillance tonight. He's a good cop."

I flop back down on the couch, bored out of my mind. "Well, why did you call me, then?"

"You know those files you took?"

Unease rises in my chest, and I sit up. "What about them?"

"I think one of them is here. First name, Greta? I hope I'm wrong."

Falling to the floor, my knees ache from the hard thud as I scatter the files around to see who is who.

I gasp, snagging her photo from the silver clip. "I have it," I answer in shock, staring at a beautiful young woman who can't be more than thirty years old.

"Yeah, I'll be right there. Talking to the wife." His voice is muffled, his words sounding distant. He probably has the cellphone pressed to his chest, so I can't hear.

"Sorry about that. I'm back," he says.

"You're a horrible liar, Zig. The town is small. Everyone knows you don't have a wife."

"I panic when I'm caught doing something I'm not supposed to be doing. Like talking to you."

I snicker, loving that Zig is a cop for the perfect reasons. He's over six feet, muscular, and is afraid of being caught when he *is* the authority.

"I think one of two things is happening, Sanchez. One, someone knows this group of people and is taking them out one by one. Two, this person knows you're looking into these case files and is doing this *for* you."

I pause drinking my beer. "For me?"

"Yeah, maybe he thinks he is doing you a favor. I don't know, but as the detective, I thought you needed to know the information. I think it's time to build your own case against the person who is killing your suspects, but don't tell the sheriff I told you."

"Zig. You're a cop telling another cop information

pertaining to a case I'm allowed information on. I'm just not allowed to leave the house," I remind him.

"Right. I know that. I'm making sure you know that. I got to go. I'll talk to you later."

"Wait! Wait, Zig," I try to stop him from hanging up the phone.

"Yeah?"

"How did she die?"

"I don't know. It's like she was burned from the inside out, but that's impossible, right? The deaths in this town are getting weirder by the day. The weirder thing is her bones are missing. We only know who she is due to the other two bodies we found. What's left of her...it's pretty gruesome."

"Send me the crime scene photos," I mumble, getting lost in thought. "I'll text you. Later, Zig."

"Later."

I toss my phone onto the couch, thinking about the victims lately. They have nothing in common except the fact that they are criminals. Other than that, they have nothing tying them together for the suspect to kill them like he is.

Opening the coffee table drawer, I grab the tape and hang Greta's photo on the wall. I scribble on a Post-it with how she died.

"Burned to death," I whisper as I write it out, then stick it to her photo.

Next, we have the taxidermist, who, according to the forensic pathologist, was eaten alive by beetles.

I place his photo next to Greta's, writing down his cause of death. While he isn't directly connected to Greta or Fireopal, his business was next to the park that Fireopal lived near, and where her body and a few others were found.

Taping Fireopal's picture in sequential order of death next to the taxidermist, I put her cause of death as a question mark. Parts of her body were flattened, while bones stuck out of her skin.

Who would be next?

I stare at the last three photos on the table, debating which order the killer is going in. He isn't going by age, or height, or hair color.

My eyes round when a thought occurs. It's impossible.

"No jodas!" There's no fucking way this person was able to get into my house without me knowing, but I think he is killing in order of how he saw the files laid out on my coffee table.

"No, there's...there's no..." My thought trails off when the reality hits me like a cold bucket of ice water on a freezing day.

Someone broke into my house. Studied these files. Broke my fucking bed somehow, which really pisses me off because my mattress is on the floor now, and wrote on my bathroom mirror.

And let's not forget my fucking fridge being stocked and my couch broken.

Who the hell is this guy? A murderer with a conscious who takes care of me? Maybe he is feeding me before killing me.

I gasp again.

What if he is trying to eat me?

I press my palms against my forehead and take a deep breath. "You sound like Zig. Everything is fine. If this person wanted to kill you, they would have by now."

I double-check the lock on the front door and windows before running to the back.

Locked.

So are the windows.

I haven't had time to install a security system yet since I am new to town. That will have to change. I'll have to ask to see who can do that for me.

I check all the bedrooms that I don't use. They are all fine except the room closest to mine.

I stand in the doorway, shivering from the cold draft drifting in through the open window. The original frayed curtains sway and dance. Leaves trickle in, sliding onto the hardwood floor as if this is a ballet and I'm the spectator.

Roots have made their way through the window, veining across the wall, overtaking the ceiling with their long twig fingers, with small dark blue berries growing amongst the lengths.

"Qué carajo?"I whisper harshly to the empty room, wondering what the fuck is happening in my house.

Gripping the window, I push it down just as another cool breeze brushes my cheek, carrying a song that I've been hearing all day.

"Lula-lala-la-la-laa."

What was that?

"Hello?" I peek my head out of the window, my curiosity getting the best of me. "Is someone there?" Glancing left and right, all I see is pitch black night.

The darkened shapes of the tree line come to life, playing tricks on my mind like a ventriloquist tugging the string to cause the shadows to move.

"Nothing is there," I say to myself, swallowing the lump of unease building in my throat.

An owl hoots in the distance, a lonesome, eerie note carrying across the yard. A creak coming from the side of the house makes me peer to the left, another trick causing me to see what clearly isn't there.

The roots are moving, stretching, becoming longer, and continuing to grow through the window. I rub my eyes, blaming exhaustion when it comes to the environment coming to life.

Pushing myself back inside, I clutch the lip of the window to close it. A few roots snap in half from the pressure, but the thicker ones don't budge.

"Come. On." I grunt, using all my weight and strength to close the window. "Fuck." Stepping back, I place my hands on my hips and stare at the problem I can't seem to solve.

Even being a detective, there are some things that don't have solutions.

"I could get a knife and cut them. God, that's going to take forever. And a ton of clean up. So much for my night off," I grumble, lacing my hands and placing them on top of my head while blowing out a breath.

Groaning, I bend down and pick up the berries that have fallen off the roots, wondering if they are edible.

"Lula-lala-la-la-laaa."

I freeze when the deep voice slithers down my spine. The gravel to the edge has goosebumps peppering over my flesh, my body's natural way of telling me that I'm in danger.

"Lulaaa," he breathes the end of my name, a haunted hiss mixing with the wind howling through the window. The floorboards creak under his weight when he takes a step forward, his shadow swallowing my own.

This can't be real. This can't be real. This can't be real.

I chant over and over again in my head. The feeling of being watched lately comes to mind, and the same sensations overcome my body. The same sense of danger, the same yearning to know who is responsible for awakening the need for thrill.

A hot flush rolls over every inch of my body. From head to toe, I feel his presence, yet there's a buzz of safety, security, and protection. Whoever this is, whoever has been following me, breaking into my home, even going as far as killing people, he doesn't scare me.

"You don't want to do this. I'm an officer with Cove Police Department and—"

"—I know what you are. I know *who* you are." His voice rumbles like the depths of an earthquake, sending tremors through my every bone. "I don't care."

"Killing a cop will only make this worse for you. You'll never get out of prison."

His shadow becomes bigger, towering over me as he takes a step forward, engulfing me in its sinful cloak.

"Do you think prison could keep me away from you?" A growl from him calls to me, my body reacting in ways that don't make sense. "Do you think anyone could keep me away from you?" He takes another step forward, the warmth radiating from his body seeping into my back. "Do you think that anyone who came between us would live to see another day?"

I still can't move. Fear immobilizes me, my brain unable to communicate with my body when I see the reflection of the intruder in the window.

He's part of the unknown I can see. He's massive, his head nearly touching the ceiling. His skin reminds me of leaves on a spring day.

He's my favorite color and, for reasons beyond me, I want to know what he'd look like against me. I want to fall against him. I want him to catch me and wrap me in his oversized embrace.

A reaction I've never felt before with anyone.

Roots slither over my shoulders, the dark blue berries catching my eye that are scattered across them. A hazy memory tries to come forward. I remember him from the night of the accident, I think.

The monster I thought I saw above me in bed, which I blamed on a nightmare. I'm either dreaming right now, or I'm truly in a terrifying situation that I have no chance of escaping.

Not when it comes to the size of this beast.

I stand no chance.

I'm pinned against the wall before I have a chance to blink, a large palm is nestled between my shoulders, applying enough pressure to keep me still, but not enough to hurt me.

A chittering sound comes from him, mixed between a purr and a click. The clamor is quick, awakening an outcry of need in my soul as if he is calling to me, *for* me, only I don't know how to answer.

"Not even death would keep me away from what I desire most." His breath is warm against the shell of my ear as his roots bind me to the wall. "You cannot escape me, Lulaaa," he whispers my name in a way that would travel with the autumn leaves on a brisk wind—hushed with a soft crackle as the tones travel to find the perfect place beneath my bones.

"What do you want?" I whimper, wondering why the trail of his lips against the back of my neck only has me agonizing for more.

"Is it not obvious, My Dream?" His gargantuan hand curls around my shoulder, the tips of his black claws biting into my skin.

My breath comes out in shaking bursts. Lust is a partner

to thrill, dancing inside my soul, and fighting for who takes the lead. A sensual battle that I know thrill will lose.

"Take what you want and go then." I swallow, my throat dry as my breath becomes faster.

A sharp pain drags down my arm. Pushing through the fear, my eyes peer down, inhaling when I see his fingers rake down my arm. Thin red lines appear on my skin.

Easing the pain, he changes his touch. He flips his hand, the rough caress gone and replaced with the ease of his knuckles gliding up my arm, a gentle curiosity as if he is touching a person for the first time.

I'm transfixed.

I'm trapped within his roots.

Bound in his grasp.

And there's nowhere for me to run.

I can't turn around. I can't see him for what he is. All I have is the wall holding me and the hope that whoever this man is, this creature, that he decides to let me go.

"Taking what I want isn't so easy," he says, grabbing the length of my dark brown hair.

Any attempts at moving are gone when he sniffs the strands, groaning, sounding like he has never smelled anything better.

I swallow, afraid for my finger to twitch because it might remind him that I'm here, that I'm alive, and listening to his every move.

His every breath.

With every intake, there's a slight growl that follows, one that is pleased, one that climbs down my spine, one that allows lust to pool between my legs.

"You smell intoxxxicating."

A tear breaks free from the pools filling my eyes.

"What's wrong?" He drags his nose across the top of my

head. "Are you afraid, Little Dream?" His wet tongue slides up my cheek, gathering the tears that have fallen. "You should be." Finger by finger, each one curls around my throat until he has a firm grasp on me. "As I am your damnation." One arm cages me in on the right side, his large bicep filling my vision.

"Your salvation." The other arm locks the cage, pressing against the wall on the other side of me, trapping me further. "Your mutilation." The sharp claw growing out of his thick, long finger cuts open the scab that was the healing scratch on my cheek.

It reaffirms that he has been here already, and the scratch that was there when I woke up to the sheriff banging on my door was caused by the monster inside my house.

He licks the blood from the wound, and damn it all, I lean into his touch, bending my head back to expose my neck for him.

His lips graze my throat, full and softer than I imagined a beast's mouth to be, and two sharp points threaten to break my skin. "Your curse."

Roots tighten around my body, securing me so I can't escape. This should feel like a curse. I should be screaming for help, begging for him not to hurt me, fight for my life, I should do something, anything!

But this is exactly what I crave.

"You like being in the hands of someone who might kill you, don't you?"

"You won't," I manage to mumble between my incoherent thoughts.

"I might." He runs his claws through my hair.

"Do it, then," I grit through my teeth. "End me. End whatever you're doing if all you want is me."

"End youuu?" The familiar hushed breath travels across my cheek. "That would end me."

I close my eyes, relishing in the thrum of my heart, wondering if I'll die tonight. The thrill alone might kill me, waiting to see if I'll make it until tomorrow.

I don't know why, but I can trust this brutal beast.

"Why aren't you screaming? I smell your fear, Little Dream." In a rough grip, he palms my breast, squeezing until I gasp from the sharp point of his nails teasing my nipples. "And yet I smell your desire."

"You terrify me," I admit, licking my lips, wishing he'd allow me to look at him. "I love that."

"Why?"

"Mi alma me lo dice," I reply, submitting to his hands exploring my body.

"What does that mean?"

"My soul says so."

He falls silent. I only know he is still here because I feel him. He is still standing behind me, radiating heat, a fire brewing between us that I would happily give in to, to experience more of whatever *this* is.

Because what if I wake up and this was all a dream? I know most women would want that. Most would be crying, begging to be set free, fighting against the restraints, and I can't.

His roots loosen their grip, allowing me just enough space to turn around so I can finally see the monster who has invaded my home. The moment my back is against the wall, the roots bind me again, keeping me still so I can't run.

His fingers slip under my chin, the digits wide and calloused, and they lift my head.

"Look at me."

I didn't realize I had my eyes shut, too afraid to know that maybe he isn't real. I'm still not convinced that this isn't a dream.

"I am your worst nightmare," his voice softens for the first time, "and you are my sweetest dream."

Opening my eyes, they widen in shock when I have to tilt my head all the way back until I hit the wall, my gaze migrating from the chiseled abs to his wide chest, broad shoulders, and a sculpted jaw. His eyes are pitch black, and he has horns in the middle of his head like a mohawk. Black veins and roots appear all over his body, slithering like snakes as if they are their own entity.

"What are you?" Another tear breaks free from my lash line.

"I've already told you." He tilts his head, the light gleaming from his nose piercing.

He has an eyebrow piercing and two massive bone gages in his ears. His nipples have small bones through them too.

I wonder who they belong to.

"So you've said. That is what you have labeled yourself as, but what are you?"

"I am no longer a man, but a DNA experiment," he says, pinching his brows together. "I am part rhino, nightmare, nightshade, vampire, and anglerfish."

My eyes dart all over his body, trying to see each and every part that belongs to what he has named, but I don't see them all.

"I-I-I don't unders-stand," I stammer, confused about how that is possible.

"I don't understand why you can see me and no one else can."

"I can see things that others can't. I have always been able to."

He cages me in again, the pitch black of his eyes shining like polished onyx, and he leans down. If I could melt into the wall, I would. More distance between us would be best. I don't trust myself around him.

Roots tighten around my body again, this time pinning my arms and legs to the wall and leaving me vulnerable.

"You want to see where my monsters hideee?" The chitter his back, his fangs gleaming, and a large black shadow with the consistency of smoke begins to emerge from him.

It swirls around his body, hissing and clicking with excitement.

Flowers begin to bloom along the roots, a sweet floral scent invading my nose. My fingers and toes begin to tingle, white static moving throughout my entire body.

"Let me in." He grips my jaw, prying my mouth open. "And I will show you why your soul has led you astray."

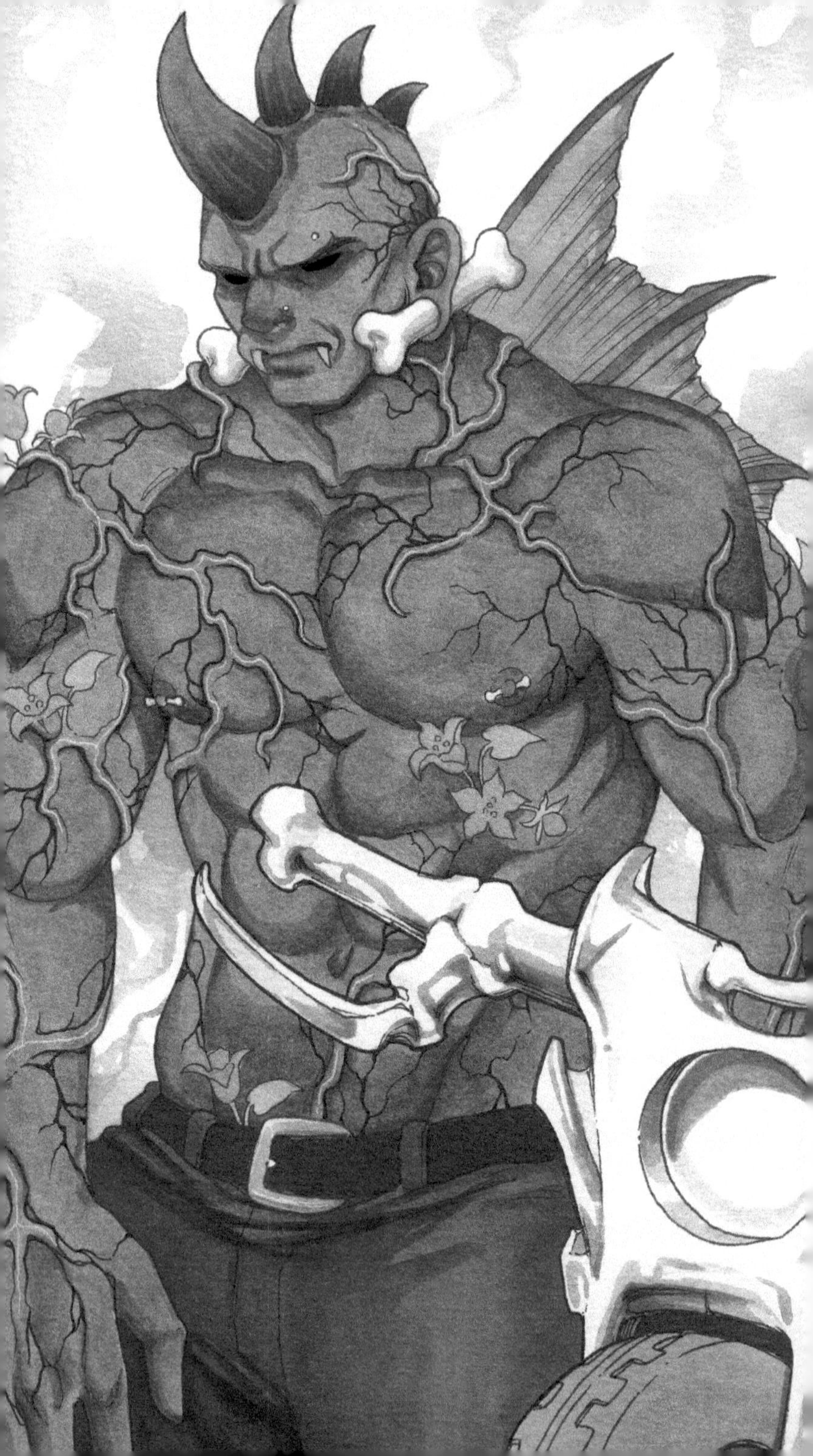

The longer I stare into her eyes, the more I want to fall into them. I want to explore her insides to figure out what makes her so unique compared to all the others.

There isn't a moment when she locks into my gaze, and her sense of consciousness drifts. The hypnotic state I use against my victims does not work on Lula. My vampire influence has no effect on her. Will anything else? Will finding her fears be impossible?

A thunderous growl of frustration builds in my chest, followed by a slight whine of not knowing what she fears most. I want to experience her terror and soothe her pain. I want her screams, yet I want her moans.

I get lost in the feel of her trapped within my roots, her skin rubbing against the rough vascular tissue that allows me to feel every torturous inch of her silken skin.

She's softer than I deserve.

Without breaking eye contact, I kick off my boots and unbutton my jeans.

"What are you—" She stops mid- sentence, closing her eyes to focus on speaking. The nightshade poison is beginning to work. "What are you doing?" Lula manages to slur, the poison taking longer to take hold.

"Taking what's mine, Lula. I should have done this much sooner." One claw drifts down her chest, plucking the first button free. "But I've been busy making sure no one else has your attention."

"The killings?" Her eyes hood. "It's you?"

"It's always me. It will always be me."

"I can't..." She swallows. "I can't allow you to do that."

I pop another free, her blouse parting to show her cleavage, a white laced bra peeking through.

"Allow me?" A full belly laugh is unknown to my own ears since I can't remember the last time I found something truly amusing. I rip her shirt free, her body on display to sate my disgusting tendencies. "I do not need permission." Raking my nails down her pants, blood sticking to the underside of my claws.

She screams the moment her skin tears from the sharpened points.

"Mmmm," I hum with satisfaction, lifting my nails to the light.

Her blood glistens so beautifully. It's the perfect color. Not too dark, not too bright—the exact shade that I love the most.

I smell them, inhaling the rich citrus that reminds me of a refreshing drink on a hot, unforgiving day.

"You smell..." My voice deepens with arousal. "Divine."

She watches me intently, calculating, as if she's trying to figure out a way to set herself free or give in to the monster who has been breaking into her home for the last few days.

Without her knowledge.

"Look at me when I taste you." I grip her chin with one

hand to give her stability since she is losing all feeling in her body.

Her long lashes blink in wonder, seducing me with every flutter.

I suck my index finger between my lips, never breaking eye contact with my mate. My tongue dips into the crevice of my nail, her blood exploding over every supernatural taste bud, allowing me to experience her in ways that barely scratch the itch of the cravings I have for her and her alone.

Fireworks of screams I've ignited from so many others burst in my eyes as her blood travels down my throat. I can taste her terror, a bittersweet undertone that adds to the spice of her want for me.

Such a confusing mate, finding herself wanting yet fearing me. I can give her the best of both worlds.

"Do you want to see what you do to me?" I rumble, sucking a second finger into my mouth, needing every fucking drop so none goes to waste.

I'll drink her by the time the night ends and the sun rises. She will be bound to me as the first rays of light pour through the window. For all eternity, for all futures, her soul hexed to be mine.

What I'm learning is that it is me who is in her cage, never wanting to be set free because freedom only exists if I can see her. Every choice I make, every life I take, every nightmare I inflict, it is all for her. She wields the key to every decision made, and I regret nothing.

"Who are you?" The words are strained against her tongue.

I suck all my fingers clean before stepping into her space, until her breasts push against my abdomen.

"How rude of me not to introduce myself." I flatten my

palm over my heart. "After all this time, I had forgotten that while hunting you, you don't know me." I push down my jeans, tossing them to the side, licking the tip of my left fang.

"What are you going to do to me? Are you going to leave me in nothing but pieces like you did Greta? Fireopal? The taxidermist?" A fresh wave of sadness deconstructs her face, her wet cheeks reminding me how thirsty I have become for her.

Mesmerized by her beauty, I skim my fingers over her cheek, across her lips, over the tip of her nose, needing to recite every line and curve that creates her.

"You have hollowed out a part of me that I am afraid only you can fill." My brows pull together, hating that she thinks that I would ever disrespect her body like the others. I find myself mourning at the thought of her needing to be put back together, something as similar to me, and it is the last thing I want for her.

The pain of being transformed is not what I want for her.

I'm mourning at the thought of finding her pieces, the imagery too strong.

"I am Shade Hellström." I nuzzle her cheek, marking her with my scent. Every threat needs to smell me on her, knowing she's taken, knowing she's mine.

"Shade," she repeats in a slow, struggling exhale, but a wave of content ripples between us—a scent I could get used to.

Hearing her say my name has an electrical river of ecstasy buzzing in my veins.

"And I want you to see what you do to me." Gripping the back of her neck, I force her to look down at my cock. "Watch what you're chained to."

The anglerfish mouth parts, the teeth bearing themselves to her for the first time, showing off how sharp they are. My long, thick cock begins to lengthen at last, aching due to being trapped for so long.

Her lust fuels the air, sparking it, so all that it would take for me to come is a simple exhale of her breath against the shaft.

"Oh god—" she wheezes, lifting her worrying gaze up to meet mine.

"I said to watch what you do to me." I force her head back down, my fingers digging into the muscles of her neck.

My hard length weighs so much that it can't stand straight.

"You're—" She whimpers, squeezing her eyes shut as she continues to fight the poison. "You're pierced."

I have a Prince Albert through the tip and a Jacob's ladder down the shaft. The metal bars gleam from the precome leaking from the tip. I'm dying to be inside my mate, literally. The vampire needs her blood in massive waves, to drink is to claim, and I've been so focused on killing her suspects to have her to myself—that I haven't fucking had her *to* myself.

That will change going forward. She is too important to allow another day to slip through my fingers.

My hard cock falls to my knee, the precome smearing against my thigh.

I bare her to me, stripping the remaining shreds of her pants off. She's in her bra and panties. The simple white lace against her tanned skin has an insatiable need come over me. I'm reminded of the night I fucked her with a root and came all over her chest, marking her as mine and mine alone.

Too much time has passed, and now I'm afraid that

what I will do next will take her to the edge of death. Killing her is impossible now that she has my blood inside her.

"What do yo—" She stops speaking, the poison finally doing its job. Her eyes widen in horror, and the amount of fear pouring from her gets me a little tipsy.

She tries to speak, but nothing but noises come out. More tears fall when she realizes her predicament.

Lula can't cry for help.

She can't scream.

No one will be able to hear her.

Her misery is mine.

I growl, my cock bumping into her thigh. The teeth surrounding the base of my cock try to bite, wanting to lock her to me while I fill her pretty cunt with come.

Before, I wasn't sure if I wanted children with her, but the thought of her carrying my offspring, smelling of me, branded, proof of my claim, now I want nothing more than to see her belly round.

My tongue drags over my teeth as my eyes linger on her body that I'm about to invade. Grabbing her by the neck, I bend down until I'm eye level with her, more tears escaping her eyes, but she can't fool me.

She loves this.

Lula loves me.

Even if she doesn't know it yet.

My claw slices through her bra, freeing her breasts that fit perfectly in my hands. Her nipples become tight as I drift my fingers down her chest, then her trembling stomach, and cup her pussy.

She gasps, mouth wide open, just waiting to be filled by my rhino cock that will no doubt choke her from the size.

Puncturing the material of her panties, I fist them in my hand, ripping them from her body so she's naked before me. Unable to stop the dying need to smell her sweet cunt, I bury my nose into her underwear,

I growl, inhaling deep. Anger consumes me when my lungs won't expand any further. I could suffocate myself just like this, infiltrated by her, and I'd die a happy beast.

"I'm going to be saving these for later." I toss her underwear on top of my jeans, a reminder not to leave them behind when this night ends.

Another wave of lust penetrates the air, making me turn to Lula with a raised brow. She's still crying, but I'm no fool. She squeezes her thighs together, the evidence of her arousal shining on her tender flesh.

I crash to my knees, the floor cracking under my weight, and the walls shaking from the force of me. I'm nearly her height now. I skim my hands up her thighs, her muscles trembling under me.

Bending down, I flatten my tongue across the marks I've left behind when I ripped her pants free. Lifting my own hands, I school my face when I notice a tremble.

I'm...nervous.

I've never been nervous a day in my life.

Inhaling her again, needing to know that this *is* my mate before me. Flattening my tongue, I lick up her leg, her blood fusing to my cells. Her essence binding to me.

The bond between us becomes stronger, the tendrils of fate strengthen the ropes our souls are tugging on to pull us together.

My mate.

My one.

My only.

My dream.

My beloved.

I have never wanted a woman the way I want her.

When I was the enforcer for Shallow Sinners, the biker bunnies were easy when or if I ever wanted them. They knew the drill. I wanted nothing to do with them afterwards—not because I didn't like or respect them—but because I didn't have the emotional capability to give them more of whatever fucking life they wanted.

As for giving Lula what she wants emotionally, I know I'll fall short there too. I was not created to love. Love complicates life, twisting the choices usually made into something better.

I don't *do* better.

I want messy. I want death. I want blood on my hands.

Bad decisions are what fuel me. What kind of monster would I be if I did good deeds?

Her whimper when my tongue swipes close to her cunt pulls me from the path my thoughts were going down.

I will never be good for her, but I will always try to be. Everyone else though, can die by my hands. Their blood can rain from the clouds, and I will drown myself in every drop.

Her scent is too much for me as I continue to lick the wounds I've created. They slowly heal, from my blood, from my saliva; she will never need to worry about being hurt when I can heal her.

She impatiently grunts since she can't speak, urging me for more. Lust drips down her thighs; the sweet treat smells too good to ignore. Gripping the inside of her legs, I yank them apart, ordering the roots to bind her ankles to the wall.

I want all access.

She gasps, her stomach rising and falling with every heavy breath. Her eyes are glazed with confusion, and her lashes are still wet from all her delicious tears.

Hopefully, she has more for me later.

Unable to stop myself, I lick up her inner thigh, gathering the liquid heat dripping from her cunt. A loud, rumbling growl vibrates my chest when the citrus perfume permeating from her blood is alive in her precome.

Groaning, I tilt my head back with my eyes closed, taking a moment to marvel at the delicacy of Lula.

"You taste so good, Little Dream. Sweet and bright like the sun upon my skin. I don't think I'll ever be able to get enough." Opening my eyes when she fades from my tongue.

Since I'm nearly the same height as her while I'm on my knees, looking at her is simple. Saliva drips from her lips, the ability to swallow hindered by the nightshade.

Opening my mouth, I catch the string of spit dangling from her bottom lip, needing to quench my thirst for every type of liquid she possesses. Stretching out my tongue, I catch the next droplet that falls, clutching her thighs with my claws.

She whimpers again, which causes me to tsk.

"Ah, ah, ah, so impatient. Let me discover you, Lulaaa," I say in a hushed tone, the nightmare inside me clawing at my throat.

Lula whimpers again, doing her best to struggle against the roots. More flowers bloom across them, adding more poison to the air for her to inhale.

"Relax, Little Dream. I'm only the worst thing to ever happen to you."

The wind blows through the window again, allowing her scent to wrap around me like a warm blanket. A purr trills in my chest when my thick, long tongue slips through her lips, rolling over her clit.

Her thighs tremble from the touch. I do it again and again, the worst of me expanding beyond my body, engulfing her in my shadow. It's as if the moon slipped in front of the sun, casting us into darkness.

I feast, sucking her clit in between my fangs, loving that my poison keeps her still, yet she can feel every pleasurable thing I do to her. She has no control over herself. In time, I hope she learns to relinquish herself to me, and I'll give her everything she's ever yearned for.

"You are everything I desired, and nothing will keep me from having you." I dive my tongue inside her, plunging it in and out.

Sucking each lip into my mouth, I groan, nibbling the sensitive flesh with my fangs. Breaking the roots holding her down, I lift her legs onto my shoulders, allowing me to bury my head between her legs, getting lost in her beautiful cunt.

Her taste is a peaceful river, flowing endlessly into my mouth and sliding down my throat the way water drips upon the skin. A primal hunger surges through me, a heat I can't explain. Every nerve-ending is on fire for her, my beasts growling and clawing at my insides to claim her.

She will be claimed.

Whether she likes it or not.

By the time the sun rises, she will wear my mark on her neck for all to see.

I'm not that dumb. I know there are other monsters here. I see them, and I know they can sense me. I can't have my mate walking around without my mark or without my scent! What kind of man would I be if I allowed other males to think she is available?

I would have to kill so many. As much as I would love that, I'd rather have her smell of me. I want to know I've done everything in my power to bind her to me, and now that I have her here, naked, bared to me, I want nothing more than to breed her.

I think it's the only way for my beasts to calm down. My skin crawls with need. I feel the monsters that make me stretching my skin, pushing at my bones to consume her.

Gliding my nails up her inner thighs, I push one finger inside her slick cunt. One finger is three of hers, wide and long, and even finger fucking her won't be enough to prepare her for my cock.

Reaching between my legs, I stroke myself, giving into the need to relieve the ache. I twist my palm over the tip, gathering the precome with every stroke that brings me closer to devouring her.

She whimpers again, this time it's higher-pitched, as if she's trying to scream. Glancing up, her lips are parted, and her eyes roll to the back of her head as her orgasm has her thighs tightening around my head.

Knowing she came because of me has my own orgasm threatening, but I hold off. I want every fucking drop to go inside her. That's where it belongs—where I belong.

Standing, I don't wipe my mouth. I want her to see how my lips shine from how wet I made her.

Roots travel up her body, twisting around her nipples, pulling gasps from her, and I place one arm against the wall while the other wraps around her neck.

"Let's see what you fear the most, Little Dream. Let me in." I smash my lips to hers, wanting her to taste herself, wanting to feel the give of her pillow-soft lips against mine.

Maybe one day, when she won't run from me, and I won't have to use my nightshade against her, she'll kiss me because she craves it.

"Let me in," I whisper against her lips, my nightmare drifting into her lungs with every breath I give.

I close my eyes, allowing my mind to travel to her subconscious, wanting her fear more than I have ever wanted anything else in this world.

"Interesting," I say to myself in a soft, curious rumble.

I'm not sure what I expected, but it wasn't this.

I'm in a deserted city. Cars are in the middle of the roads. Some have crashed into one another; others are parked with doors open and windows busted. Weeds have overtaken the city. Vines have crawled up traffic lights and lamp posts, slithering, haunting greenery that is slowly taking over the city.

Everything is empty.

There are no children.

No pets.

No wild animals.

It's as if everyone has vanished.

The skyscrapers get lost in the low-hanging clouds. The windows don't even shine from the buildup of dirt and dust.

I begin to walk, curious as to why I am here, why her subconscious would take me to such a desolate place.

The first ice-cold chill seeps into my skin. I pause, flipping my palm over to catch a snowflake. When it melts, I gasp for the first time when I hear a child scream.

I wipe the water onto my jeans, questioning why the scream has made my chest hurt. I clutch my heart, wishing I could rip it free from my chest from the amount of pain that singular scream brought me.

I had forgotten that the snowflakes are memories, forgotten or not, allowing my nightmare to feed and decide what to scare them with next. It's information. It's survival, but with Lula, it feels...like an invasion.

"Hello?" Lula's voice has me lift my head.

She's distant. I can't tell where she is.

"Hello! Is someone there?" she cries out again. "Anybody? Hello!"

I follow the sound of her voice, that is twitched with panic. Speeding to her in less than a few seconds, I duck behind a large truck, peering out its window. My eyes find her spinning in a circle every few steps, hoping to see someone behind her.

"Hello?"

Her fear smells...impeccable. I inhale, the nightmare strengthening in a way I've never felt before. Her fear not only feeds me but empowers me.

Looking down, I grin when I see a loose stone. Grabbing it, I throw it over the car, and it lands behind Lula.

She spins around so fast, she loses her footing, catching herself at the last second.

"H-Hello?" Her voice sounds so small, so fragile, and there's that fear again, quaking her voice. "Is someone there? Anyone? Please! Call out. I'll come to you. You don't have to fear me." She waits for anyone to reply, but all that meets her is the light patter of snow falling.

"No." She shakes her head, whispering in denial.

Lula dashes into the store, shouting at the top of her lungs. "Is anyone here!"

Crashes sound from inside, the chaos making me grin. Her fear is unlike anything I have ever tasted. It's as if I've pressed myself onto a live wire, allowing the buzz and electricity to flow through my veins.

The window of the business shatters, and when I peek around the truck, I see Lula standing there, heaving, and a chair lying in broken glass on the sidewalk.

Her fear slides down my throat like a burning shot of vodka, *warming my stomach, invigorating my veins. I've never felt such power.*

"Where is everyone!" She falls to her knees, the aroma of her blood stinging my nose.

My enhanced vision focuses on where she fell, the glass digging into her skin.

She's harmed herself.

I don't like that.

Even though her sadness tastes better than a pig being roasted for long hours, dripping in juices and tender, the meat falling off the bone—the thought alone makes my mouth water.

Yet.

I find that I do not wish for her to be sad. I don't like it. It's an odd realization. I hate that my need for her fear requires her to be in pain. What kind of mate does that make me?

And why do I still hide behind a truck, soaking in her sadness as if I am the desert waiting for a wild rain?

"Lula-lala-la-la-laaa." The nightmare sings for her, her name echoing in the emptiness of this abandoned city.

She jerks her head up, hissing from the pain in her knees as she stands. "What are you? What do you want!" She yells until her voice breaks, stumbling out of the open window, the glass crunching under her shoes. "What do you want from me!"

Bending down, she picks up a shard of glass, her gaze darting left and right to see where I am.

She runs, sprinting down the road, zigzagging between cars while yelling, "Please, call out to me! Is someone there? Anyone?"

I follow her, keeping a safe distance, allowing her to feel my presence without seeing me.

This nightmare could end now. I'm full. Her fear has sated me, but I'm addicted. I want to soak all of it up until there's nothing left for me to eat.

I bump against a car hard enough for the alarm to go off, the loud siren causing Lula to jump, weaponizing the shard of glass in her hand by holding it in front of her.

"Who is there! Stop being such a fucking coward and come get me!" she roars, her bravery masking the scent of the terror I love so much.

I would come out, but that would end all the fun.

And there's a quiet part of me that I'm wrestling with that is whispering that it isn't fun anymore because she is our mate. We shouldn't want her to be afraid.

"I'm alone," she begins to sob. "I hate being alone."

My eyes widen in realization that her worst fear is dying alone. I'm torturing her for my own enjoyment.

The fear in her eyes shifts, and so does the smell. Her eyes have turned from angry, readying herself to fight, to withdrawn, and from here, I can hear her heartbeat slow.

"What are you thinking?" I mutter to myself, unable to take my eyes off her.

"I hate being alone," she repeats, falling to her knees once again.

She readjusts the long shard of glass in her hand that reminds me of an icicle during a frigid storm. Without hesitation, without any doubt, she angles the point of the piece of glass onto her wrist.

I hold my breath, wondering if she is baiting me.

"I can't live in a world where I am the only one," she says, another tear escaping. "I'd rather die than be alone."

She digs the glass into her skin, slicing into her beautiful, tanned skin. Blood pours from her forearm, the ground unable to drink it like I wish to. Lula moves the makeshift blade to the other hand, smearing blood on the glass, and repeats the same cut from her wrist to her elbow.

My blood that I had her consume won't heal her in her dreams. If she dies in her dream, there's no coming back from that. Not even fate could save her.

Placing the glass against her neck, she begins to slice, and it's too much for me. This is no longer fun. I can't watch the only person in the world I care about die.

I'm at her side in my next breath, catching her in my arms as she begins to fall. Pools of blood grow onto the pavement, red rivers forming in the cracks of the road.

"You," she wheezes, lifting her hand to slap me.

But to my surprise, her palm rests on my cheek, cupping my jaw.

"I won't die alone." She closes her eyes, her cries pulling at the soul inside me that I thought was long dead. "Thank you."

"You can't die, Little Dream." I raise her arm, brows furrowing at the amount of blood leaving her.

Licking the wound, I moan, her blood gushing into my mouth. "This is nothing but a bad dream, Lula. The nightmare inside me couldn't help it. Your fear is unlike anything I have ever experienced." I lick her other arm, trying to stop the bleeding with my healing capabilities, but it isn't working on her. "We have to go back to reality. It's the only way to save you."

"Why? Aren't you here to kill me?"

I shake my head, pulling her closer to my chest, a protective stance as her body becomes weaker.

"No, Little Dream. Killing you would kill me. In the depths of my despair, in the cave of the hell that created me, the only spark of good is you."

She only has a few minutes left before we are stuck in her worst fear. I don't know what would become of me, but if I didn't die like I feel like I would, I would wander aimlessly through her nightmare to live alone as punishment.

"Why?" A tear rolls slowly down the apples of her high cheeks.

"Because my soul says so and fate deemed you to be mine."

"Are you mine as well?"

"Every damned part of me," I whisper, brushing her hair from her face. "And I am damned, Lulaaa," I sigh her name. "Beyond your wildest dreams."

I bend down, the endless pits of my eyes stare into hers, learning more about myself in this moment than I thought I ever would.

I love her.

With every ounce of DNA that makes me.

I press my lips against hers, uncaring if it's the time or not. I need to feel the connection between us. It's time for me to stop lurking in the shadows. I'll always follow her. I'll always protect her. I'll always kill for her.

I'll always.

OVE POLI
EPARTMENT

CHAPTER ELEVEN

LULA

His lips are a shock, bringing me back to the real world and out of the horrible nightmare he induced.

I should be furious. If I'm honest, a part of me is. And confused. So confused as to how this is happening and why, but it can wait.

All of it can wait.

His kiss is much softer than I expected it to be. It's still rough from the sharp points of his fangs grazing against my lips, and the strength he holds in his kiss alone is something new for me.

But I love it.

He is exactly what I have craved my entire life. The thrill. The adrenaline. The fear. I never thought it was because I'm meant to be more. I'm meant to belong to a monster.

To Shade.

His tongue is thicker and longer than mine, twisting around mine with dominance. The roots binding me loosen, helping me down until I can stand on my own, which breaks our kiss.

He growls with every rise of his chest, the black pools of his eyes hooded with lust. Without saying a word, he picks me up, slamming my back against the wall, then wraps my legs around his waist.

I can't focus. I'm lightheaded. Looking down at my arms, I'm still bleeding, yet I can't feel my body.

Am I still dreaming? What if the only time I can see him is in my dreams?

"Mine," he snarls, grabbing his cock and guiding it to my pussy.

If my eyes could fall out of my head from shock, they would. There's no way he is going to fit inside me. His cock is as wide as his wrist and at least two feet in length, if not more.

His claws dig into my scalp, grip my hair, yanking my head back, and Shade strikes. His fangs sink into my neck, dragging the blood directly from my vein. My body heats, an intense fever that has a sweat breaking out over my body.

I don't know what's happening to me. I can't move my arms or legs, but I can feel *everything* else.

When his tongue brushes against mine, when the tips of his claws bite into my skin, when he pulls blood from me, it's all sensations causing my brain to short-circuit.

I don't think this is real.

He retracts his fangs, a root wrapping around my throat in a tight vise. I gasp for breath, blood rushing to my head.

"One day you will want me the way I want you," he sneers, grabbing his cock and pushing it against my pussy that struggles to stretch for him. "But you will learn to."

Unable to move my head, I peer down, my stomach twisting when I see what else is down there. The teeth are sharp, retracting in a way that reminds me of a bite. Something long and wire-like unravels from the base of his cock, a bright light glowing at the very tip.

It stretches to the length of his cock, entering me as Shade does. He is too big. Too thick. Too much. I try to beg him to stop, to not go any further, but I can't speak. Whatever he did to me has rendered me useless.

"You're going to take every fucking inch of me too. It will hurt, but you won't be able to beg me to stop." He grips my chin, a smug smirk tugging his lips. "And I am glad you can't."

He drives inside me in one full thrust, uncaring that he is too big for my body. Blood drenches his cock as he tears my insides apart.

"Oh, isn't that a pretty sight?" He moans, drifting his finger across the end of his shaft. "Christening what belongs to you, Little Dream?" Shade chuckles, sucking his finger into his mouth. "As you should. I'm all yours."

And that terrifies me.

His nostrils flare. "So much fear. If you keep smelling that good, I'm not going to lasttt," he hisses the last word again, his voice being possessed by the nightmare.

I can't breathe. He stretches me beyond belief.

I feel him everywhere.

In my skin, threatening my bones, tearing any organ that is in his way.

The fin on his back tenses, spiking into sharp points with every thrust he gives me. Blood begins to pool in my mouth, and I try to scream, but I'm silenced due to the poison in my system.

He's killing me.

He sniffs the air again, growling. "You love being in death's grip, don't you?"

I whimper, hating that he is right, but if this is how I die, I can't think of a better way to fade from existence.

"Don't worry, Lulaaa. I won't kill you, but you'll come close."

My ribs break, snapping in half like a twig. I cough up blood, spewing it all over his face and chest. Shade's wide tongue licks his lips, his fangs gleaming in a red-tinted smile.

Without warning, he pulls out of me, a gush of blood following and splashing onto the floor. The roots binding me to the wall release me, and I fall onto the floor, crumbling in weakness.

I wheeze, struggling to catch my breath.

I thought he was done, but he pulls my arms back, popping them from the sockets, then mounts me from behind. His giant cock easily drives into me again, his hands gripping my hips so hard, they crack.

He's breaking me.

And the most fucked up part is that I like it. This is what I have always craved. I'm thankful I can't feel the painful parts, but I know there will be a day when I do—that I'll want to feel the pain he inflicts on me.

The poison is starting to wear off slightly. There's a tingle in my fingers and toes. That could be from losing so much blood. It's starting to pool under my body, and with every punishing thrust of his hips, we slide through the slippery puddle.

Flipping me over onto my back, the blood splashes around me, decorating my arms in droplets of crimson rain.

My vision begins to blur. His magnificent body is easily still able to be seen. He towers over me. Every limb is as thick as a redwood tree trunk. His veins are black, the roots slither along his skin like snakes, and his abs are carved bricks, tensing with every flex of his hips.

He's beautiful and deadly, the combination my soul has been starved for.

Glancing down, my stomach and chest bulge from his cock, the skin stretching, my body breaking itself to accommodate him.

"That's it. Fuck, you feel so good, Lula. You're sick for me, aren't you? Hating that you need something as disturbing as me to come." He runs his hands up my body, engulfing my breasts with his palms. "So fucking perfect for me. All of you." He glides his hands down my curves, surprising me with the ease of his touch compared to the violence he continues to deliver with every push. "All of you is made for all of me," he says more to himself with a slight confusion twisting the arch of his brow.

He bends down, snagging my lips in another kiss, his tongue slipping into my mouth.

I want to kiss him back. I want to experience what he is experiencing, and all I can do is lie here, taking what he gives me.

"Such a beautiful body for such a decrepit soul." He slips his hand under the back of my head and lifts me, slicing his throat, and his lip curls, my gaze landing on his long fangs. "Drink. Be damned to me for all eternity, and I will protect you with my life."

The blood that spills out of him drifts into the air, floating like smoke, trying to reach the clouds.

"Drink and I will give you the thrill you so rightfully deserve."

Not having to think twice, I lock my lips onto his wound, drinking whatever flows in his veins that pumps his immoral heart. Shade moans, slamming his fist down onto the floor, snapping the hardwood floors.

"Fuck, you're going to make me come. Your lips feel so good on me."

His blood does something to me. My insides feel odd, as if my organs are shifting and my wounds are healing.

"You already had my blood inside you, but you needed more. The more you have, the more you'll be able to accommodate me." He pets the back of my head, then locks his own teeth on the back of my neck, igniting a loud cry from me as his bite is harder.

The more his teeth sink into me, the more I know he is about to rip the flesh from my bones. He growls, continuing to fuck me without care of hurting me. A tug within my chest forms, filling the cavity with emotions that aren't my own.

Rage, unlike anything I've ever experienced, fills my chest, followed by obsession, possessiveness, happiness, and a hint of sadness that I can't understand. I think these emotions belong to Shade. I don't understand how or why I can sense them, and I don't mind. Feeling him within me has me closer to him. I can almost hear the whispering hiss of the nightmare inside my head.

He's right there, pushing to breach my thoughts, but can't.

Ripping his fangs free, his hand lands in the middle of my chest, pushing me backwards until the cold floor presses against the warmth of my back.

I don't feel as dizzy now that I've had more of his blood. His cock almost slips out, then eases in again, only to not go as deep. The bulbous light that slipped into me with his shaft illuminates my insides. He continues to inch forward, the light acting like a guide.

I gasp when I feel a pinch. Watching in both horror and fascination, the light glows bright, revealing my womb to Shade. A low guttural sound thunders in his chest, becoming louder the deeper he enters me. Roots keep my legs spread.

"You'll be a good girl, Little Dream, and take every fucking drop of me. We won't leave this room until you're bred and your cunt is overflowing with my come. You'll be claimed, mated, and owned by me." He slips his hand up my thigh, up to my stomach, and outlines the thick ridges of his cock stretching my belly.

"Lulaaa," he hisses, the sinister shadow within him pulsing from his skin with every stream of come that fills me. "Can you feel it? My little parasite is swimming around in your womb, gobbling up my come and your eggs. Just wait until it latches on."

The bulb's brightness fades when his come encompasses it, extinguishing the light.

And when it does, there's a pinch of pain before the most intense orgasm courses through my body, my muscles clenching around his girth, drinking in his come with every spasm.

A vicious primal snarl twists his mouth, his fangs flashing at me with a threat. Without warning, the anglerfish mouth around the base of his cock bites down on me. The top row of teeth sinks into my lower abdomen while the bottom jaw slices below the curve of my ass, locking us in place.

I cry out from the pain, the nightshade no longer able to camouflage numbness in my body.

Shade roars to the ceiling, his claws digging into my thighs, raking down the lengths of my legs, and tearing the flesh from the bone.

I heal due to his blood inside me.

"Mine." He yanks me against him, closing the few inches of space we had between us. "All mine."

He curls over me, trapping me within the makeshift cage his arms create around my head. I've never felt so small before, my body so insignificant and breakable compared to Shade.

And I love it.

"You are the undoing of darkness." He kisses me, and this time I'm able to meet every movement, every turn, every slip of the tongue.

"Me? Why?" I break away from his lips, my vision tumbling into a blur when exhaustion grips me.

"Because my soul says so, even if it doesn't understand it."

We stay locked like this, my body forced to drink his come since his warmth has nowhere else to go.

I'm still not sure if he is a dream, one I haven't decided if it's good or bad. Unable to fight the demand of consciousness, my eyes fall shut.

I'm led into a darkness that is no longer my own.

I'm in a place I don't recognize. If my mamita were here, she would call this place 'Lo Desconocido."

The Unknown.

It's very cold in here. I can see my own breath with every exhale, a cloud leaving my mouth to drift to the sky. Reaching my hand out, I flip my hand over, the white flakes settling in my palm.

Snow.

When the snow melts, an electrified zap of pain embeds itself in my skin. I grip my wrist, crying out from the surprise of it. Another snowflake falls and screams echo in my mind, nothing exact, nothing I can remember experiencing myself.

My hand continues to tingle, the petrified screams reverberating in my mind can't be forgotten. I feel the pain as if it is my own trauma. Looking around for any signs of life.

A room forms ahead, and a middle-aged man is standing over a woman, screaming at her, his greying brown hair falling into his face. I pause a decent distance away, not knowing if what I'm seeing is real or not.

He pushes her so hard, she falls to the ground between the bed and a rocking chair that is nestled in the corner.

I don't know these people. I've never seen them before in my entire life. My Mamita taught me that everything happens for a reason. Whatever the explanation is as to why I'm here, I accept it.

"You fucking bitch! How dare you try to keep him from me!" the man yells, leaning down to point his finger in her face. "He is my son!"

She has tears staining her face, her mascara ruined from being so scared. The woman raises her hand to keep him at least an arm's length away.

"He shouldn't have been!" she yells. "He deserves better than you. He is better than you. I can't believe such a wonderful boy is able to exist in a world that you sour with your existence!"

My brows raise, surprised she would stand her ground like that, given their positions.

He takes a swig of whatever clear liquid is in the bottle he has gripped by the neck.

"If he didn't have a slut of a mother, maybe he'd end up being a real man. There's no way that runt of a kid is mine." He takes another long swallow from the bottle. Sweat glistens off his forehead which has his hair sticking to the moisture. "I regret *marrying you," he sneers. "I only married you because you were pregnant, but if I had known he wasn't mine, I wouldn't have wasted my time with you."*

"He is yours! How many times do I have to tell you! He is yours!" she cries.

A small boy is crouched in the next room, knees tucked to his chest, and his arms wrapped around his thighs. His face is half hidden behind his knees, but I'm able to see the dark, wet lashes that frame his eyes.

He only has a pair of shorts on, and I'm able to see all the bruises left on his body. He's a little underweight too. My heart breaks for the unknown child. No kid should experience fear within their own home.

I sit down, huffing hot air into my hands as the temperature drops.

"Where is he? Where's that waste of fucking space?" his father slurs, stomping out of the room to find the boy.

Standing in alarm, I step forward. "Don't you dare! He didn't do anything to you!"

The drunken, sorry excuse of a man has a stained white tank top on that looks like it hasn't seen the washer in days. He stands in his underwear that has me curling my lip in disgust with the holes around the waistband and the grimy yellow dimming the material.

He notices his son curled up in the corner of the room, then slams the door, locking it so no one can enter.

"No!" I scream, sprinting across the floor. "Open the door!" I try the handle, jiggling it with all my strength. The whimpers leak out from under the door every time his fists make contact.

Patting my hip for my gun, I groan in frustration when I notice I'm not wearing my holster. I have no weapon in this dream, which only irritates me further.

I bang on the door again, pounding it with all my weight. "Open the fucking door!" I yell just as my surroundings change.

The door is gone.

The floor vanishes from under my feet, and I fall, screaming at the top of my lungs since everything is still so dark. Snow continues to fall, and I'm still able to hear and feel the screams of pain.

But these types of wails aren't just from physical pain. These are brutal, soul-wrenching cries, the ones that steal breath from your lungs. It brings tears to my eyes. All I want to do is soothe the poor soul they belong to.

I land, the snow-covered ground breaking my fall. I groan, pushing myself up until I'm standing. This time, I'm in what looks like a backyard. Beyond the property line is all black, reminding me that this is a dream.

"I said to fucking stay out here until I'm ready to let you in." That hateful yet familiar voice has me turn my head, seeing the man who calls himself a father open the sliding glass doors and toss his child outside. "Maybe you'll think twice before interrupting me while I'm talking to your mother. She needs to learn her lesson just like you do."

The child in question is a little older in this dream than the last. I'm not sure who he is or what this dream is supposed to tell me.

He cries, banging on the glass door. "Daddy! Let me in," he begs. "It's so cold. Let me in! Daddy!" He presses his forehead against the glass, the warmth of his body fogging it. "Mommy!" He tries for her next, but from the slaps coming from the other room, this poor kid is stuck outside.

"Hey! Hey, you aren't alone!" I run to him, wanting him to know he is safe.

Before I can get to him, the dream changes again.

I take another ride, another fall through the endless pit. This time, when I land on the ground, the snow has only just kissed the ground, lying directly on top of the dead grass in a thin sheet.

The trees are shadows in the night, the stars twinkling above to remind me that there's beauty, and the moon is full, casting a bright glow onto the same house.

I duck behind a nearby tree, rolling my eyes at myself when I remember no one can see me. Leaning against the trunk, I smile to myself when I see the boy, who is clearly older now, sit at the living room table with his mom. The blinds are open, and I'm able to see through the glass of the sliding door.

My heart warms knowing that, despite everything he had been through, he was able to find happiness. I cross my arms to watch them, smiling when the teenage boy tosses his head to laugh.

His head is shaved this time, and he is clearly older. He has a defined jaw now, broader shoulders, and, sitting down, he is taller than his mom. His smile, as quick as it arrived, disappears when the loud shake of the front door slams.

His mother's hand reaches for her son's arm, clenching it.

I gasp, stepping forward, wishing I could help, but I'm forced to be here. I'm forced to watch the scene unfold before me, and there's nothing I can do. I hate feeling hopeless. I became a cop for a reason—to be there for others when no one else can be.

When people find themselves alone and in a situation they can't escape from. Being in a dream where my hands are tied is now considered one of my worst nightmares.

"Who the fuck do you think you are having dinner before I get home?" the abuser yells.

I grind my teeth, curling my fingers until my hands are tight fists.

Watching through the door, the father grabs the salad bowl and throws it against the wall. The glass bowl shatters, the teenage boy lifting his arm in pain as a shard ricochets off the wall, embedding itself in his arm.

"Fuck!" the boy shouts.

"Don't talk to me that way!" His father backhands him, sending the young man to the floor.

I gasp, taking another step forward, twisting my restless hands together as I watch the violence unfold.

"You act like you run this household," he slurs at the mother. "I work. I provide. What the fuck do you do?" He rips her from her seat and, to my surprise, throws her through the door.

The glass shatters from the force, the sound of the door breaking has goosebumps pimpling on my skin, and the air frozen in my lungs.

Blood tints the layer of snow on the ground. She whimpers, pieces of glass sticking in her arms, her face. Nothing that will kill her, but enough for her to be in a lot of pain.

I sprint to her, forgetting that I'm useless. I fall to my knees, skidding across the thin layer of ice, and try to help her up.

"You have to move. You have to get up. Come on." I try to grab her, my hands sinking through her as if I'm a ghost.

I suppose in a way I am.

"Come on, please," I beg for her to hear me. "Please, move." I gesture my arm out to the road. "Run. Run as far as you can. Don't look back."

She stands on trembling legs, her jeans stained with fresh blood as those sharp shards stick out from various parts of her body.

"Shade," she wheezes for the boy. "Shade, run, My Love. Run!"

I gasp, turning my head too fast, and I become dizzy when I stare at him trying to push himself to his feet.

"Shade?" I mutter to myself in confusion, wondering why I'm able to see such an intimate, horrible memory.

"Shade!" his mother screams at the top of her lungs when her husband flips Shade over, grips him by his shirt with one hand, and with his other, begins to hit him.

I cover my mouth with my hands, tears brimming in my eyes. "Shade!" I scream so loud, I taste blood in my throat, hoping to cut through the barrier the dream creates.

Every punch to his face has my stomach turning. His father's knuckles become bloody, and rage burns bright in his father's bright blue eyes—the piercing ice color that sears into someone's soul.

"No! Stop! You're going to kill him!" I run inside, doing my best to grab his father's hand to stop him, but I can't touch anything. None of my attempts work. I'm left to watch the scene unfold.

I fall to my knees, tears wetting my face.

"Shade!" His mother stumbles into the house, needing a hospital more than she needs to stop her abuser. She grabs the nearest thing, a plate, and smashes it on her husband's face.

It stops him from hitting Shade, whose face is beyond recognition. Blood is everywhere. His nose is broken. Shade coughs, spewing blood onto his chin.

"Shade. Shade, I'm here. You can't see me, but I'm here. I'm right here." I try to take his hand, the phantom of my touch sliding through his. That only frustrates me further. "You aren't alone," I yell at him through tight teeth, my jaw clenched in so much rage that if I had my gun, I would shoot his father dead without a care in the fucking world.

I'd make sure the last thing he ever saw was the abyss of my nine millimeter barrel staring him in the face.

"Don't fucking touch my son again." His mother grabs a fork from the table, stabbing his father in the neck.

Anything can be used as a weapon when one is desperate enough.

"Shade. Shade." I try to shake him awake, to get him to hear me. "Your mom needs you. Please, wake up. Please." More tears fall, hating to know all the abuse he went through in his life.

"Marrying you was the biggest mistake of my life." Her husband yanks the fork from his neck, tosses it over his shoulder, and it clanks to the ground behind him. "Both of you have made my life so miserable that every day, I hate you more. I wish neither of you existed. I dream of your deaths with a smile on my face."

I curl over Shade to protect him, even knowing that I can't. "I have you. You aren't alone," I whisper into his ear. "I'm right here. I won't let him get you. I'll do my best to protect you. I'm so sorry this was your life. I'm so sorry, Shade, but I promise, it gets better. While it might not seem like it, it does. I have you." I pet his buzzed head with reassurance, knowing he can't feel it, but it makes me feel better—like I'm actually doing something to make this situation better.

Shade coughs, more blood spearing into the air, and he bolts forward, spitting red wads onto the floor.

"That's it. You'll be okay. Get it all out. I'm right here. I'm not leaving you." I pat his back, trying to let him know he isn't alone.

"You were always right," his mother sneers. "He isn't yours. He can't be. He's too good to have any of your DNA."

I knew in my heart those would be her last words.

His father launches himself at her, effectively steering him away from Shade by betting her own life in return.

He tackles her out of the broken door, slams her against the ground, and frees all the hate he has kept inside his rotten soul.

I flinch with every hit he gives her. The wet sound of blood, skin slapping, the loud cracks of bones breaking, her gasps for air, the way her legs kick, and her nails try to claw at his back tell me her fight is almost over.

She's almost free.

"You are by far the worst mistake of my life," he roars, rearing his arms back, taking turns with each bloody fist as he punches her over and over and over again.

"Mom," Shade wheezes, grabbing for the wall to help himself to his feet. "Mom!" he yells for her with no response.

I know the moment she dies. Her legs stop kicking. Her arms stop trying to wrap around his neck, everything about her fight falls limp. I close my eyes, my bottom lip trembling as I try to control my emotions.

"Fucking bitch. Rot in Hell." His father stands, spitting on her body.

Shade grabs a knife from the table, wiping the blood from his mouth with the back of his hand.

"You'll be the one going to Hell," Shade says, clutching the blade tight within his hand.

His father turns around, stumbling from how drunk he still is, and laughs, pointing a blood-soaked finger at Shade.

"And what are you going to do? You're just as weak as she was."

"She's been the one holding me back."

I see it, then. This is the moment that changes Shade forever. The light that brightens a child's eyes is gone, replaced with emptiness and fury. He lunges, ducking low as his father tries to wrap his arms around his son. Shade is smarter, not wasting any time, and stabs the man who was supposed to raise him with love.

The blade vanishes into his father's side, the man's eyes widening in surprise when Shade pulls out the knife, only to plunge it into his gut again. Shade throws the knife to the side, wraps his hands around his father's throat, and drags him to the ground.

He straddles him to get more leverage, the vein popping in his neck from the amount of force he is using to strangle his own father.

I don't attempt to stop him. It's not as if he can hear me anyway.

"She deserved everything!" Shade cries. "She deserved more than you were ever willing to give her."

I squat next to him, trying to brush the tears that are making streaks through the blood on his face.

That's when I notice his eyes. They are the same bright piercing blues as his father's. This might not be the moment he became a monster, but it is the moment he became a beast.

His father struggles to breathe, slapping Shade's arms to free him.

Shade holds on tighter every second, finding more strength within him until his father's last breath finally leaves him.

When he stops fighting and is dead, Shade checks for a pulse.

"Good fucking riddance." Grabbing the knife again, he plunges the knife into his father's chest—right through the heart. "I fucking hated you too."

Falling to the side, he scrambles to his mother's side. Her eyes are open and unblinking, pupils blown.

"Mom?" he calls for her in a small, child-like voice, one full of fear and vulnerability. "Mom?" Shade tries again, slipping a hand under her head and dragging her to his lap. "Mom!" he shouts with all his might, clutching her dead body to him. "No, no, no. No." Shade shakes his head in denial, the snow beginning to fall again.

Every flake holds the same screams that I heard throughout his life.

"Mom! Come back, Mom. Come back. He is gone. He won't hurt us anymore. He's gone. Please." Shade clutches onto her shirt, dragging her closer to his chest, embracing the one person

who loved him more than anything in this world. "Mommy," his voice breaks. "Please, come back." He tries shaking her again, even going as far as to place his ear next to her mouth to hear for any signs of life.

"No." He continues to be in denial, placing her on the ground gently. "No!" His hands lie over one another and begin compressions. "Come on, Mom. Come on. Don't let him win. Don't let him win!" he screams so loud, his voice echoes through the air.

Even with his attempts, she lies motionless.

"Mommy. Not my mommy." The young voice of a child is back as he clutches onto her for dear life.

He holds her dead body, sobbing into her neck, and I cry with him, wishing I could help.

"I love you. I love you. I love you. Please, come back to me. I can't do this without you. I can't face the world without you. I can't face this nightmare alone."

The pounding of boots has me turn my head, my vision blurry from the tears, when I see very large men with black cuts on running through the house. Their cuts say 'Shallow Sinners' and the one that has the 'Prez' patch, kneels by Shade.

"Oh, shit," one of them says.

"Damn. We're too late," another echoes their disappointment.

"Hey, Kid. Your neighbor called us and said they heard fighting over here again. We came as soon as possible." He presses his hand against his chest. "I'm Ryker. My friends call me Prez, though. Who are you?"

Shade doesn't say anything. He only continues to silently cry while holding his mother.

"Can you tell me what happened? The neighbor said your dad wasn't a very nice man. Is that what happened here? You tried to save your mom?"

Shade's fingers somehow clutch onto her harder, his knuckles turning white. When he blinks, a fresh wave of tears breaks free.

"Tell you what, we will take care of his body, and we will give your mom a nice funeral on our property if you want. You can stay with us, and you'll be able to visit her anytime."

"Mom," Shade's voice breaks, eyes pinching shut as he buries his face into her neck, and sobs.

His shoulders shake, his sobs become roars, he cries until he can't breathe, and Ryker wraps his massive arms around Shade and his mother.

"I know, Kid. I know. Let it all out. You're safe now."

All Shade has known is trauma his entire life. As a child, as a teen, and then as a man, when he was turned into a monster.

These dreams I was forced to see weren't dreams at all.

They were nightmares.

And they all belonged to Shade.

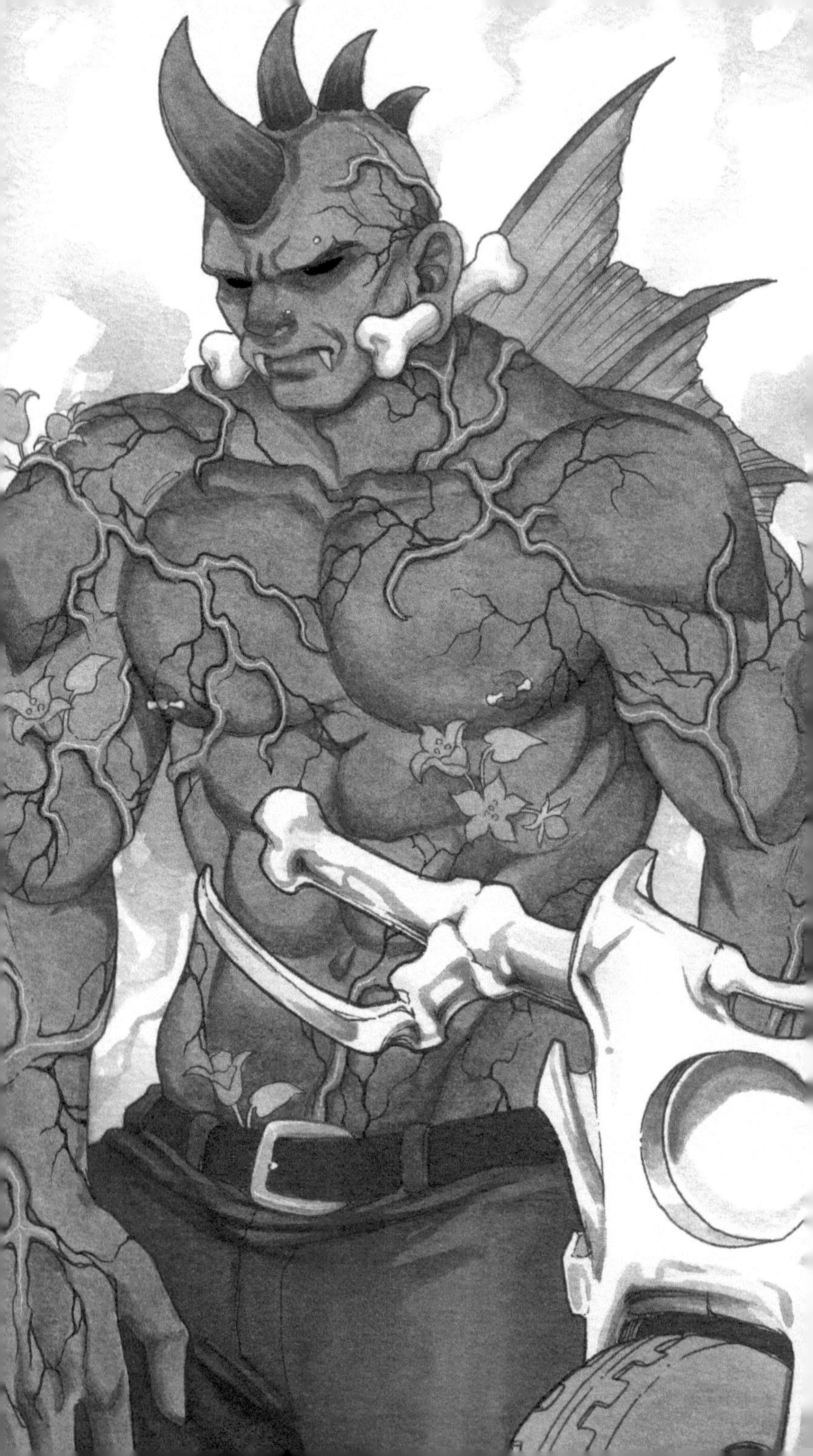

CHAPTER TWELVE

SHADE

I step out from the silhouette of the trees, confused as to what I'm seeing. The snow crunches with every step, my deep, rushed breaths causing my shoulders to rise and fall.

Anger spreads through my chest like a hot blaze, my green skin darkening from the flush. Lula isn't supposed to see this. She isn't supposed to be here! No one was supposed to see into the most shadowed corners of my mind. I have locked these memories deep within my mind. I don't even dare to go where they can be opened.

They sadden me.

"What are you doing here?" I growl at her, staring at the small, weak version of myself clutching my mother. "You aren't supposed to see this!" The memory fades away, leaving us standing in the backyard of what used to be my home.

My parents' blood stains the snow. The broken glass still lies there, reminding me of the fear on my mother's face when my father pushed her through the sliding door.

I hate this memory. It is the one that shaped me into who I am.

Into what I am.

"I don't know." Lula stands, holding snow where my teenage hand used to be. "I saw so much of your childhood." She lifts her eyes from the bloodied ground, filled with tears.

"Don't waste your tears on me, Little Dream. I am not worthy of them."

Lula runs to me, her hair dancing over her shoulders with her movements, snow sticking to the strands.

Lost memories.

"Not worthy?" She stands in front of me, stretching her arm to touch my face, but she can't reach—not even when she tries to stand on her tiptoes.

I bend down when I realize I crave her touch—even if it is due to pity.

Her fingers skim the rough hide of my green flesh, tracing the edge of my jaw. Lula's eyes soften as her gaze darts all over my face, lost in contemplation.

I grunt in response, finding the rage and violence drifting away from me as her fingers explore me.

"Mmmm," I hum, a peace settling over me for the first time in ages.

I lean into her palm, pushing my cheek closer into her hand. I want more of the sweetness that doesn't deserve to touch me.

It's been so long since I've experienced a touch that was filled with care. I forgot what it felt like—what peace feels like.

"You deserve good things, Shade. You've been punishing yourself all these years?"

I close my eyes, knowing I had to do what I had to do to survive, but the entire point of survival was saving my mother— and I failed at that.

"You did what you had to do. You were just a boy."

I fall to my knees in front of her, still slightly taller, and she has to stretch to reach me.

"A boy who loved his mother, who wanted to save her, and

she wanted to save you too. She always wanted to save you. I noticed that. In all these memories, that was the common denominator."

My hands fall to Lula's hips, her small frame appearing so fragile in my embrace. I'm so much bigger than her; it's astonishing she's able to take me and survive.

"If there ever came a time where I couldn't save you, death would be my only answer at peace," I say, relaxing when her hands glide down my neck to my chest.

"Death isn't the answer for everything, Shade."

"It is when it comes to you," I state, a guttural purr vibrating from me as she caresses my abdomen.

My stomach clenches from how sensitive I am. My muscles tremble, my cock awakening from the delicate touch. I can't believe how good she feels. Her touch is the only peace I've ever felt—I've ever known.

And if anything, that terrifies me the most.

What if someone tried to take my peace away from me? Tried to take her away from me?

I would go on a mission to kill everyone in the world. Death would fear me for the destruction I'd bring to the world. The idea of peace would no longer exist. I would pull the world into a dystopian nightmare. The rivers would run with blood, and the oceans would be red from my madness.

"You are beautiful," she breathes in wonderment, continuing to explore the body that belongs to her.

"I am a monsterrr," The nightmare possesses my voice, the vulnerability shaking the words.

I've never felt more exposed.

"No." She steps closer, sliding her soft fingers across my collarbone, then up the thick muscle of my neck. "You are mine."

My skin reacts to her words, to being claimed by a woman who deserves a better fate than me.

There isn't hope for me. I can't change.

I am violence. I am murder.

I am the bringer of sorrow and pain.

I wouldn't have it any other way.

Except for when it comes to Lula. She is the exception. I want to be more for her. I don't know if it's possible.

Even right now, with her hands on my body, exploring with awe and fascination, I want to have her bleed for me.

How can an animal like me overcome the catastrophic urge to bring her pain?

"You're so massive," she compliments, dragging her palm down my bicep.

I watch her face, completely enamored by her own will, her own want, to touch me and get to know me.

"It's the rhino," I explain, wishing my dream would take us anywhere else but here.

She shakes her head. "No, it's you. You must have been a big guy before the experiments happened."

I nod in agreement. "I was, but I wasn't like this. I can't remember what I looked like before," I say with a shoulder shrug.

She reaches for the horn, pausing as her eyes meet mine. "May I?"

I lower my head for her to reach the horns in the middle of my head. "I'll never say no to your touch, Little Dream."

Her eyes soften, filled with care and love. Probably not the type of love I feel for her already—being my mate—whatever that means. I know it's significant. I feel that in my soul. There's no other for me.

I love her more than the fear I taste when I kill someone in their dreams. I'm not sure she could ever feel for me the way I feel for her.

Her lithe fingers drag from the base of the horn, skimming up to the point. Lula wraps her hand around it, studying it with more enthusiasm than I ever felt for my new features.

I moan, my eyes closing from how good her hand feels. I had no idea my horns were sensitive.

"Oh. I'm sorry. I didn't know—" She pulls her hand away, and I snag her wrist before opening my eyes, staring into her light brown irises that remind me of a darkening sunset.

"Don't stop. I love your hands on me." I lift her hand to my horns again, wrapping my arms around her waist to lift her up so she no longer has to stretch. "Explore all you want. I am yours," I state with no room for argument.

Her hands skim over the top of my head, tracing the veins and roots that are part of me now.

"Do they hurt?" Lula's fingers are back to rubbing the horns.

I shiver, the sensations traveling down my spine to my cock. If she keeps touching me like this, I'll be taking her in the dream too. We're locked together in reality. My teeth have sunk into her body, keeping me against her with nowhere to go, so she drains me of every drop.

"No, especially right now," I say, lowering her back to the ground. Her body dragging down mine, and I'm able to feel every soft curve of her. "You're cold," I notice, wishing I had a jacket to give her.

Our frozen breaths mingle as we stare at one another. Her eyes fall to my lips, and I become nervous. I've kissed her before. I've taken from her. I've done things no man should be proud of —to her.

It's a good thing I'm no man.

"You're gentler here," she whispers, tapping my temple. "When I'm in your mind. Why?"

"It's the only place where a part of who I used to be lives," I answer honestly. "I wasn't a good man though, Lula. I killed then just as I kill now. I was part of a motorcycle club. I was the

enforcer. I did things that you would have arrested me for—that you could still arrest me for."

"I don't think my cuffs will fit," she giggles, using both of her hands to lift one of mine into the air because I'm so big. "It doesn't bother me—what you do. I notice your pattern. You kill people who do bad things, I don't disagree with that."

I lift my pierced brow. "Most cops would."

"I'm not most cops." She raises her hand again, touching my piercings along my brow and nose.

"I've noticed."

"I love your rage. It thrills me."

"I've seen your tattoo," I growl, wanting to see it again.

Lula blushes, breaking our gaze in embarrassment. "I got that when I was nineteen. I thought I was so clever, but it still fits." She nibbles her bottom lip, grinning.

My fingers slide under her chin, forcing her to look at me again. "It does. I can smell when you're scared and underneath that delicious scent that feeds me—" My voice deepens at the thought "—there's the delectable aroma of lust. Like when you were in the alley that night looking to save someone, I could smell how aroused you were."

She inhales a sharp breath, eyes wide, her scent shifting to embarrassment that has a strong sharpness to it. It almost hurts to breathe in.

"That was you? You've been following me since that day?"

"I discovered you that night," I answer, tugging her against me. "The moment I scented you from the woods, I knew I'd follow you to the ends of the earth."

To my surprise, she wraps her arms around my neck, her eyes once again falling to my lips. "You broke into my house?" she asks.

"I broke into your house," I growl in satisfaction. "I've climbed into your bed. I've fucked you with my roots. I've studied the cases you're working on and took care of them for you. I've filled your fridge." I wrap a hand around her throat, bringing her face closer to mine. "And I'll continue to kill the people from your case files. I need to feed, Lula. My nightmare demands fear."

"What if I helped you?"

To my surprise, her lips find my neck in a bold move I wasn't expecting. My eyes roll to the back of my head when she places a gentle kiss on my jugular.

"Help me?" I rasp, tilting my head back to give her more access to my throat.

"I can't have you go hungry. My fear won't be enough, will it?" Her fingers play with the bone ring piercing my nipple.

"Your fear is the best I've ever tasted. You fuel me like no other."

"So you don't need more?" She pulls back with a smirk. "Am I enough? Or does my lust cloud my fear?"

"I might need more," I admit. "But I can live without anyone else's fear as long as I have you."

"But what if you had more?"

"Why would a detective help me?"

"Bad people don't hold any sympathy from me. I've seen what the worst of the worst can do. I don't mind feeding you. It's what you need."

I tighten my grip on her neck and pull her back, keeping her sinful lips from toying with my body. "How about we find out?"

"What do you mean?"

"Run," I growl, shoving her away from me before I lose control. "Run as hard and fast as you can."

"You'll chase me?"

I chuckle at the childlike word.

"No, Little Dream." I lean forward, licking a fang. "I'm going to hunt." I can't hold in the growl.

Her eyes widen, fear permeating the air, followed by the delicious perfume of her desire.

My eyes roam her body up and down. "You don't seem to mind that idea."

"But, I-I-" She spins around, stretching her arms out. "I don't know where to run. Everything is dark except this yard and house."

"Afraid of the dark, are we?"

"A little," she admits, taking a step away from me.

"Just run into the dark. It's endless since it's my nightmare —well—a dream now that you're here."

"Don't sweet-talk me when you're about to hunt me. You're going to give me a head start, right?"

"Lula-lala-la-la-laa," I sing, a warning that I am no longer in charge, but my nightmare is.

"You're the song." True astonishment has her walking backwards, trying to put more space between us. "I've heard you for days now."

"It's one of the waysss I get into your head." I tap a finger on the side of my skull. "And I do love getting into your head, but you're in mine now. That's a very dangerous place to be. It's worse than the dark." I fall to all fours, blowing out a breath that turns to fog in the night. "Tick Tock, Lula. You'd better run. I'm becoming impatient."

She turns, launching herself into a sprint. Her hair flows behind her, wild and untamed. Looking over her shoulder to see where I'm at, I paw at the ground, the rhino fueling my veins to charge.

I give her such a large head start that she disappears into the night just like I told her to. My blood heats with the anticipation of catching her. My cock extends from its mouth, already dripping with precome. My claws extend, digging into the cold, wet surface of the earth, my muscles trembling and ready to launch.

Do I play with her emotions? Do I tease her? How long should I scare her?

Reaching between my legs from the thoughts, I swipe a finger over the flared thick crown, gathering the precome, then suck it into my mouth. I shiver when I allow myself to think about being connected to her in reality. She's still wrapped around my cock, her tightness gripping me as more orgasms take over her body.

I don't only want her in reality.

I want her in my nightmares too.

This nightmare, especially, is the darkest one I have. And already, she's making it feel like a dream.

When I can no longer hear her breathing as she runs, I take off, running full speed into the darkness. The further away I get from the house that holds my mother's and father's murder, the better I feel.

The emptiness of the abyss of space morphs into a forest. The trees are tall with massive trunks that can easily be hidden behind. She has no idea how I've set her up to fail. I can easily find her now by her scent, hearing her breathe, hearing every step she takes, her heartbeat, everything is working against her.

It's a few degrees cooler within the thick of the woods. Fog hovers over the ground, drifting in slow motion. Lifting my head, I inhale, allowing her aroma to seep into my lungs to tell me where to go.

With a quick jerk of my head to the left, I run again, tearing down trees that are in my way with one solid swipe of my arm. The ground shakes with every step I take, the leaves shaking from the vibrations traveling through the ground and up the roots of the trees.

When I'm close enough to her, I slow. I don't want to give away my position. She's up ahead, twisting and turning to find me. Even from this far, her fear smells like a fresh rain at night with loud thunder and hot, intense lightning. There's a warm undertone to it, a bitterness that reminds me of licorice.

Lula is my sweet treat, even when she's afraid.

"Lula-lala-la-la-la," I sing, dashing closer to her with my enhanced abilities.

I hide behind the tree next to her, remaining quiet and stealthy. My heart is fucking racing. I press my hand against the middle of my chest, needing to feel the strong beat bumping against my ribcage.

Taking a moment to wonder what I'm experiencing, it dawns on me that I'm excited.

I'm...happy.

She's allowing me to hunt her. She accepts me, for me. What I need to survive, to thrive, she's willing to give.

My mate deserves the sun, but unfortunately, she is damned to the moon.

I peek around the tree trunk, my mouth salivating when the salty air of her sweat lingers. A growl works its way up my throat, but I hold it in, needing to remain quiet.

"Lula-lala-la-la-la." I dash to another tree, dig my claws into the bark, and climb up it.

"Shade!" She twists and turns, that wonderful smell of her fear feeding my sinister soul.

I climb higher into the tree, hiding myself in the snow-covered branches. Our surroundings are so dark, it's impossible for her to see me unless I'm directly in front of her. A chitter clicks within my throat, the nightmare singing its happiness.

Jumping from one tree to another, the snow jostles from the branches and falls. Lula peers up, trying to locate where I'm at before taking off running again. I laugh to myself, finding her effort to escape me adorable.

"Lula-lala-la-la-laaa."

She pumps her arms, sprinting as fast as she can, but she'll *never be as fast as me. Lula stops again. The woods in my dream are never-ending. This hunt could last forever if I wanted it to. I could have us live inside my mind for all eternity.*

Hooking my claws into the bark, I use gravity to allow me to slide down, engraving my mark on the tree.

She spins when she hears the grating of wood, and I blur to a spot directly behind her. Bending down, I smell her hair, the citrus scent causing more precome to leak from me.

She steps forward, curious and careful, not wanting to spook me if I am waiting for her behind the tree.

Adorable.

"This isn't funny anymore," her voice is ridden with emotion. "I don't know where I am."

Of course, she's afraid. She's running through someone else's mind. When something is new and unknown, it's scary at first, but over time, she'll realize the safest place she'll ever be is with me.

Growling so close to her ear, I speed away to another tree, watching her spin around to find that no one is behind her.

Oh, toying with my mate is so much fun.

"Shade?" Her bottom lip quivers, another fresh wave of terror hanging thick in the air. "Shade, this isn't funny. I'm ready to be caught."

I don't like my food to surrender so easily.

That's too fucking bad.

Using my vampire speed, I run right in front of her, having her wonder if what she saw—she actually saw.

"Shade? Is that you? Shade!" she screams for me, my name echoing into the void. "Shade!" Lula desperately tries to call for me, all while I'm right here, five steps to her left.

I chuckle, amusing myself as her panic rises. Such a big, empty space for a delicate human. And no matter what she says, Lula is delicate, compared to me, she's as soft as a flower petal.

Standing behind her again, I move to the left and right, dodging her gaze when she turns around to find me. She can sense me when I'm that close.

"I know you're close. I can feel you." Her frozen breath puffs past her lips. "You're not far. I bet your hair is standing on its ends, warning you that a predator is close."

I hide behind her, lifting strands of her hair with my claw. I press them against my nose, closing my eyes to sink deeper into the place her scent brings me to.

Peace.

I rub the ends against my cheek, so soft, so silky. I want them to drag over my body as she kisses her way down my stomach to suck my cock.

Screeching at the top of her lungs when she feels me, she turns around to catch me red-handed, but I'm gone before she makes sense of what she thought she felt.

"Lula-lala-la-la-la," I sing, running around her in circles so she has no idea where the song is coming from. "Lula-lala-la-la-laaa."

She spins and spins, left and right, trying her best to locate me, and she becomes dizzy. Lula loses her balance and collapses in the snow, groaning. She's on her hands and knees, taking a moment to gather her breath, but all I can think about is ripping her pants free and splitting her open with my cock.

Gripping her by her hair, I yank her head back, her eyes glazed with worry and arousal. Her pheromones are so strong, an orgasm threatens to paint the fake forest floor.

She inhales, her lips parted, open and inviting, but I'm not done hunting her yet.

I tug on her hair again, forcing her to get to her feet. She hisses, reaching back to where I'm gripping her by the root.

"Run. And don't look back, Lula."

"You have me now. Do what you want with me."

"Oh, I plan to." I push her forward, falling to all fours again. I crack my neck, left, then right, the sound eerie within the silent forest. "Run."

She's confused, but it doesn't stop her from listening. Lula runs, sprinting hard and fast. She jumps over the trees I've ripped from their roots. My mate doesn't look back. She doesn't trip. Her strides are long and fast, taking her further and further away from me.

And we can't have that.

I leap into the air, my hands and feet thunderous against the ground like a stampede of wild animals. I jump onto a tree trunk, using it as leverage to launch myself through the air.

Landing on all fours, a sly snarl curls my lips.

I could use my enhanced speed to finally catch her, but where's the fun in that?

Lowering my head, I smash into another tree, using my horns to rip it in half, and wood chips scatter on the ground. I use another log for support, slicing through the air and gaining so much ground. I stretch to reach her, and my claw drags across her shirt, ripping a large hole in the back.

Landing on one arm, I slide against the ground until I come to a stop, snow hitting my face.

"Oh, that is exactly what I want, Little Dream." I wipe the snow from my face, watching her fade into the distance. "Make me work for it."

Rolling my shoulders, I fall back onto my hands and feet, lowering my head, and run, grunting and snarling the closer I get to her. My horn tears into another tree, then another, bulldozing them down to clear my path.

Roots begin to spread across the ground the closer I get to her, wanting to bind her so she can't move, but I want to be the one who holds her within my arms. I want the satisfaction of knowing that I caught her.

She looks back, realizing how close I am, and she whimpers, pushing herself to run harder.

But Lula can't.

When I'm close enough, I jump into the air, my claws hooking on her shoulders, and I tackle her to the ground. Without a word, I rip her clothes off. Not that she's truly wearing any, this is a dream after all.

Blood drips from the wound in her back, her blood practically begging me to drink as it rolls down the divot of her spine.

Becoming impatient, I tear her pants off, baring her to me. She trembles from the cold, the snow sticking to her skin.

Flattening my tongue at the base of her spine, I lick up to her shoulder, gathering the sweet liquid from the cut.

Flipping her onto her back, she looks up at me with those amber-hued eyes, her teeth clattering together from the cold.

Gripping her by her throat, I lift her, my cock inches away from her mouth. "Suck."

"I ca-ca-can't," she shivers. "Too cold."

"I don't give a fuck. I said suck," I growl with impatience, wanting to feel her mouth around me more than I need my next breath.

Opening her mouth, that familiar scent of her fear hardens me more. She stares down the two and a half foot length, eyes widening when she sees the mouth and sharp teeth around the base. The light is wrapped around me, waiting to place the bulb within her womb again.

Her mouth stretches wide to accommodate me, those big brown eyes watering. Lula's tongue is cold, but it feels good against the heat of my cock. Teeth try to clink together from the tremors, the sharp pain adding to the delicious sensation of her mouth.

"Good girl," I praise, watching my beautiful mate suck me down the best she can.

Lula hums, licking and sucking each of my piercings, which has me groaning. I like that—no—I fucking love that. She wraps her hand around my shaft, trying to stroke me in tandem every time she hollows her cheeks. She pinches the Prince Albert between her teeth, the rod clicking against her front teeth. Lula gives it a tug, gaining a loud grunt from me. Her tongue flattens along the ridges of the Jacob's ladder, my eyes rolling back from the pleasure.

Using her free hand, she cups my large sack, one orb filling her palm. She massages, tugs, and twists before moving to the next.

"Fuck," I growl in approval. "You're too good at that. I'm going to need to find all the men who have felt your mouth and kill them."

Her arousal soaks the air as she moans, the vibration traveling through the hard length. It causes me to stand on my tiptoes, tossing my head back from how good it feels.

She takes about six inches, the tip touching her throat, before she chokes and gags.

"Little Dream," I tsk, clawing into her scalp again. "You can do better than that." Thrusting my hips forward as hard as I can, punching through the back of her skull.

Blood and bones soak the shaft, dripping off my cock to stain the snow.

She whimpers, her scent of pleasure switching to fear. I don't think I've ever smelled her so afraid.

"It's okay. You'll be fine. We're mated now. You're made for me. Your body will give me exactly what I need." I move, thrusting in and out, the warmth of her blood thawing the cold within.

A tear drips down her cheek. She's frozen, unable to move, yet underneath all that fear is the lust.

"You feel so good." I continue to thrust, using her head in the way I need so she can fit me.

The squelching sounds become too much. The way her blood coats me like silk, I can't take much more.

"You're being a very good girl, Little Dream. Now, drink every drop of me so I don't go to waste."

She whines in response.

My pace quickens, my hips flex harder, her tongue drags across my piercings. She finds a way to flick the tip of her tongue over the crown when I pull back, and that's all it takes for me to explode.

"Lula!" I roar so loud, the dreamscape vibrates to the point it begins to shatter like glass.

I paint her throat, giving her so much, it begins to drip out of the back of her head.

"Mmm, you're a filthy cock sucker, aren't you? You love what I do to you." I smash my mouth against hers, gathering my come from her tongue so I know what I taste like marinated in her spit.

The dreamscape finally shatters, darkness crumbles around us...

And I wake up with Lula in my arms, more come pumped into her womb, stretching her stomach. The hole in the back of her head is healed, making me smirk.

At the reminder of what she has seen, the broken, vulnerable side of me, I pull her close, her back against my front, and I kiss the graceful curve of her shoulder.

"Forever, My Little Dream. Mi alma me lo dice, Lula." My soul says so.

OVE POLI
EPARTMENT

CHAPTER THIRTEEN
LULA

"Refill?"

I look up from my case files, studying who I think the next victim will be. Her name is Christina, and she has been found innocent of embezzlement charges in the past, but she is currently being investigated for the same crime, and I don't think she's innocent.

"Detective?"

I blink away my thoughts, rubbing my exhausted eyes that I can't seem to keep open. I ache everywhere. My head hurts, my body, my legs, and especially between my legs. The pain is the only reminder that what I experienced was real.

It had to be right? No one just wakes up like they have been broken into pieces and put back together without a little pain.

Maybe it was a dream. When I try to remember, the details are a little fuzzy. I can't remember everything, truly; it's as if it were a dream. Shade trapped me against the wall, my body paralyzed and unmoving, yet I could feel *certain* things he did to me. Like anything that brought me plea-sure, I could feel.

And then, I think reality meshes with the dream I had. I saw Shade's worst memories, the moments that give him nightmares, and it made me understand him a little more.

The way I acted, the way I didn't care about how he is killing people, made me realize I would do anything for him. Even if it means committing crimes myself.

"Lula?" Demi sits down across from me, placing the fresh pot of coffee on the table. "Are you okay? You seem very distracted, a bit pale, and exhausted. I've never seen you like this before."

I blink away my thoughts again, getting lost in the confusion of what has happened to me.

"I'm fine. Tired. Working overtime to catch this person who is killing all these people." I don't even feel guilty knowing that I know the person—monster—behind these crimes. Granted, the taxidermist wasn't a bad person, from what I know so far, just someone who was in the way.

If I ever see Shade again, I'll ask him.

I take a sip of my third cup of coffee, which is doing nothing for me. All I want to do is crawl back into bed, hopefully, with Shade wrapping his massive body around mine. I go back to reading the case files of Greta, wondering if she was the very first victim.

According to her coroner's report, there were no bones left at the scene.

So what did Shade do with them?

"You're lying."

I swivel my gaze from hot pink-haired Demi to Caden, someone I hadn't had a chance to meet yet.

He sets my plate down in front of me, right on top of my case files, and the scent of crispy bacon has my annoyance falling away. The hashbrowns are perfect, and the eggs are over-easy with fresh toast. Holt, the cook, makes the bread fresh every day, and it is worth it.

I'm addicted.

I bite into a piece of bacon, watching Caden take the spot next to Demi. I've never seen a creature like him before. I doubt anyone has been able to see his true form. I think back to the book my mamita had while I was growing up. Every night when I was a little girl, I would ask her to read me a bedtime story; instead, she would pull out this giant leather-bound book.

Inside were hundreds of old, discolored pages with sketches and explanations of every creature my ancestors had ever come across, because they could also see the unknown. Every page held a mystery, a curiosity that I had only begun to see in my young age in the real world.

I have that book at home, stuffed in my nightstand, and I'm trying to remember everything about Caden's monster.

All of the thunderstorms make sense now. There's a storm kitsune sitting directly in front of me. His eyes crackle with constant lightning. To regular humans, I'm sure they see someone normal, but not me. I can see everything he is trying to hide.

Kitsunes are fox spirits; the more tails they acquire, the older, wiser, and more powerful they are. They can have a max of nine tails, and when they reach that, their fox form will be at their most powerful.

I know, in general, kitsunes have a lot of power, but I can't remember them all off the top of my head. I'll have to look when I get home.

Caden, by the three tails he has, is young. Probably around three hundred years old. His fox is almost like a shadow emerging from him, but he glows a beautiful black with eyes the color of lightning, and a dark green hue surrounding him. His ears are tall and pointed, the fox's jaw defined and square, reminding me of a super soldier. His tails fix behind him as his fox stares at me, tilting his head, knowing that I can see him for what he is.

"You can see me," Caden states, folding his hands on top of the table.

Rain begins to pour outside, followed by a loud crack of lightning.

I lean against the booth, taking a sip of my coffee. Kitsunes are very intuitive creatures. It doesn't surprise me at all that he caught onto my ability.

"I can," I answer honestly.

Demi waves her hands in the air, then makes a 'T' with her hands. "Time-out. Wait. You can see"—she leans in and whispers—"you can see him? You know what he is?"

I mimic her position, placing my cup down first, then crossing my arms on the table. "I can. It's a gift that has been passed down from generation to generation. My family calls the gift the ability to see The Unknown."

"Gift? Or curse?" Caden asks, another strobe of lightning cracking so loud, the lights flicker.

"Caden," Demi hisses his name, scolding him.

"No need to show off, Caden," I say with a twinge of a smile, pushing through the pain my body is in.

I hope that over time, I will become used to Shade and his needs. I'm not sure if this amount of agony is something I can live with forever.

"I know how strong you are based on how many tails you have."

"Tails?" Demi whips her head to him. "You have tails?"

"You know about the tails. I've told you. I just haven't shown you. I find comfort in my human form."

"Which isn't uncommon for kitsunes," I add, biting into a piece of bacon.

Caden taps his fingers on the table. "It isn't."

His skepticism makes me laugh.

"You can trust me with your form, Caden. I would never tell anyone or anything."

Caden takes her hand, his eyes softening at her, the lightning in his irises bolting around his pupils. "I know. It isn't about not trusting you. It's about comfort. That's all. I'm comfortable around you, but I'm not like that with everyone here, even if I've known them a long time. A storm kitsune can only claim one region at a time, but it is possible for another kitsune to steal a region from another. They would have to collect my tails to do that. It's more paranoia, I guess. I don't want others to see my real form. Trouble usually spreads when that happens."

He turns to me, the softening in his eyes gone, and the wind forces the rain to bullet against the window.

"So much rain lately," I begin and add a bit of sugar to my coffee, stirring it with a spoon. "Are you feeling okay, Caden? I know sometimes kitsunes can feel a lot of loneliness, especially with your long lives. I remember reading about the storm kitsunes that the more rain that pours, the more their heart aches."

"And?" Caden's jaw is tight, tense, and his fox is clearly unhappy with me by how his tails are flicking behind him.

"Caden," Demi says his name with worry and sadness. "Does your heart ache?"

Caden grips the edge of the booth, and by the way his fox grows above him, his power is going to be directed at me any minute.

The skies darken with his rage, the inside of the diner cast in the storm's shadow. Customers who were on their way out decide to stay, sitting down in their booths again to wait for the storm to pass.

"That's none of your business," he seethes at me, the lightning in his eyes becoming bolder as his power increases.

"I'm not trying to start a fight with you. I'm only trying to have a conversation. You're upset that I can see you, but I can't help that, Caden. I can't help what I am, just like you can't help what you are. I wouldn't tell anyone. I haven't whispered anything to anyone about the creatures I have seen, except to my family, since they have the same...affliction as I do. And if I did tell, a regular person would call me crazy."

Bolts of electricity begin to crackle across Caden's fingertips, his veins lightning up with his power.

"Caden." Demi reaches to touch his arm, and before I can tell her to stop, her fingers graze his bicep, shocking her instantly. "Damn it!" She sucks a finger into her mouth, bringing it away to see the damage.

It's red but fading fast.

The fox must care for Demi because his ears lie flat, his eyes becoming wide with panic. Caden's power recedes in an instant, and he snags Demi's hand to inspect it.

"I'm so sorry. I didn't mean to. I didn't...I didn't mean to hurt you. Oh my god, are you okay? Do you feel okay?" Caden checks her over, even going as far as to press two fingers against her throat to check for a pulse.

Which is funny, considering she is obviously alive.

"Caden. I'm fine. You shocked me. It isn't a big deal. See? It's gone already."

Caden flips her hands over a dozen times to check for any sign of injury.

"Because you're mated to Creed. That's the only reason

you're alive right now," I state, dipping the toast in the runny egg yolk. "That's why he is freaking out. One shock from him can stop someone's heart. He isn't all rain, wind, thunder, and lightning like he puts on."

"The storms help me keep my power in check."

"Caden, that can't be good for you. It storms here all the time. Every day, nearly all day."

"Because his heart aches," I add. "If it weren't for the storms, he'd lose himself in power."

Caden narrows his eyes at me, not liking what I have to say, when finally, he puts his defenses down and sags against the table. "Yes, she's right," he says to Demi. "It's hard seeing all of you find your fated mates. I want mine too. I don't think you realize how big a deal it is to paranormals, to creatures like me, like Creed, to find someone destined for them. Some paranormals wait their entire lives and never meet the other half of their soul, someone meant for them, created to make their soul whole again, someone to spend eternity with. I know with Creed it was hard because of all the DNA he has, but at least his vampire would have only lived two hundred years, and he would have died if he hadn't met you," Caden explains, and a large realization slams against me.

I'm Shade's fated mate. Everything he said last night makes sense. How he would protect me for all eternity, how I am his, and he is mine. He didn't go into detail about fated mates, and I don't think he knows *why* he needs me.

"So yes, I want that, and my fox is sad with every day that passes that we don't meet the one meant for us. I'm so happy for you, Rhett, and Fitz. I love seeing your families grow. The way Creed would kill anyone for you, Demi, that's how any paranormal would react. We kill anyone we see as a threat to our mate. If I ever met my mate and she was in danger, I would create the most dangerous hurricanes and tornadoes. I would rip cities to pieces if it meant protecting her. I'm young in kitsune years. I have plenty of time to find my mate, but living three hundred years already—"

I knew it.

"—It's just a long time to not have anyone."

Demi doesn't say anything. Instead, she wraps her arms around him, embracing him in a tight hug.

His fox becomes smaller, relieved that he doesn't feel the need to have to protect himself.

"I didn't mean to start anything," I say between chewing. "It's hard not to talk about it when I can see things for what they are."

"Must be hard to see things like us and not know what will happen to you," Caden steals a piece of my bacon off my plate.

"I've never come across anyone who has wanted to hurt me before. I have found that a lot of creatures are like humans. There are good ones and bad ones."

Caden nods in agreement.

The bell to the diner door rings. I look up to see Creed, followed by a few others who look similar to Shade. Monster DNA experiments.

"Can no one see what they look like? I find it hard to think they can walk around like that and not get noticed," I ask, never taking my eyes off the chaos that just walked through the door.

"Spelled rain. I know a witch. People see the versions of us we want them to see. They just see normal people," Caden explains.

"Spelled rain. Makes sense," I mumble, taking a large gulp of my coffee.

"So that's Creed, you remember him." Demi sighs as if Creed is the dreamiest thing to ever exist. "Then, that's Rhett behind him. He owns the garage, and he is part crocodile, but that's not really my place to say. Then, that's Fitz, who is human, and that's his mate Holly, who is very pregnant. Rhett's mate is off today; her name is Mickey, but it must be a kid's day out. I'm surprised they have all of them. I can't wait for you to meet them!" Demi stands, waving her arms to gesture them to us.

Creed frowns when he sees Demi with us. It's a bit hilarious to see him wearing a baby sling in the front, pushing a stroller, holding hands with one, while the oldest one bites his pant leg, growling and snarling with every step Creed takes.

I hide my smile behind the mug. The little creature babies are actually really cute. I want one.

My eyes widen as a memory slams against me from last night. My hand flies to my stomach, wondering if I'm pregnant.

"You smell weird."

Caden groans. "You can't be going around telling people they smell weird all the time, Creed."

"Well. She does. Do you want me to lie about it?" He stands there, calm and collected as his oldest child growls, continuing to tug on his leg.

"That's Storm. Don't mind him. He's a bit...feral." Demi grins, like the proud mom she is. "And then the youngest, Chaos. Then, the second youngest is Pain. The one that is the most well-behaved is Strife—surprisingly—he is the one holding Creed's hand. Aren't they so cute?" Demi beams with pride.

They are adorable. I'll give her that. "They are lovely, Demi. All boys too. Goodness."

"We will have a girl. We're working on it. We worked on it this morning. Twice."

"Creed!" Demi blushes, hiding her face in her hands.

"You still smell weird. Even if you did say my kids are cute."

"Caden is right, Creed. You can't say people smell weird. I'm Rhett, the one with the most humanity of the monsters." He holds out his hand to me, and I'd have to agree, he does seem more human than the others I've met. "And these are the twins, Agonie and Havock." He has a baby on each arm. "Aggie is a daddy's girl, isn't that right, princess?" He blows a raspberry on her crocodile-skin neck.

"I'm Fitz. Regular human, this is my mate, Holly."

Holly sits down next to me, groaning as she gets off her feet. "This kid could come out right now, and I'd be happy. Eight months. I can't believe I've had a human pregnancy," she sneers. "And Creed is right; you do smell weird."

"You know, Mickey smelled weird when she mated Rhett," Creed remembers, grabbing his kid by the wings to stop him from tugging at his pants.

Caden snaps his fingers together. "And Demi smelled weird because of you," he points to Creed.

Creed growls, smoke drifting from his nose. "I'm going to take your smelling abilities away if you keep talking."

Caden smirks. "I'm just saying. People around here tend to smell 'weird.'" He quotes with his fingers. "When they mate someone."

I feel every single pair of eyes on me and my entire body becomes hot, the truth sizzling underneath my skin. I don't know how much to share. This would be the safest place to share my secret.

But do I say that the killer in this town is my mate?

And that I'm not going to do *anything* to stop him.

My phone rings in the nick of time. "Sorry. I have to get this. It's Jake," I tell them which makes Caden and Demi pout because they wanted to know who I was mated to.

"Sanchez," I answer, wiping my mouth with a napkin.

"We have a robbery and a homicide at Harold's Jewelers. I'll need you there."

I finish off my hashbrowns and wash it down with my lukewarm coffee. "Finally need me there?"

"Get your ass here, Sanchez."

He hangs up the phone and I wince, digging out some cash from my pocket to pay for breakfast.

"Sorry everyone. I have to run. Homicide."

"Another? Interesting, they tend to skyrocket when new monsters come around." Caden eyes stop on each beast at the table.

I lift a shoulder, wanting to keep my mate to myself since it's so new. After breakfast, my body begins to feel better. My head doesn't hurt anymore, my bones don't seem to ache, and I'm ready to figure out how the hell I'm going to balance being a detective mated to a monster who needs to feed off fear and kills people.

Hay, Dios mío.

I'm in such a normal healthy relationship.

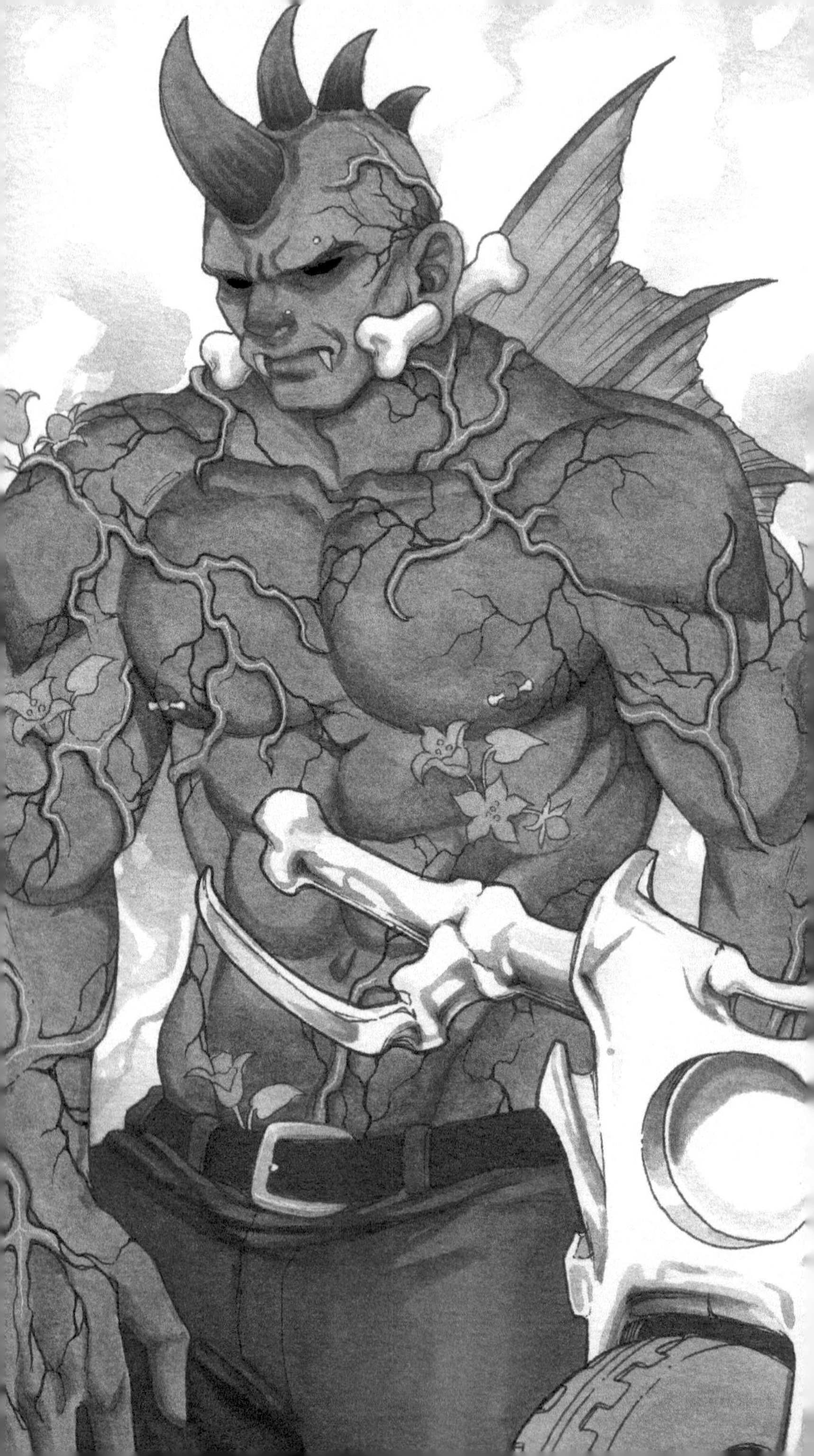

The wind and rain are pissing me off.

Now that I know these storms are because of that little fucking fox inside, I'm going to kill him. There's no reason to have it rain this much all of the time.

When Lula takes her phone call from Jake, my sour mood disappears. There's been a homicide at a local jewelry store, and I'm excited until I remember I haven't killed anyone in a few days because Lula has been able to satisfy all of my violent cravings.

At the same time, I don't like it when someone is one-upping me in murdering others. I'm the monster. I do the murdering.

Holding my palm out, the roots grow together, making a small stalk. A nightshade flower blossoms on top, the purple shades giving a hint of beauty in the gloomy day. I set it on her windshield, wanting Lula to know I was here.

I'm always here.

Wherever she is, I'm never far. I can either always see or hear her. When the distance between us grows too much, my monsters become unsettled.

Taking one last look at the small gift I left on her windshield, I'm across town at Harold's Jewelers in the next minute, the rain finally easing.

Sheriff Holland and Officer Waylon are here, talking to witnesses a few doors down. I survey the parking lot, doing my best to hold in my growls. The audacity of someone else ruining my killing spree only has the nightmare inside me roaring with fury.

I duck behind the Sheriff's car, doing my best to hide my massive body and listen to the Sheriff's conversation.

"You didn't see anything out of the ordinary? Or hear anything, Ms. Trudel?" He questions the middle-aged woman who seems to own the boutique just a few stores down.

"No," she answers, clearly upset by the emotion in her voice. "I only heard the gunshots. I'm sorry. I didn't come outside when I heard them. I locked my door and hid in the backroom with my loaded shotgun—which I have a permit for," she adds with a bit of attitude.

"Thank you, Ms. Trudel. I appreciate your time today."

"Sorry I couldn't be more help, Sheriff," she says.

She walks back into her boutique while the Sheriff and Officer Waylon stay outside. Sheriff Holland clicks his pen over and over again, staring at his notepad.

"Someone had to have seen something. We have a few more businesses to hit," Waylon tries to sound positive.

"That's not what's eating at me," Sheriff Holland sighs. "This murder isn't like the others. The others were brutal, gruesome, and almost filled with hate. You could tell by looking at the bodies or what was left of them."

Pride swells in my chest. *That's the nicest thing anyone has ever said about me.*

"This is a clear robbery and homicide. Three gunshot

wounds to the chest. Harold didn't stand a chance. This is another killer, Waylon. If I can't stop these murders or start catching the fucking killer, this entire town will be after my badge, and they might elect someone else."

"The killings always stop," Waylon states, pointing out a small bit of hope. "They happen, yes, but then they stop. That's good for us."

"No, Waylon. No, it isn't. Because not once have I arrested anyone over the years for any of these killings," his voice a harsh, inpatient whisper. "This is bad for me, and something needs to change." Sheriff turns around and walks away, heading to another place of business.

Waylon blows out a heavy breath, following his boss, but not before he turns to peer at the car I'm hiding behind, as if he can see me.

I stay crouched, wishing the one ability I had was to be invisible.

Shrugging his shoulder, he hurries to catch up to Jake.

That leaves me all alone until Lula gets here.

Bright yellow crime scene tape creates a border around the outside of the jewelry store, warning everyone to stay away, but the scent of that old man's blood calls to me, especially when fear still hangs heavy in the air.

I roll my eyes when thunder rolls above, the clouds darkening again, and rain threatening to fall.

Again.

There are two places on my body I like wet. My mouth from eating my mate's pussy and my cock from when my mate comes on it.

Making sure no one is around to see me, I'm inside the jewelry store before the next flash of lightning strikes.

"Messy," I snarl in disgust when I see the mess this amateur made. They didn't even take all of the jewelry.

What is the fucking point of robbing someone if you don't take everything?

I squat, picking up a large diamond ring that would look beautiful on Lula's hand. The shape is familiar, but I can't remember the word off the top of my head. It's almost like an oval, but skinnier, and the ends are pointed. Black diamonds frame the main one that makes me think Lula would love that part the most—hopefully because they remind her of me.

Seeing as the place was robbed already, I tuck the ring in my pocket, kicking the dead guy's leg.

To make sure.

I sniff him, trying to understand the heavy scent of fear that still lingers. It doesn't belong to Harold. This smell belongs to the killer. My mouth waters at the excitement of finding the suspect. Lula might be proud of me if I do.

I've never had anyone be proud of me before.

"Shade." Lula's voice has my skin reacting, thousands of pebbles arising on my skin, my cock twitching from the panic and worry clinging to her throat. "What are you doing here?" She grips my arm and tries to drag me towards the back of the store. "You can't be here right now, Shade. What if Jake sees you? You're at a crime scene. Anything you're doing could be disrupting it."

"I have the scent of the person who did this." I try to whisper, but my voice is too deep, and it carries. "I can find them. I think they're still close too with how strong their fear is."

Lula holds my hand, which is unusual for me. I don't hold hands. I never have. It seems intimate and important. I don't understand why people do it, but her palm against mine soothes the violence inside me, as if it's a baby that needs to be put to sleep.

"Okay. Go. Let me know somehow that you're okay. They have a gun, Shade, and they could hurt you—"

Picking her up, I silence her with a kiss. She sighs against me, relaxing when our lips meet, and her palms skim up my bare chest.

"You are real," she whispers into my mouth.

I lean back, curious as to why she would think I wasn't.

"Last night is a blur. I thought maybe you were a dream. I couldn't decide."

"Very real, Lula. That bite on the back of your neck means something."

Her hand flies to her neck, gasping when her fingers trace the indents of my teeth. "Because I'm your fated mate."

I nod, remembering the conversation I heard her having with Caden as he explained mates. It made more sense to me when I heard him tell Lula the importance of mates. Everything inside me clicked due to the massive possessiveness I feel for her. The way I need her builds into a dangerous emotion in my chest—similar to rage.

It's consumption.

"Is the damn forensic team not here yet? Harold's body needs to be taken to the morgue. He doesn't deserve to be lying in his own damn store for so long."

Lula's eyes widen. "It's Jake. You have to go. Go! Find them."

"If I find them, I'll kill them."

"I don't care. You do what you have to, and one day, I'll help you get what you need." She places her palm on my chest again, right where my heart beats, and I grunt, my skin reacting to her once again.

"You're cold," she whispers, dragging her finger across the expanse of my chest.

"No. I'm yours." I kiss her on the cheek, Jake's footsteps getting closer, and a low rumble vibrates my chest at the fury of leaving her with other men.

"Go," she urges, her anxiety poisoning the air between us.

I'm outside behind the business, standing in the alley before she can blink again.

I'm ducking by the dumpsters, I tilt my head back as I take a deep breath in to find the trail of the killer. I would have hunted and killed this person anyway, but having Lula's approval? It has my entire body on fire. My cock is semi-hard, pressing against the sharp teeth.

Later, I'm going to fuck her all over again. Now that she wears my mark, there's nothing her body won't be able to take from me.

My head slowly turns to the right, catching the scent of the killer's trail, and a sardonic laugh escapes me just as the rain begins to fall. I take my time walking down the narrow dirt road, knowing I have all the damn time in the world because the person who killed Harold isn't in a hurry with how strong their scent is. Even with the rain, the fear and anxiety are potent.

A chittering sound clicks within my throat, the nightmare swelling inside my skin to be set free.

I'm starved to hear screams of someone begging for their life.

My arm stretches out, my claws lengthen, cutting into the metal fence that is on my left. On the other side is a huge field with tall grass, the wind swaying it from side to side.

I pass a guy with a round stomach, wearing a greasy apron, and he has a cigarette hanging out of his mouth, tossing a large bag of trash in the dumpster.

He gives me a nod, and I stop in my tracks.

"Can I get one?" I ask, tempted to take his entire pack if he says no. By force.

He doesn't say a word. He takes the pack out of his back pocket, opens it, and offers it to me.

"Thanks." I take one, then snag another. "For the road." I tuck it behind my ear, lean forward, and lock eyes with him. "What you're about to see, hear, or witness is not your concern. You won't remember meeting me. You offered a stranger a light. That's all."

He nods, digging out the lighter from his pocket. "Yeah, okay. Whatever," he grumbles.

I light my cigarette and leave the man there to live another day, the trail of terror becoming stronger. I'm going to guess they have never robbed or killed anyone before. People who are seasoned professionals at being rotten to the core don't give a fuck what they take or who they hurt to get it.

Like me.

The fact that Lula doesn't care if I kill these people pleases me in ways that can't be described. I know with her job, the balance of toeing the line with me will be difficult.

And she doesn't care about difficulty.

Lightning cracks in the field right next to me. The heat radiates over my skin, and my ears ring for a split second before the damage heals itself.

"Fuck you, Caden."

Lightning spreads across the sky like it's traveling through the clouds in response.

I continue walking down the dirt road, the trail becoming stronger until I'm two blocks away from the jewelry store. Stopping at the edge of the busy road, staring at the alley between an Italian restaurant and a computer repair shop.

"Idiots," I mumble around my cigarette, blowing out a cloud of toxic smoke.

That's where they are. I can't believe they didn't have a better getaway plan? Who the fuck taught them? Did they even try to get away with this? At least I'm assuming it is 'they' because the scent I'm following, too much anxiety for it to belong to only one person.

I cross the street, looking over my shoulder to make sure no one is watching me. Walking down the alley reminds me of the days I used to be the enforcer for Shallow Sinners. Many times, I would deal with business in sketchy alleys or mold-ridden rooms where no one would ever find me. Dumpsters line each wall on either side, cardboard boxes stacked, and a dark green van is parked at the very end.

Smoke spills out of the exhaust, telling me they haven't been here very long. By the smell of it, they are nervous. Regret and guilt hang heavy in the air, and sniffles come from inside the van.

Aw. My bleeding fucking heart.

I don't care.

"La-lala-la-la-laaa," the nightmare within me sings, wanting to start the process of infiltrating their minds. I don't want this to take too long.

I have a mate to see, to fuck, to breed, to claim. I'd rather be with her, learning her body, her sounds, her wants, her fear, than to be here.

Stopping in my tracks, my emotions mix on that recent thought. I'm not sure how that makes me feel.

Lula's fear has a sense of safety to it. There's no judgment, no harshness, no hate.

Only love. Understanding. And thrill.

Oh, the thrill she is so desperate for, I'm more than happy to give her. Her enthusiasm for pain, for adventure, for the fear I so desperately crave, she gives.

No one could ever compare to my mate. She was created for my body, which only makes me thankful that I am what I am. If I had remained human, I would have never been able to meet her.

And what a damn fucking catastrophe that would have been. I would have missed the most beautiful, remarkable woman I have ever laid eyes on.

Yeah, there's no way I would turn back the clock to be human, not if it meant losing the one person in the world who understands me more than anyone ever has. She barely knows anything about me too, since we haven't known one another very long, but she knows more than most of the people who have ever been in my life. She knows the worst parts, the dark, bloody, sad, unforgivable parts that warped my soul into who I am today.

If my mate told me she doesn't care who I kill, that only heightens the freedom I've always felt.

"What was that?"

I smirk as I stand behind the van. I knew there were two of them.

"What? No one. It was probably a stray dog or something," her friend replies.

Or something.

"Christina. I'm serious. It sounded creepy. Like a song from a scary movie."

"You're just freaking out because you shot someone, Becca."

Beccaaww. I wonder if her friend is the same Christina in Lula's files. The embezzler. That would be fucking fantastic.

I snicker at my inner thoughts, then frown, because I've never been funny. I'm not a funny guy. I don't make jokes, not even to myself. Enough of that. Being funny ruins my fucking mood.

I listen to their bickering while I have my cigarette. Becca's panic and anxiety smell bitter and rancid to me, nothing like Lula's. Hers almost makes me cough, which would give away my position.

"Because I shot someone!" Becca screeches. "I didn't just shoot *someone*, Christina."

"I killed someone! And he wasn't just anybody. I shot Harold. Cute, old, happy Harold who offered me a fucking job last week!" Her voice becomes higher with emotion, and my eyes roll while I blow out smoke.

"He was old as fuck anyway," Christina tries to reason. "His days were probably numbered. If anything, you did him a favor."

"I can't believe I did this. I can't believe I killed some-one. I'm going to go to prison. My life is over. I'm—"

"—Oh, shut up!" Christina yells. "You aren't going to prison. There's no proof of who did this. Our faces were covered, the gun isn't traceable, and Harold didn't have any security cameras. We are fine. No one saw us either. We are rich." Christina cackles, and the clinking of hard materials clinks together.

She must be dipping into her bag of gems.

"We can go wherever we want," she continues. "Be whatever we want. Do whatever we want. Rich people get away with anything and everything. All we have to do is get out of town after we remove the plates from this van and add another set."

Christina makes valid points. Her mind is twisted, a

little similar to mine, which I respect, but they are forgetting one major detail they weren't expecting.

Me.

"You're right," Becca exhales, her heart rate calming. "I still don't like that I killed him, but he came at me, and I panicked. I didn't mean to do it."

"I know you didn't, but I'm not mad at you. We did what we had to do."

"La-lala-la-la-laaa," I sing, frowning when I see my cigarette is nearly gone.

The ladies fall silent, causing a crooked grin to tilt my mouth when not only Becca's fear skyrockets, but Christina's too.

"You heard it that time, right? Right, Christina? I'm not losing my mind because I killed someone?"

Christina's heart rate kicks up a notch. "I heard it. Stay here, Becca. I'll go check it out."

Oh, this should be fun. I've never had them come to me before. I'm standing directly behind the van, but the windows are so tinted that they aren't able to see me standing just in their rear view.

Tsk. Tsk. Tsk. Reasons like me is why windows should never be so dark.

"No, what? Are you kidding? You can't go out there. We are safer in here. Where he, it, whatever, can't get us."

Sweet little Becca, in the van, out of the van, it doesn't matter. Nothing will stop me from killing them. Not even a weak lock on a 1998 van that has seen much better days.

"It's probably some kid being an asshole." A familiar click of the safety turning off has me blowing out the rest of the smoke and tossing the butt of the cigarette on the ground, then stomping it out with my foot.

"Don't go out there. You're going to get yourself killed," Becca warns.

And how right she was.

"Look at this gun," Christina says, then I hear the twisting of metal. "And this silencer? No one will hear a thing, and this person will be so afraid, I won't even have to pull the trigger. They will run away. I probably won't even fire it."

I hope she does. I do miss the taste of gunpowder.

If there is one thing I will never do, it's run away.

"Don't. Don't go," Becca begs, her pathetic attempt to save her friend. "I don't like the sound it's making."

"It?" Christina cocks the weapon. "*It's* a person, Becca. That's all."

Debatable.

Becca begins to cry. Soft cries, nothing loud or dramatic. The kind of cries that are full of the kind of emotions that get my dick hard. Becca's fear is so strong, so potent, that her cries can barely form sounds. The air becomes so thick, I could swim through the hot waves of the horror-drowned ocean.

"It didn't sound like a person," Becca whispers just as Christina opens the driver's side door.

"La-lala-la-la-laaa," My voice deepens, allowing the nightmare to peek through.

"Don't go! Didn't you hear it again?" Becca screams.

"Yes, and it is pissing me off." Christina climbs out of the van, and I'm disappointed with how loud she's being.

Her feet are heavy with every step, kicking dirt, rushing to me.

I stand there, leaning against the back of the van, and it groans from my weight, the bumper touching the ground while the front tires lift in the air.

Becca screams so loud, I hear a blood vessel pop.

The fear is quite delicious.

"Stand up! Stand the fuck up! Or I swear to fucking God, I will kill you! Put her down!" Christina shouts, threatening me with the gun.

I stand, and the van crashes onto the ground, Becca still screaming for her dear life.

"Get out of our way so we can leave, and I promise I won't shoot you. I only want to leave town," Christina tries to bargain with me.

"I can't do that. See, you've done something very." I step forward. "Very."

She inhales a sharp breath, thrusting her weapon forward. "Don't come closer."

I come closer. "Very."

"I'm warning you!"

"Very." Her fear slips down my throat, more bitter than what I prefer, but it will do.

She pulls the trigger, and I'm able to hear the bullet leave the chamber, regardless of the silencer. The bullet pierces my chest, black smoke drifting free.

"Bad," the word is pure venom, mixed with all of my beasts.

Christina's eyes round knowing she is up against something so much more. She empties the clip into me, firing one shot after another into my chest, shoulders, neck, and head.

"What the fuck?" Her entire body trembles, scurrying backwards until her back hits the wall, and the gun falls from her hand.

Becca is still screaming.

"What the fuck are you?"

The bullets are pushed from my body, clinking one after another after another onto the ground.

I step into her space until my shadow is suffocating her against the wall. My roots are quick, slithering up her body and pinning her to the wall.

Becca doesn't even take a breath to continue screaming.

It's driving me insane.

Urging the roots around the van, they creep inside and cover her mouth so I can finally have some fucking peace.

"Let me show you." The stygian cloud infiltrates through her lips, nose, and ears, conquering her body.

She tries to scream, but it gets caught in her throat, choking her as she tries to call for help.

"You're noticing that you can't feel anything. You can't see anything but the emptiness of your own mind. Don't worry. I'll be there soon," I warn. "You are paralyzed, Christina. You can't feel a thing. You can't speak." Another darkness fills my mind, and that's when I turn to look at the van. I'm inside Becca's mind too. The nightmare has taken her as well.

"Oh, this is going to be fun," I whisper, diving into my two-for-one deal.

I'm standing in a typical room. Nothing special. There's a couch against the wall. A lamp in the corner. A family photo hanging on the wall to my right. The floors are hardwood, not old or original hardwood, but new—looks cheap.

To my surprise, both ladies are sitting in chairs that look like they are from a dining table set, with a high back and big cushions to keep them comfortable. They are tied to the chairs with barbed wire, the sharp metal cutting into their skin. Blood drips from every wound, and Becca is still fucking screaming.

"Shut up or I'll rip your fucking tongue out and shove it down Christina's throat."

Becca shuts her lips immediately.

"What are you?" Christina asks, her voice a discombobulated whisper.

"I'm...many things, but what I want to know is, why both of you are here." I bend down, taking my time to stare at Christina before turning to look at Becca.

Their cheeks are wet with tears. Snot runs down their nose. Christina seems a little braver. Her lips tremble while she holds her head high to look at me, daring me to try anything, while Becca stares at the floor, accepting her fate.

"You must be very close if both of your fears are connected." Being inside their mind, I can taste their pasts. "You are best friends. No. More like sisters. Your fear is to live without one another. There's no specific death you are afraid of; you just don't want to lose your best friend. Well, isn't that fucking sweet." I shove their chairs over, and they fall onto their sides, the wire digging deeper into their flesh.

Lifting Christina up by her hair, I set her chair on all fours, forcing her to stare at Becca. "Tell me, how do you want me to kill her?"

"What? No. No, please. Don't hurt her. She is good! She didn't do anything. She wouldn't have done anything if it weren't for me. I talked her into it. I'm the embezzler!"

I press my nose against her cheek, inhaling all that terror she's trying to hide.

"Oh, but she did. She killed him. She had a choice."

"So do you." Her face morphs into a hopeful smile, as if she has found a way to twist my words against me to save her life. "You have a choice. You can let us go, and we won't tell a soul. We won't," Christina shakes her head.

"What's the worst way you'd want to die?" I ignore her attempts because they annoy me.

"Please."

Impatient, I wrap my hand around her throat and lift her into the air, the chair coming off the ground. "I said, what is the worst way you'd want to die!" I roar, the monsters within me taking hold.

"A shark!" she answers, another sly little grin threatening her lips.

She sees no water. Christina thinks she has outsmarted me.

"A shark? That's not that bad. I've killed people in more brutal ways than a shark ever could." I grab her face and turn it with a hard push, nearly breaking her jaw with my strength. "And I think you forget who runs the show here, Christinaaa," I breathe the end of her name, the nightmare becoming one with my skin.

Becca becomes locked in a long, square tank that seems endless. She is no longer bound to the wire or chair, but banging on the inside of the glass for Christina to save her.

There's no way out of that tank. Shark or not, Becca is dead.

"Becca! Becca! No!" Christina struggles against the barbed wire, cutting open her skin in her attempts to save her best friend. "Becca!" Her scream echoes into the neurons.

Becca swims, banging on the glass in hopes it will break. Her hair floats behind her, a silken scarf drifting through the raging seas.

I point, bending down to be eye level with my new friend. "Look. She has company."

Christina's spike of fear is like a drug to me, a shot into my veins that soaks into the chambers of my wretched, sick spirit.

"Becca! Becca!"

Poor Becca tries to swim away, away into the endless ocean I've created for her. She should be struggling to breathe any minute.

The shark swims fast, coming from the deep blue shadows. A great white, the white belly unmistakable. Bubbles flow from Becca's mouth as she screams.

Even in the damn water, she screams. It's never-ending.

The shark plays with her, snapping onto her leg, then letting go, then her arm, and letting go.

Red begins to bleed into the water, drifting through the current.

More sharks begin to come, and Christina screams when they attack Becca all at once, ripping her head from her body.

"No! No! Becca! Becca." She sobs and shouts, shoulders shaking from how hard she's grieving her friend. "You're fucking sick." Her angry eyes narrow at me through wet lashes.

"Oh, you have no idea." I curl over her, burying my nose into her hair to breathe in the fucking fright. "My cock is aching to be set free, but I'd never allow you to see me. I belong to my mate."

"No one could ever love you," Christina says, her fucking chin held up high. "No one could love anyone who does what you do. What you look like. You're a freak of nature. An abomination. Someone who shouldn't exist. You're a waste of fucking space!"

I know she's wrong. Lula doesn't care what I am. I've shown her all of me. Christina's words bother me still, and instead of enjoying another kill, I become impatient and charge at her.

My head is down, my horns are sharp, and I spear right through her heart, then swing her into the shark-filled tank. I watch as their sharp teeth rip into her flesh, tearing away her muscles and bones. Pieces of her mix with what is left of Becca while I search for the peace Lula gives me.

OVE POLI
EPARTMENT

CHAPTER FIFTEEN
LULA

I stand on the sidewalk, staring at my new home with my mouth open. I'm not sure if I'm imagining things with how exhausted I am from yesterday's events and how long this day has been trying to 'find' the person who killed Harold.

I never met the man who owned the jewelry store, but apparently, he was very beloved in this town. Jake had grown up knowing Harold his entire life, so he is taking it hard and is on a mission to find who killed the defenseless man.

The wind blows into my eyes, reminding me to go inside and get out of this weather. It's wet, cold, and dark minus the glow of the street lamp. The light is enough to show my yard covered in roots. They are even creeping up on the side of the house.

The nightshade flowers bloom, adding a touch of color. The roots form an arch down the pathway, and there are small glowing lights now that I don't remember ever seeing on any of his roots.

I walk forward, needing to make a pot of coffee to get

through the next few hours. I need to talk to Shade. I haven't seen him since the crime scene.

In my hand, I hold the small plant he left for me on my car, embracing it against my chest because it's from him.

Traveling under the archway, I lift my hand to touch the light, realizing it's the lure light that illuminates my insides when he is fucking me. Paired with the flower blooming, there's an ethereal beauty, like I'm walking under hundreds of stars.

When I open the front door, I expect to see Shade here, but the house is empty. I frown, doubt creeping in, and wonder if he was a figment of my imagination after all.

The couch is still snapped in half, bringing a smile to my face, knowing that anything that is broken is because of him.

Except me. All these years of feeling so different, for craving what Shade could give to me.

I stare at the pictures on the wall from the case files, knowing I need to take them down, but I'm not sure that I want to. Yet. They seem to be like trophies, in a way. I'm not ready to part with them yet.

Checking the time on my phone, I blow out a breath when I see the clock has just struck midnight. I'm tired, but I'm starving, and decide while I wait, I'll make us Bandeja Paisa. It's one of my favorite comfort dishes when I have a lot on my mind. I grew up with my mamita cooking it. It's a traditional Colombian dish with Colombian Chorizo, blood sausage, sweet plantains, shredded beef, arepa—similar to a tortilla—eggs, rice, beans, and avocado.

Thanks to Shade stocking my fridge, I have everything I need to make it. While cooking the meat, I get started on the plantain and brew a small pot of coffee while everything is cooking. My eyes are so heavy, but my stomach is grumbling, and I won't be able to sleep without eating.

I chop the avocado, then pour myself half a cup of coffee. Just enough to keep me from face-planting in my food. I pour in a dash of creamer, give it a quick stir, and take a sip.

"Mmm," I hum, closing my eyes as the warm drink awakens my soul a bit. "That's the stuff." I tug my badge from my neck and drop it on the table, the gold shining against the dining room light.

I don't feel like I deserve the label of detective, considering the series of events.

"I'd be jealous of that coffee if I didn't know you were consuming me too."

The sound of Shade's voice has me lifting my eyes from the swirls of coffee in my mug to him standing in the living room like an intruder hiding in the shadows.

"Shade!" I set my coffee down and run to him, flipping on the light so I can see him. I gasp when I do. He has black dried blood on his body. "Oh my god! What happened? Are you okay?" I skim my hands down his torso, touching every wound that is healed over, but I can still see the shadow of a hole.

He hisses.

"Sorry. Still healing. I'll be fine in another few minutes," his booming voice rumbles.

"How many times did they shoot you!" Tears are in my eyes, counting so many bullet holes, that I lose count and have to start over.

"Until the clip emptied. I'm okay. It takes more for me to die, apparently." He makes an odd face, then plucks a crushed bullet shell from his mouth.

I don't know why, but something about that has my breath catching, and my thighs pressing together.

Shade inhales, his pierced nostrils flaring. "You like me getting shot, Little Dream?"

"What?" Entranced by the bullet he is holding, a small spike of fear jumps in my heart from being caught. My hands are pressed against his stomach, his warmth soothing the chill in my palms. His skin is rough, thick, similar to leather, maybe—or a rhino. Small goosebumps appear on his tough flesh when I begin to track the black veins, the roots, amazed at how different he is. "No, no. You took the bullet from your mouth, and something about that," I nibble my bottom lip. "It was hot."

He growls, somehow his onyx eyes darkening further if that is possible. "Why?"

My heart rate kicks up, and I instinctively take a step back. He doesn't allow the distance to be between us. "I-I don't know." My knees hit the edge of the couch cushions, and a part of me wants to vanish into it or lie down so Shade can do whatever he fucking wants, however he wants. *To me.*

His roots wrap around my waist. "I think you dooo," his creature controls his voice, the one that slips inside my mind to create my worst fear. "But you might burn the house down if you do."

I gasp, running to the kitchen and turning the oven off. Looks like I got here just in time. Thankfully, Shade has those paranormal senses.

"You need to eat before I rip you to pieces tonight. You'll need the energy to help you heal."

"Oh?" I gulp while I make our plates.

A shadow falls behind me, completely covering the light and casting me into darkness.

"I've only barely begun to explore you," he says, his arms wrapping around my waist with a gentle caress I didn't know he could possess, given his natural strength.

I blow out a breath to calm my nerves. My hand shakes as it scoops the rice onto the plates. There's no way he can't hear the wild beat of my heart racing from his nearness.

"I can't focus when you're so close to me," I admit, needing a certain amount of space.

My hands are full with our plates as he turns me around, caging me in by placing his arms on either side of me. Shade bends down, growling, the inky pools of his eyes somehow filled with so much lust, it's hard for me to catch my breath.

"Being close to you is the only thing that tames me." He leans in, his lips inches away from mine. "I'm not sure I like being tamed, Lulaaa."

I swallow hard, gasping when I hear the creature barely contained.

"I...I...well...you..." I stutter, and his lips tick to the left to form a sly grin. "I made my favorite dinner. Bandeja Paisa." I thrust the plate out for him to take to try to put a little space between us because I'm ready to starve, take him to bed, and let him have his wicked nightmare way with me.

Shade's brows furrow as he looks down, the edge of the plate against his stomach. He takes a step back and, with awkward hands, he holds the dish, just...staring.

"You don't have to eat it." I feel ridiculous. Of course he doesn't want it. "You don't eat food, right? I can save it. It can be my leftovers." I spin around, not wanting him to see the embarrassment on my face. Muttering under my breath, "Eres tan tonta."

You're so dumb.

Why would I cook food when he clearly only eats people's fear and my blood?

"What did you just say?"

I spin around, shocked by how small and soft his voice is. I've never heard him speak like that. He's still staring at all the food piled onto his plate.

"I called myself dumb for cooking because you don't—"

One moment, he is leaning against the dining room table, and in the next, he is standing in front of me, anger pinching his features while he presses his giant body against mine.

"Don't ever speak about yourself that way or I will give you nightmares for your entire fucking life, Lulaaa," he warns, his cock hard and pressing against me through his black jeans. "I love that you cooked for me. I was shocked." He kisses my forehead, a tender moment I save in my mind.

Shade is far from sweet, but he has his moments.

"Why?"

He grabs his plate off the table. "The last person who cooked for me was my mother," he admits on a deep breath, not bothering to take a seat since the chair will break under his weight. "You're right. I don't *need* to eat food. I eat *you*, instead."

The way he is looking at me would have me melt in a puddle onto the floor if it wasn't for me gripping the ledge of the countertop.

"But I can eat food. I just...haven't. And I haven't had a home-cooked meal since *that* night."

"That was so long ago, Shade."

He nods, picking up the fork that is way too small for his hand. It's awkward, and I can tell he is struggling. The metal bends from his strength, eventually snapping in half, and sends the rice splatting to his plate.

He huffs, snarling, showing those sharp fangs that I miss in my neck, my thigh, just on my body in general.

"You're more than welcome to feed from me, Shade," I tell him, wanting him to know there is no pressure. "Every day. All of the time. Whenever you want."

Those tormented eyes heat when they glance down at me. "As much as I love feeding from you. Your blood, your fears, they sate me in ways food never can, but you made this for me. I want to eat it."

I snag our plates. "Come on. Let's go to the living room. Follow me."

"Why?"

"Don't question me. I'll get my gun," I tease with a smile.

His hard cock strains his jeans, the length traveling down his leg, and I'm able to see the thick ridge of the crown pressing against the denim.

After food, I'm going to ride him. I want to feel his piercings inside me, his lure light illuminating my womb— I want it all.

"Sit," I order him, as I take a seat on the broken sofa.

He grunts.

To me, it takes him forever to take a seat because he is so tall. It has me rolling my lips together to keep from laughing. The couch moans under the threat of his weight —*I can relate*—and his half of the sofa begins to dip in the middle, threatening to break again.

"We will make you a silverware you can hold, but until then," I say, picking up my fork and getting a little bit of everything on it. Rice, meat, avocado, and then I get onto my knees so I can reach him. "Let me take care of you, Shade."

His eyes widen, those black eyes shining more than

usual. I thought he would fight me on this, but to my surprise, he leans back.

Grinning, I snag the plate and straddle his lap, so I'm closer, inching the fork to his mouth.

He stares at me so intensely that I have to focus on not dropping the fork. I have to spread my legs as far as they can due to how big his thighs are. His hands settle on my waist as I continue to feed him and take bites in between.

"It's really been that long?" I ask, breaking the silence.

He chews, eyes closing, and he groans in approval. "That's delicious. Thank you for making me a dish that brings you comfort." His lashes flutter, the expanse of space beaming into me again. "It now brings me comfort."

Before I give him the next bite, I lean in, pressing a gentle, easy kiss against him. "I'll always bring you comfort, Shade. In any way. In every way." There's no way I gave him enough food, but learning curve; I've never fed a giant.

We fall into another comfortable silence, but I can tell something is on his mind.

"Even when I was with Shallow Sinners, the motorcycle club I was a part of when I was human, I ate food that was easy and quick. Homemade meals would take me back to that night, the last time I had my mother's cooking, and I know how that sounds. I sound like a child—"

"I've seen that memory, remember. You don't sound like a child. You sound like someone who has been traumatized. You had to do a lot that night, Shade. You had to do something most people will never do." I drop the fork onto the empty plate and set it down instead of grabbing the other plate of food. Scooting closer to him, I realize that maybe I'm not that hungry anyway now that I have this green giant in front of me.

I slip my hands up his chest, my fingertips grazing over

the tendons in his neck, and finally, I cup his face. "It's okay to avoid the things you are protecting yourself from."

He leans in, his arms circling around my entire body to haul me closer. "I don't want to protect myself from you," he says, the earnestness in his tone has me become a little dizzy. "I've protected myself from everyone my entire life. Even Shallow Sinners. They were so good to me, but I didn't let them get to know me. I mean, it's good I didn't, right? Look at me now. They probably would have tried to burn me at the stake."

"Cállate," I snap, silencing him by placing my finger over his mouth.

"I don't know what that means, but I like it when you talk to me in Spanish," he rumbles, his chest quaking with a growl.

I giggle, pressing a kiss against his lips. "It means shut up."

"You would have never let them get close enough to you to kill you, Shade. You would have torn them all apart if they tried, and I would have helped you burn down the clubhouse."

Those roots I love so much wrap around me too, almost like they are wrapping me in a hug.

"Your lips taste like coffee," he says out of nowhere, kissing me again. His tongue slips across mine, and he moans, digging his fingers into my sides.

"I needed some before you came home. I was tired."

"Good. I can smell me in your blood."

I cock my head, confused. "What do you mean?"

He smirks. "I crushed some of my roots into dust and poured them into your coffee container."

I gasp in horror. "No! Hay Dios mío, Shade. I made my coworkers' coffee! They drank it."

"They don't need to know."

"What's that do? Will it hurt them?"

"No, they didn't have enough for it to matter, but you drink it every day." He buries his face against the side of my throat and inhales, inhaling me as if I'm the air he needs to breathe. "I love how you fucking smell, and the best part is, our scents are combined. No one can make the mistake of you not belonging to me." I let him explore, his nose dragging across my neck, then he fists my hair, bringing it against his face, and rubs the silky strands across his cheek. "I could feel and smell you all day."

I've never had anyone who liked to sniff me as much as Shade does. I love it. It's his love language, I think.

"Talk to me in Spanish, Little Dream," he says, reminding me of his request.

I giggle, skimming my fingers from shoulder to shoulder. "I really love your body," I compliment, loving that I have a chance to truly talk to him, to get to know him. Even though we are fated mates, there's so much I want to learn about him.

Even though I've seen the darkest parts of his mind, I want to know what makes him happy.

"It's green," he mumbles as if he isn't the most gorgeous creature I've ever seen.

"Green is my favorite color." I continue to drag my fingers back and forth across his shoulders. "You're the most beautiful man I've ever seen." I change the tone of my voice, wanting him to know how serious I am. "I love all the things that make you different." His shoulders are so wide, it takes me a few seconds longer than normal to get to one side.

"Hombros," I finally say, my voice slightly husky with

need, the longer I touch him. I'm getting distracted by his nipple piercings. God, no one should be this good-looking.

"Hombros," he repeats as the slight scratch of our skins touching sounds in the silence of the living room. "What's that mean?" His words are spoken with a growl, his roots begin to move on their own accord, every part of him needing to touch me in some way.

"Shoulders. I love how wide they are. How strong they are. How big." I lick my lips, hoarse with lust, and it's pooling between my legs. I begin to rock against his long, thick, hard, solid cock.

I gasp, my clit dragging along his length. Shade's nostrils flare, and his claws bite into my skin when his hands slip up my shirt.

"All of you is…big," I say, rocking against him even harder.

My skin ignites with heat, a sheen of sweat draping over me, which causes my long hair to stick to the back of my neck.

"You like that? You like that I'm big?"

"So much. I love everything you do to me. The fear you give me, that thrill I seek, the pain, I crave it. You're everything I never knew could exist. I know what happened to you was terrible, and maybe you can talk about it with me one day about the experiments, but I'm happy you're here, and you're…*you*."

"I'm glad you're you too," he whispers, eyes dropping to my lips at the same time my palms skim down his chest.

It's such a nice chest.

Never in my life have I ever seen muscles like this or a frame so wide. His pectorals are defined, strong, his dark green nipples hardening when my thumb caresses the piercing.

"Pecho," I force my dry tongue to peel away from the roof of my mouth to speak.

"Pecho," he repeats with flared nostrils. "Translate for me, Little Dream."

"Chest," I nearly whimper. "The most perfect chest I've ever seen."

His claws ruin another shirt of mine, ripping through the material just to tear it from my body, along with my bra.

"Hmmm," he growls.

I'll never get tired of that sound. "I love your chest too." He palms my breasts, sparks flying through my abdomen. "Maybe I'll fuck them one day, drown you in my come, make you choke on it."

I throw my head back and moan, imagining his come filling my throat so much that I can't breathe.

His pants rip, the sound causing me to look down. The seams tear down the sides, his cock hardening even more, growing to the point his pants can't contain him.

This is the first time that I get a proper look at it. I'm not delirious and out of my mind in a nightmare or paralyzed by his nightshade flower. I'm coherent, nervous, and excited.

"Your heart is beating so fast," he says. "But you're not afraid."

"I'm never truly afraid. Not with you," I admit, still taking my time admiring his chest. "Yes, you scare me, but I want it, and you know that. It's like..." I lean forward, pressing a small kiss to his expansive chest. "I don't know." I can't seem to find the words.

"Like we were made for one another. Because we are. Do that again."

A sly, knowing smirk ghosts my face. "This?" I press another kiss on his chest. Nothing special. I'm just enjoying touching him. "Or this?" I scoot back, lowering myself to kiss him on his abs. "Abdominal, I'm afraid, is the same in English. There isn't a translation for it."

"Sounds better when you say it," he says on a moan, his claws digging into the couch. "Your touch is gentle."

I kiss his lower abdomen. "I'll stop if you don't like it."

"You better not," he snarls. "I didn't know I could like gentle, but your lips, they set me on fire when they touch me."

The roots begin to travel, getting a mind of their own, spreading across the living room floor as I continue to kiss down his stomach. I move to the left, nipping and dragging my lips across his ribs. The way his body moves when I kiss that last rib, the way he moans, I think I found a spot he very much enjoys.

I do the same on the other side. Shade is struggling to catch his breath, heavy, broken gasps escape him as I drag my tongue down to the shreds of his pants.

He rips them off, tossing them behind the couch, and there's a pleading look in his sinister eyes, one that is begging me not to stop.

I have a big, bad monster subdued on my broken couch. Why would I stop? I have him where I finally want him.

I gasp at the large anglerfish mouth that's open, allowing his gargantuan cock to be free. The lure light is at the base, glowing brightly, and waiting for its moment to shine.

Kissing his thigh, I whisper, "Muslo."

"Translate, Little Dream."

I grin against his leg. "Thigh. And yours are very impressive."

If I'm not mistaken, I think his cheeks deepen to a

darker shade of green. Is my big bad monster a little shy when it comes to compliments?

"I like it when you praise me," he admits. "I've never had love like that before."

Something inside me breaks because I've seen his memories, and the saddest part is that I believe him when he says that. He hasn't ever had love.

"I'll love you forever if you let me." I drop to my knees on the floor, inserting myself between his legs.

The piercings on his cock shine from the precome leaking from his wide shaft.

"Love," he repeats, and it sounds like a foreign word, something he has never said before. "I do. Love you. I think you're the only person in the world that I love. I would kill everyone else, slaughter them, feed off their screams, if it meant you got to breathe for another second."

I'm surprised how this evening has gone. I expected the monster to walk through my door, and he is a dangerous killing machine, but right now, he's letting me see a side that's been buried for a very long time.

Not wanting to say another word to ruin the moment, I decide to try to tackle the beast of a cock. I know there's no way I'll be able to take him fully.

"Let me do this for you, okay?"

His fingers slide across my cheek, tucking a wavy piece of hair behind my ear. "You better wrap your lips around me before I take matters into my own hands, Lulaaa."

A shiver trickles down my spine when his nightmare emerges. I grab his cock, my fingers not touching, and guide him to my mouth. The salty liquid of his precome awakens my taste buds.

I'm not able to take very much of him, but I do my best. I swirl my tongue over the piercings, playing with the bars of the Jacob's ladder. I suck the Prince Albert, rolling it between my teeth.

"Fuck!" he roars, his roots beginning to climb up the walls as he loses control.

I hollow my cheeks, sucking him harder, bobbing my head fast in tandem with stroking up and down his cock.

His hands wrap around my neck and picks me up, lifting me from my knees.

Was I that bad?

He flips me around in the air, rips my pants from my body, and buries his face between my legs while my head is pressed against his cock.

Oh.

I lick down him, wondering how the hell I've survived a monstrous fucking by him. I gasp when his tongue plunges inside me. I do my best to suck him in return, but spit leaves my mouth, dribbling on his inches, and I'm unable to do this skillfully when he is bringing me so much pleasure.

"Lulaaa," he moans into my cunt.

God, the wickedness of the nightmare stings my insides, clawing at my organs to possess me. I wish he could. I would let him take over my body and do whatever he wanted to.

The position is a little awkward. I'm upside down, and his cock is so big, I barely have the time to appreciate it. I lick, stroke, kiss, and suck, but my favorite thing to do is play with the piercings.

He seems to like that too.

Shade raises my hips, and I shout loudly when he begins to rock me against something. It's hard, but I turn to look over my shoulder to see that the longest and thickest rhino horn is rubbing against me. The sharp point rubs against my clit, and I'm an absolute fucking mess. He isn't gentle with me when he pushes two fingers inside, pumping without a care in the world.

I shout around his cock, and the heavy weight slips from my mouth, slapping onto his thigh.

"Oh god, Shade! What are you doing? I can't focus. I can't...I can't..." I can't finish my sentence. "You feel so good. Don't stop. Don't stop." I press my forehead against his thigh, my nails digging into his muscles for some form of support.

"I've been wanting to fuck you with my horn. Be a good fucking girl and take it. Even if it hurts. Even if you bleed."

I push back, seeking what he is threatening, and I become dizzy with need for him. I scratch my nails up his leg when his horn penetrates me, then bite into the muscle of his thigh until I taste his blood. His cock tenses, and that's when a black spurt leaves him, the head angry, the veins protruding, aching to come, but Shade must have controlled himself.

The animalistic noises that escape him as he drives his horn into me only heighten my senses. He hurts. With him, sex always hurts, and I never want it to stop. I heal now, and I'm thankful because I feel the blood dripping from me and onto his horn.

Looking back, red stains this face. It drips down his eyes and cheeks, a murderous scene.

"Shade. Shade!" I cry out his name when he increases the pace.

I cough. Blood spurting from my mouth as his horn inflicts more damage.

Shade flicks my clit with his claw, and that's all it takes for me to clench around his rhino horn, a life-threatening orgasm ripping through me.

Flipping me right side up, blood drips onto his cock

when I'm settled against him. In a few seconds, the bleeding stops, the pain in my belly subsides, and I'm good as new.

Shade isn't.

His chest his heaving, his fangs are showing, tinted in blood. Streaks of crimson roll down his face, and he isn't focused on that at all. He leans in, licking my mouth free of blood.

I moan, his claws raking down my back, only to cause me to bleed again.

"You better fuck me." He settles his cock between my legs. "I'm not going to last long."

The teeth around his cock look so sharp, and I'm reminded of the scars I have where they clamp around me when he comes. I love it. I want to feel that pain again.

Inching down on him until I hiss and can't take anymore, I ride him. His shoulders are perfect for leverage. Rocking my hips, his piercings touch that spot inside me that has stars explode in my vision. My body feels so different. I accommodate him now. I can take him.

"You're so fucking beautiful," he praises. "That's it. Take my monster cock. You're so fucking sick for liking me, for liking what I do to you. Don't get used to this treatment. Tomorrow, I'm going to fuck with your mind and give you dreams that will make you ill. You'll scream alone in darkness, begging me to save you, and I won't. You'll be locked in your own mind until I decide what to do with you."

I grab my breasts, moaning. "Yes, Shade. I want that. I want anything you give me. You feel so good. Oh, god. Fuck. You're so big."

"I love that I can see my cock bulging inside you. Such a little body fated to me when I can easily break it."

I come so hard, my entire body trembles. My ears ring

from how loud I scream. I sway from dizziness, wondering how the hell sex could ever be better.

The mouth clamps around me, his lure light illuminating my womb again, only to reveal something I didn't expect. Shade shouts his own climax, his hand falling to my belly.

"Seems a little parasite has attached itself to the wall of your uterus," Shade informs, rubbing his thumb back and forth over it. "Male anglerfish lock onto the females. Maybe it's a boy." I've never heard him sound so gentle and sweet.

I'm wrapping my head around the fact I'm pregnant, which wasn't something I planned any time soon, but with how Shade is looking at my belly, his lure light still glowing onto my womb to watch the very small embryo, something softens in his eyes.

"I wonder if they will look like the old me, the new me, or you."

"I don't care who they look like as long as they are healthy," I admit, placing my hand over his.

"I thought I'd want you all to myself," he admits, the first real smile stretching to meet his eyes. "Sharing you wasn't an option, but now...maybe I can have the family I never got to have."

I press my forehead against his, knowing in my heart that we would have it.

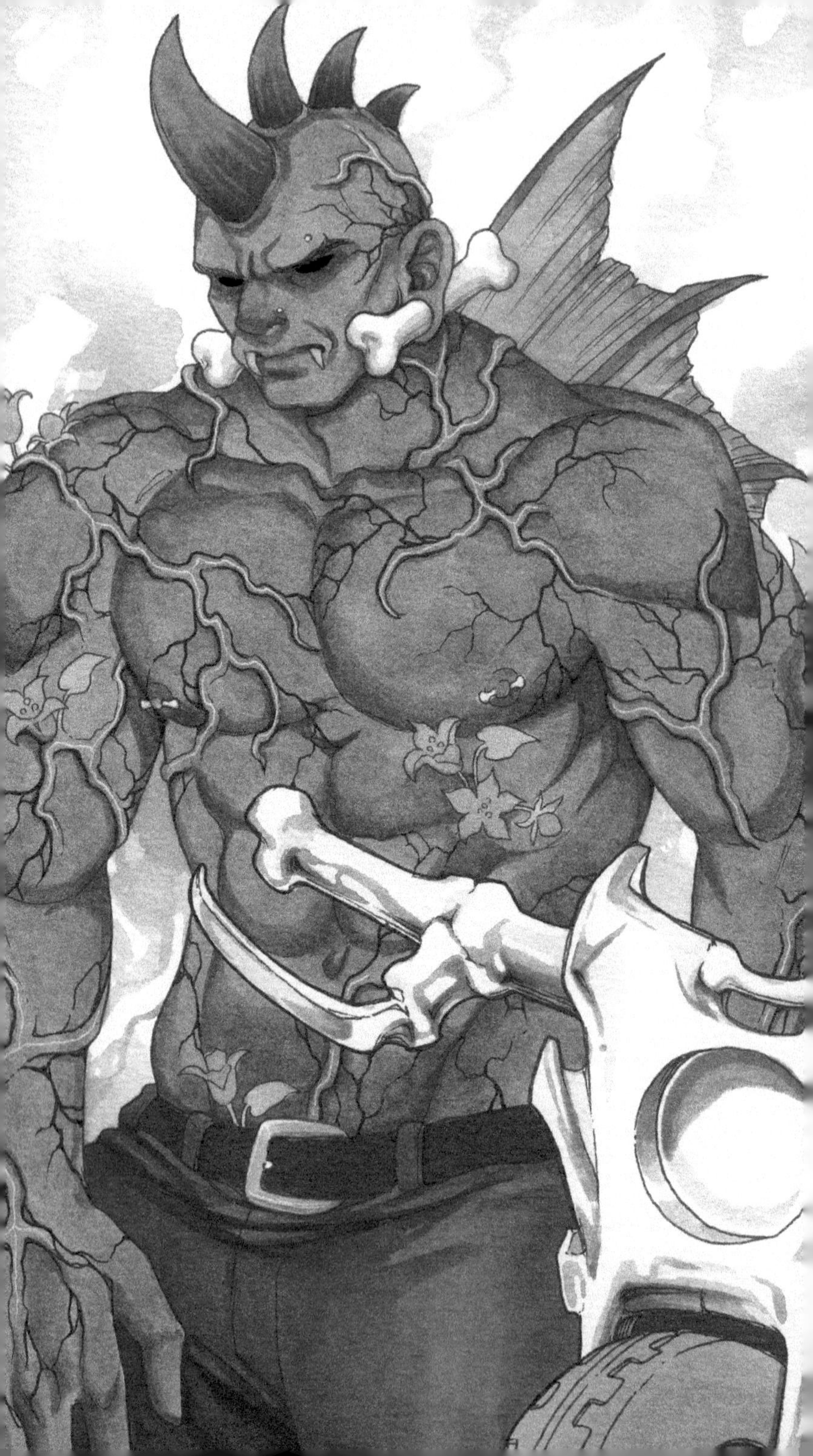

CHAPTER SIXTEEN
SHADE

A week later

I'm in Lula's garage, finally building my bike from Greta's bones.

I mount her skull where the headlight will shine through. My very first victim that led me to Lula. Such fond memories.

Her ribcage wraps around the gas tank, certain bones for the brake handles, and a few frame the seat. Truly, I'm proud of myself. It's remarkable work.

I grin when I smell my mate entering the garage. She never has to say anything when she enters a room. I always know. "Little Dream, what are you doing here?"

"Updating you. They finally found who killed Harold. Two bodies were found in a van in a nearby alley. Would you know anything about that?"

"I killed them and came straight home to you. Their fear didn't taste nearly as good as yours. No one's ever does." I crack my neck, knowing I'll need to feed again soon, more than what Lula can give me without the baby sinking his teeth into her womb.

He doesn't like it when she's afraid.

Fucking brat.

"I know," she snickers. "I was just wanting to tease you a little. You know, I never did ask why you killed the taxidermist."

"No, good reason. He was in my way of getting something I wanted," I answer honestly.

I sniff the air, growling when I smell an unwanted person on this property. Using my speed, I grab Lula and shove her behind me, protecting her as the monsters like me that I've seen around town fill the doorway.

Growling as low and as threatening as I can, the nightmare within me spreads out, the roots traveling across the ground.

"Wait! Shade, stop! They are friends. It's okay." Lula rubs my back, urging me to calm down, but I remain in my stance.

"Sorry to interrupt, but we got curious as to who Lula was mated to, and it worked out because the Hell's Harvesters are here and they are looking for you," a beast that looks like a funny version of a crocodile speaks.

There's a guy next to him who has his wings spread out and smoke billowing from his nose, wanting to fight.

"Okay, this isn't a monster pissing contest. Put your beasts away," the crocodile guy says, as if he is in charge.

"Get the fuck off my property. I've marked it. My mate is claimed. You have no business here," I snarl. "And I don't give a fuck about the Hell's Harvesters. They can get fucked too."

"Shade," Lula scolds quietly. "Be nice. These are people who are just like us. They are experiments. They have mates and families. It would be good for us to stick together.”

Looking into Lula's eyes always weakens me. My heart beats to keep her happy, so if that is what she wants, that is what she will have.

“Nice bike,” a human with a backwards cap praises. “You made that? I'm Fitz. You're talented. We could use someone like you at the garage.”

“No, thanks. I'm good here.” I try to go back to work on my bike when Lula steps in front of it, her hands on her hips, her sassy Spanish tongue is about to speak a million miles a minute.

All that is going to do is have me fuck her right here in front of them, so she knows she's mine.

I cross my arms. “Why would I work there? Have you seen me? I don't blend in.”

“Okay, let's start over,” Croc-man says with a clap of his hands. “I'm Rhett. I'm patient zero.”

My eyes widen. “Sorry to hear that.” I meant it. I remember those fucking procedures. They were torture, and I can't imagine how it felt being the first.

“I'm a crocodile, gargoyle, vampire, ghost, and jellyfish. My mate is Mickey, a human, but she's at home right now with our twins.”

“I'm Fitz. My mate is very pregnant and on bedrest, or she would have come. She is part harpy, succubus”—he blushes—“squid, chameleon, and siren.”

“Oh, you're fucked,” I blurt.

Fitz laughs, nodding in agreement. “I like it that way.”

Rhett shoves the guy next to him, the one with grey skin and purple scales and smoke coming from his mouth.

“Put the dragon away. be nice, Creed. This guy could kill us all.”

Yes. I could.

I'm dying to. It's been a week since I've killed, and I'm thirsting to do it again.

"I'm Creed," he bites through clenched teeth. "My mate is Demi, the diner owner."

"Tell him what you are."

"No," Creed argues. "I'm only here because Demi made me."

I respect him more for that. I'd be the same way.

"Listen, we don't have time for this bullshit." Rhett's concrete wings spread out in annoyance. "Hell's Harvesters will be here any minute because of your crimes. You can't go around killing humans any time you want."

I frown. "Why not?"

"It's bad." Rhett pinches the bridge of his nose. "Moving on because you're a lot like Creed, and I only have patience for him some of the day. People see you in human form due to the rain being spelled."

Ah, that makes sense.

"Sorry, Shadey. I meant to tell you," Lula says.

She started calling me Shadey a few days ago, and I love it. It fits. And I've never had a nickname. If anyone has the power to make me feel human again, it's her.

"It's okay. A lot has happened. You don't need to explain a thing." I cup her face, not wanting her to feel for one minute that it is her fault. My skin slithers with my roots, hating that they are there. "Listen, I only have so much tolerance for...people. My nightmare is clawing at my skin, and it's because of you."

"That's so fucking wild," Fitz beams.

An odd human.

"Anyway, I wanted to extend a job offer to my garage. Snapdragons. You have clear talent."

"Do I have to socialize?"

"Shade, sé amable."

"I am being nice," I grumble, cracking my neck as the nightmare slithers under my skin.

Lula's hand touches my arm, the simple, innocent touch calms me instantly, the evil only lurking through my eyes instead of trying to pry from my body.

"You're okay. You won't hurt them."

"I want to," I bite, cutting my eyes to the monster with fire, Creed. I don't like him. I wonder what he is afraid of. If he is afraid of anything.

"I know, but they aren't here as a threat, Shadey. They are here so we can be friends. It would be good for our little parasite to have friends, and they have kids," she points out.

I growl, not liking that she is right. I don't want my kid to be alone. "Fine. Yes. I'll take your offer to work at the garage. These are human bones though. Can I provide those? I already have the beetles I need to clean the bones."

"You won't be building human bone bicycles. Oh my god, you're just like Creed. Okay, you'll be building the bikes the customers want. What the humans want."

I curl my lip, take a step back, and look Rhett up and down. The audacity to come onto my property and say I have to listen to humans.

Hay, Dios mío.

That's what Lula would say. I hear her voice in my head because I hear it all the time. She says it when she wakes up sleepy, mad, laughing, stubbing her toe, whatever, she says it a hundred times a day, and if anyone ever made her stop saying it, I would kill them.

Brutally.

Lula shoves me forward.

"Fine," I mumble. "Thanks."

"You and Creed won't be allowed to interact. It's a rule."

"I'd fucking kill him anyway," Creed dares.

My nightmare is inside him before he has a chance to blow his fucking smoke. Creed's eyes turn black, but shockingly, I don't find a single thing he is afraid of.

Demi is all that is in his mind, so if I wanted to truly kill him, I'd kill her, which I wouldn't do because she's good.

Loud, sorrow-filled screams pierce the air, which has me rescinding the shadow.

"Who are they?" I question, staring down the end of the driveway.

"Uh, like paranormal police but way more dangerous," Fitz, the human, explains. "Led by Abaddon, then The Four Horsemen."

"...*the* Four Horsemen."

Everyone nods.

Motorcycles come down the driveway, their bikes bigger, made of bones too, but the screams come from within the bike. The closer they get, the more I see the souls pressing their faces against the motorcycle, begging to be set free.

Something about their nearness calms me, in a way. It's as if my nightmare recognizes them. I don't know how or why.

They are massive though. Bigger than me.

"Another DNA experiment," the leader says. "I've learned not to try to do anything with you lot. Especially now since you're mated." He stands in front of me, and a giant wave of power actually causes my beasts to still.

All but the nightmare.

He's ready to do whatever this guy tells him to.

"Abaddon," he holds out his hand.

"Shade." I shake it, a vibration passing between us.

"Well, well, well, that is interesting. I knew you were part nightmare. It was the only thing that made sense when I heard about how the victims died. Good thing I brought the reinforcement, or we would all be fucked."

"He can't be stronger than you guys." Rhett is taken aback and confused.

"Are you kidding? He's one pissed off rage away from taking over this entire town to give every person deadly nightmares."

"He can do that?" Lula asks with a terrified gasp.

Mmm, her terror tastes good.

"Oh, yeah. If he really wanted, if something really triggered it, depending on his rage, he could collapse this planet and give everyone deadly nightmares."

"What could trigger something like that?" Lula questions, her worry vibrating through the bond.

I go to her side and wrap my arms around her, doing my best to change that.

"It would need to be huge. The loss of a mate or child would do it."

I snarl low in warning, telling him in the darkest, deepest gravel I have to shut the fuck up. No one will talk about my mate or unborn child that way.

Unleashing the roots and nightmare at the same time wasn't a choice. It just happened at the idea of someone taking away my family from me.

My. Family.

I've had my family taken from me once, and I will die protecting the one I have made from scratch. A family fated to me.

"Ah, ah, ah, nightmare. I can't let you do that." A playful, arrogant tone becomes a wall, blocking the nightmare and roots from reaching the Hell's Harvesters.

Out of sand, another creature appears. He doesn't look like The Four Horsemen. Instead, he is tall, lean, but built, wearing a black-on-black suit.

He brushes sand off it.

"Think of him like the King of Dreams. Nightmare is his son," Abaddon explains.

I cross my arms, not giving a shit about who this man in front of me is.

"Yeah, he is definitely part nightmare," Dreamer says. "Not the good part either, but he's family. Nightmare isn't going to be happy."

"Yeah, makes two of us."

Dreamer smiles. "That isn't what I meant. He will not be happy that he had a son that he didn't know about."

"Well, considering the circumstances, I'm assuming someone got his DNA because here I am. You'll need to ask him how the scientists got it."

"Yes, yes," he says, thoughtfully, also wondering how. "I will. Don't go into their minds." He points to The Hell's Harvesters. "You'll be able to get inside their head, but you aren't trained for that. You'd die being in a mind as strong as theirs."

"We want to offer you a deal," Abaddon says. "We want you to be part of Hell's Harvesters. You can stay here, but when we call, you will come. You'll be able to feed off the fear you need to survive without killing any more people."

I don't like that. Killing is part of how I feed the nightmare.

"Five people. Criminals only," Lula steps up, her badge still on her hip. "Per year."

"Ten," I counter.

"Five," Dreamer states. "That's all you need since you are mated. So young too. Nightmare will be jealous. He is thousands of years old but has not met his fated mate."

"I'll send tissues. Is this done? I'd rather get back to my life."

"Do we have a deal?" Dreamer steps forward, holding out his hand. Sand twirls in the air. "Shake on it. Our entities will have to bond. If you break the bond, there will be trouble, understand?"

Growling, I slap my hand in his. "Yes."

Black smoke swirls around the sand, a small twister forming as electricity intensifies.

"Excellent." Our creatures seep into us again, the contract officially binding. "Don't call me grandpa. Makes me feel old."

"You're not my family. Lula is."

"We'll see," Dreamer hums. "So much like him," he mutters, taking a step near one of the Horsemen who is looking directly into my eyes.

"I'm Death. That's Famine. Conquest. And War." Death points to each. "It isn't often we recruit, but your skills are valuable." He tosses a black cut at me. "Welcome to the Hell's Harvesters."

I turn it over to see my name stitched across the left chest, reminding me of the days when I was part of Shallow Sinners.

"First trip we take, we will go to see your old crew. They spent a lot of time looking for you, but your scent trail ended," Famine says.

"Scent? They are—"

"Shifters. Yes. We'll get you connected," Death chimes in.

"Death might get emotional at the reunion."

"Shut the fuck up, Famine," Death snaps, the green grass wilting and turning to ash as it dies.

"Yeah, it would be good to see them one day." I get lost in the memory of Prez saving me from that situation. He did everything he promised.

I wonder where my cut went when the scientists took me. I wonder what they did with it. I wish I could see them again and ask before killing them.

"I have to go," Dreamer announces as if I give a fuck. "It was nice meeting you, Shade. I hope to see more of you."

"I hope you don't."

"Shadey."

"What? I don't. I need everyone to get out. The nightmare is clawing at me with you all here."

"You need to be trained," War informs me. "I'll come by soon. We'll get started, but for now, everyone needs to leave."

One by one, they all leave, finally leaving me alone with Lula.

"You need me, don't you?" Lula asks. "Come give me nightmares, Shadey."

"How did you know?"

"Mi alma me lo dice."

I grab Lula's hand, blurring us against the wall, and the shadow seeps into her. Those brown eyes I love so much turn black, burnt tears dripping down her face.

"Let me see what you fear, Little Dream."

The end

If you kind of like me and want to follow me for me, join my readers group on Facebook: January's Raynestormers

OVE POLI
EPARTMENT

EPILOGUE

LULA

Two weeks later

"I want to fuck you in the back seat right now." Shade's claws are lengthened, digging into his black jeans so hard that he might rip them.

We've gone through too many pairs of pants lately. At this rate, I need to buy stock in denim.

"And have your big body ruin my 1969 Chevy Impala? That's like me running over your motorcycle."

"I won't ruin it. I'll be good. I'll sit up while you ride that pretty cunt on my cock."

"You only feel that way because I'm helping you hunt someone," I add, knowing that it isn't the only reason. Teasing him is fun. He gets worked up so easily.

"No." His giant, oversized hand covers my leg, reminding me of last night, when he held onto them while fucking me on our new couch. "Because that citrus scent of yours is stronger now since the pregnancy."

My heart warms. I understand now. He won't admit it,

but I've noticed. He loves it when the lure light shines on our child. Shade is always enamored when seeing our child. A trance overtakes him, along with a big smile that I don't think he knows appears upon his face.

He watches for as long as possible, never taking his eyes away from the glowing womb. Shade talks to his son every night. At least, I feel he's a boy. I don't know how. I just do.

It warms my heart to know Shade finally has the family he has ached for his entire life. It's changed a part of him. He's...softer sometimes, but only with me. I have to stop him from killing someone at least once every single day.

He hates everyone.

Everyone but me.

And I love it that way.

"If you're good, when we get home, you can have me any way you want."

His growls shake the car, the windows vibrating from the force. I gasp, feeling the rumble in my body.

"I'm always good," he murmurs, his lips finding the shell of my ear.

That lie causes me to laugh. I turn my head, pressing my palm against his cheek. "You are *never* always good."

He kisses the back of my neck where my mating mark is, sending tingles down my spine.

"I know, but that's exactly why you love me." His fingers drop to my hip, where that dumb tattoo is hiding under my pants.

I brought up getting it removed one night, and Shade did not like that idea. He spent the entire night showing me just how much he loves it. I decided the tattoo stays. Shade said it was a reminder that I love a freak of nature like himself.

I suppose, in a way, he is a freak of nature.

My freak.

Who seems to get freakier as time passes. His abilities get stronger, and the King of Dreams guy, Shade calls him Dreamer, was right about his ability to give multiple people nightmares.

He does it to Creed, Rhett, and Fitz at least once a day.

I pull into the rundown motel just on the outskirts of town, parking it in a spot that is away from the door Reba Lynn was staying in. I have been hunting for Shade's target for a few weeks now, trying to find someone that people wouldn't miss.

The motel sign light flickers just as a rat scurries across the parking lot.

"This is where she is?" Shade asks, surveying the entire lot.

"According to one of my confidential informants. He saw her in room twelve." I pluck the mugshot photo from the file and show it to him. "She's a serial stalker murderer. I've pulled her record multiple times. She gets a restraining order against her from the men she stalks, then murders them, but she is really great at leaving no evidence behind. She's the main suspect, but no damn evidence to tie her to the crimes."

"And what is she doing so close to town?" Shade asks.

This is where I love doing my job. I become excited. Shade gives me his full attention, his intense black eyes watching me with a tilt of his lips. He loves it when I go down the rabbit hole of finding clues.

"Well, there is a man in town who filed a restraining order against her *yesterday*."

"Yesterday? Wait, how long has she been here?"

"A few weeks. I think she is doing her own hunting and has found her target. Apparently, she broke into his house, followed him at work, sent him notes, and when the police did a sweep of his apartment, they found cameras in his bedroom."

"How long before she usually goes in for the kill?"

"We have about three days, give or take a few, before she loses her patience." I gasp, gripping his arm when the door to room twelve opens. "She's leaving! She's leaving. Go, go get her. We can't have her leave."

The inside of the car darkens when his nightmare comes forward. I love the ominous, eerie creep that falls over me, a slight chill, an invisible force that I can't see, but he can see me.

It's exhilarating.

"Do you want to come with me?" Shade's voice deepens with malicious intent, a sardonic grip of his vocal cords that clicks across his throat.

"Come with you? What would I do?"

"Come see what it is like to invade someone's mind. It's quite...exhilarating."

I nibble on my bottom lip, watching Reba lean against the old, rusted iron railing and light a cigarette. Her hair is up in a messy bun, a few loose hairs sticking up around her hairline. She's definitely been planning something.

"We can be a team. Like Hemlock and Water," Shade says, and the endearment is sweet, even if he doesn't know the names.

He thinks he isn't smart, but I couldn't disagree more. I think a lot got messed up within his mind when the experiments happened. I think words get confused, stories, even memories, everything has changed for him.

I stare at him, endearingly, unable to picture what my life would be like without him. He came quick and fast, unexpected, yet welcome. He's rough, mean, murderous, possessive, and every red flag a girl can think of. There's so much people don't see when they look at him.

"You mean Sherlock and Watson?"

He grunts, giving a curt nod. "Yes, them. They make a good team. We are a good team. The best team. We are better than them."

I chuckle when he begins to growl, annoyed by fictional competition. "They aren't here, Shadey. "

"I'd kill them if they were."

I hide my smile, staring at him with the same intensity he feels for me.

I love him.

I loved him since the first time he paralyzed me, fucking me with one of his roots.

He gave me everything I needed, not knowing I would make sure he always got what he needed too.

"Let's go before she makes me run after her. I don't want to make a scene."

I open the door, allowing the cool night to wrap around me, and the red motel light reflects off my car.

He is by my side before I can double-check that my badge is on my hip. I loop my arm through his, my hand not even close to wrapping around his bicep.

Every step, the ground threatens to fall from under us from the force Shade carries himself with.

We pass a side garden to the right, walking towards the staircase, or what used to be a garden is now riddled with cigarettes and soda cans.

When we climb up the staircase, Reba is on the right. I don't hide my badge, and she doesn't seem like she is going to make a run for it.

She's confident. I'll give her that.

"I have done nothing wrong." She doesn't even look at me, never taking her eyes off the night as she smokes.

The foggy cloud escapes her lips, creating a slight mirage of her face.

"Just here to talk." I point to my badge. "I'm Detective Sanchez. I'm just here to ask a few questions."

"You can try, but I won't answer them. Not without a lawyer present. Don't waste your breath. I know my rights."

That's fine. She won't be needing rights tonight anyway. She will never stalk and murder anyone again by the time Shade is done with her.

God, I can't wait to see him in action. I'm excited. I've only ever been the star of the show, never a spectator.

"That's okay." Shade steps forward, his gaze locking onto hers.

I wish he could mystify me like he does others. Vampires aren't allowed to use their influence on their mates.

A real fucking buzz kill. I would love for him to force me to do whatever he wanted, as I obeyed his every command.

"You won't be needing a lawyer tonight, Reba Lynn." Shade plucks the cigarette from her, taking a long hit off it before blowing the smoke into her face.

She doesn't even blink.

"I don't?"

"No." His hand steers her to her room. "We're going to play a little game."

"I love games!" She brightens, giving him a smile.

"We're going to have so much fun," Shade lies. "Open the door, Reba."

She listens, completely entranced, and inserts an old gold key with a keychain attached to it. The door swings open, and Reba steps inside. The room is dark with a lamp in the corner, glowing a dim yellow light. There are stains on the carpet from years of not having a deep cleaning, and cigarette smoke hangs heavy in the air.

"What game are we playing?" Reba spins around to Shade, smiling widely.

It's hard to believe I'm looking at the face of a killer. She doesn't seem like the type, but evidence doesn't lie. She's good at what she does, but Shade is better.

I shut the door behind me and lock it, then close the blinds, not wanting anyone to know what was going on.

"We are going to play, 'What's your favorite nightmare?'" Shade replies, his roots sliding across the floor.

It's always amazing to see his abilities come to life. The roots inch from his body, going where Shade wants them to. They move like arms or legs, smooth and natural.

"How do we play that?"

"It's easy. You tell me your worst fear first." The room darkens even more, the presence of the entity within him wanting out, wanting to feed.

The roots begin to wrap around Reba Lynn, binding her arms and legs together until she can't move. Flowers begin to bloom, purple petals sprouting, and I know he is seconds away from releasing the poison.

"And then I'm going to make you relive it."

"But I'll be scared. That would be...a nightmare." Reba's eyes become sad, a frown tugging on her lips. "I don't think I like this game."

Shade grunts, the space darkening even further. Smoke releases from his skin, black and heavy.

"Let me see what you fear, Reba," Shade growls, the nightmare diving down her throat to possess her.

Her eyes turn black, and her mouth parts to scream, but the poison releases, pushing its way into her system with every ragged, desperate breath she takes. Her shout gets caught, her eyes bulge out, and her face turns red. She stares at Shade in shock, and tears begin to drip down her face.

Fear.

And I don't know how I've never noticed it before, but Shade tilts his head back, groaning as he drinks it in. I almost see it, an energy that hums around him, and if I'm not mistaken, he seems...bigger.

If that's possible.

My throat becomes dry watching him, my heart racing with adrenaline while he absorbs all the fear he can.

Liquid heat pulsates between my legs, my clit throbbing from the unnerving sight. This. This is exactly what I wanted, what I needed, what I've craved my entire life.

I gasp when I feel the fear enter my body, and I have to grip the TV stand. My stomach warms, and a drowsy sensation causes me to feel like I'm floating, like I've had too much to drink.

Shade looks over at me, his gaze latched onto my stomach. It would make sense that our child would indulge in fear too. He is part nightmare after all.

"Take my hand." Shade reaches for me, and I don't think twice; I take it, allowing him to pull me under.

Reba's eyes turn black, and I'm cast inside her mind. The suddenness of it reminds me of the fall of a rollercoaster from up high.

"Interesting," Shade says, slowly spinning in a circle.

"Wow." I don't know how to explain where I am.

When I look up, something similiar to lightning veins and crackles.

"Neurons from the brain," he explains. "We're in the part of the mind where she holds everything she fears, but this, this is what she fears most."

All that is around us is just a vast desert. Sand is beneath our feet. The sand seems endless.

"Being deserted?" I blurt, wondering how the hell this is her worst fear.

Don't get me wrong, it wouldn't be ideal to be lost in the middle of nowhere like this, but maybe there is more to it than that.

"No. It's always so much more than the obvious answer."

"Help me!" Reba calls out from somewhere. "Help! Someone!"

Her voice echoes across the never-ending pastures of sand. I can't tell where her cries for help are coming from. Her voice surrounds me. Reba's call for help should have me running to her. That's my job as a cop. I should protect and serve, but Reba has done very bad things, and I think she deserves worse than prison—or anything the justice system could give her.

"This way," Shade directs, taking my hand so I don't get lost.

What would happen if I did get lost? Would I be stuck here forever? Would I die with her?

"I feel him. Our child. He loves the taste of fear."

"He could be a she."

"Either way. It seems they won't be human."

"Being like me will only cause hardship for them," he says, still following the shouts from Reba.

"I would rather them be like you. Absolutely fearless and bold."

"That's you." He pulls me against him, lifting my chin so I

look at him in the eyes. "You're everything I'm not. I might feed from people's fear, but you soothe mine."

"You're not afraid of anything."

He doesn't say anything. His eyes lose their intensity and become a bit sad.

"I am afraid of losing what I thought I'd never have." His hand rests on my stomach.

"Help! Is anyone there? Please, I don't have much time. Oh god," she cries, her voice becoming louder the closer we get.

"She doesn't taste nearly as good as you do."

"Shadey, no one better."

We stop at the edge of a hole. It reminds me of a grave for a coffin, dug perfectly to fit a coffin, but deeper. So. Much. Deeper.

There's no way Reba Lynn can get out.

"Oh, thank goodness," she laughs with a bit of hysteria. "I didn't think anyone would hear me."

"I heard you." Shade kicks sand into the hole. "But I'm not here to save you."

"What?" Reba and I say in shock at the same time.

Shade's lip twitches and he turns to me. "Her worst fear is being buried alive."

My lips form an 'O'.

Of course we aren't here, inside her mind, to save her. Cop habit, saving people.

"Please, don't do this. Please, I won't stalk or murder anymore. I couldn't help it, but I'll stop. I'll never do it again."

Shade takes a deep breath, inhaling the fear again, and I do the same, wondering if I'll be able to feel it again.

I do.

My child loves it and wants more.

"Keep going. He likes it." I rub my still flat stomach, wanting my unborn child to get all the nourishment he needs.

Shade's face becomes something different. The light he has

when he looks at me is gone. There's no happy emotion except rage and terror.

I flinch when something tickles me on my cheek. I reach, confused, when I pull my hand away to see a snowflake.

It's snowing.

In the middle of the desert.

"Memories," Shade explains. "Sometimes you feel them, and others you won't." He pushes another pile of sand inside the hole, another scream ripping free of Reba. "So interesting what people are afraid of. Being buried alive is specific. I think people think of the worst thing that would never happen."

"And now you exist." I help by kicking in my own sand, wanting to contribute since this is a family matter now.

"Please, please, don't do this. You aren't like him! You're a cop, right? You'll help me. You have to help me."

I peek my head over the hole, staring down at her pressed against the edge of one of the walls. "I'm off duty," I pout, sticking my lip out. "Sorry." I gasp, my hand flying to my throat when it holds the same eerie undertone as Shade.

"Mmm, my son wants to come play." I've never heard Shade sound so happy before. "You are beautiful all the time, but pregnant? I'm going to fuck you into darkness when we are out of here, Little Dream."

I'm surprised it doesn't bother me to push sand in as Reba screams at the top of her lungs. Shade is faster, using his abilities and strength to gather more sand, pouring it into the hole.

Her cries for help soften, and when I leer over the edge, all that is left is her face peeking out from the sand. The sand around her eyes is wet from tears, but she is no longer fighting.

She knows her fate.

"I've nearly drained her of all the fear she can feel," Shade explains, pouring in the last bit of sand.

The hole is covered. Reba is officially buried alive.

"Her heart is slowing." Shade taps his ear, explaining he can hear her heartbeat.

When I blink, I'm pulled into reality again, standing by Shade, and staring at a very still, pale Reba. Her eyes are open. Pupils blown. And sand spills from her mouth.

Shade tackles me onto the bed, kissing my lips with hunger and desperation. "I fucking love you," he says between kisses, ripping my shirt over my head just as the alarm goes off on the nightstand, blaring one of my favorite reggaeton songs that has me grinding myself onto his very hard cock. "I'm taking you inside every nightmare from now on." He sucks a nipple into his mouth, causing me to arch my back, then his fangs scratch over the sensitive edge of my collarbone. "I need you," he murmurs, the only warning I have before he bites me, dragging my blood down his throat.

I hold his head to my neck, my orgasm getting closer with every pull. "I love you too, Shadey. So much."

He kisses my neck, whispering so low he probably can't think I can hear him. "How do you know?"

"Mi alma me lo dice," I whisper, and those words have him bite me again, harder, deeper, growling, his teeth hurting to the point of pain.

He might be a nightmare, but he is my absolute dream.

My soul says so.

The end

If you kind of like me and want to follow me for me, join my readers group on Facebook: January's Raynestormers

ACKNOWLEDGEMENTS

First, I'd like to say thank you for reading! I truly hope you enjoyed it! This story was a big challenge for me. Shade is darker than any other character I wrote. He challenged me in ways that no other character has. Lula was challenging in another way because I knew I wanted to incorporate Spanish, and I really wanted to make sure I represented Colombian Spanish correctly, which leads me to thank my friend and sensitivity reader, Luna S., for helping me perfect the Spanish in this book. You educated so much, and I honestly cannot wait to learn more! I couldn't have done this without you.

I'd like to thank my Kickstarter Backers who wanted to die a gruesome death in this book. Greta, Christina, Fire-opal, Becca, and Reba Lynn, thank you all for making the choice to not only support me, but happily become victims at the hands of our Shade.

Thank you to the ARC readers and influencers who decided to take time out of their lives to read this! I truly appreciate your support and love!

Nothing is ever done alone. Inspiration always comes from somewhere. For Shade, I want to thank my team, as always, for helping me create my characters, especially Shade. Bryckk came up with the idea to make him part nightmare (and so many other off-the-wall ideas that I can't even remember them all), which had my mind roaring!! Tiff for always sharpening Shade's abilities to make them work within the story. Carolina, for working her butt off on graphics and giving the readers the teasers of Shade and Lula. I love you all so much. Success is a team effort, and I love my team so damn much. I hope you all know how much you mean to me. You all have so much patience for me cause I know I'm a mess.

To my friend Nick H.! Thank you for wanting to talk weird creature ideas with me a year ago, and gave the suggestion of the anglerfish! I had to modify the DNA in this book because only female anglerfish have the light! That was a fun fact. That idea alone inspired this story! I knew it would be perfect for a monster stalker book.

To my friends, my family, and to all who support me, thank you so much. I love you.

My husband, Adam, you are by far my biggest supporter, my cheerleader, my everything. None of this would be possible without your support and love. The way you love me inspires me to write fated mates because I have no doubt in my mind that you are my fated mate. I love you so much. Thank you for believing in me. I wouldn't have gotten this far without you.

I love you with all my insides.
XOXOXO,
January

About the Author

January Rayne is a paranormal fantasy romance author who lives in Buffalo, NY with her husband, son, two dogs, and two leopard geckos. Buffalo is freezing, but January loves when it snows as it gives her the perfect atmosphere to write a book for you to get lost in.

Scan here for easy access to follow me on social media: